SILENCING THE SIREN

SONGS AND STORMS BOOK 1

SARA REYNOLDS

Copyright © 2022 by Sara Reynolds

All rights reserved. No part of this publication may be reproduced, stored or transmitted in any form or by any means, electronic, mechanical, photocopying, recording, scanning, or otherwise without written permission from the publisher. It is illegal to copy this book, post it to a website, or distribute it by any other means without permission.

This novel is entirely a work of fiction. The names, characters and incidents portrayed in it are the work of the author's imagination. Any resemblance to actual persons, living or dead, events or localities is entirely coincidental.

Sara Reynolds asserts the moral right to be identified as the author of this work.

Sara Reynolds has no responsibility for the persistence or accuracy of URLs for external or third-party Internet Websites referred to in this publication and does not guarantee that any content on such Websites is, or will remain, accurate or appropriate.

Designations used by companies to distinguish their products are often claimed as trademarks. All brand names and product names used in this book and on its cover are trade names, service marks, trademarks and registered trademarks of their respective owners. The publishers and the book are not associated with any product or vendor mentioned in this book. None of the companies referenced within the book have endorsed the book.

Book Cover designed by Sara Reynolds

First paperback edition published July 2022

Published Independently

I would like to dedicate this book to everyone who believed in me. Specifically, I would like to dedicate it to my husband, whose support and encouragement was endless. I never would have gotten this far without him or the friends who helped me pick out chapter titles and other random details at all hours of the night. To Caleb, Alex, Colton, and Marcus—thank you.

"I say you're asking me to follow you into Mordor, which—if I'm totally straight with you—I think is a really bad idea. But 'the shire... the shire is burning.' So, Mordor it is."

—Eddie Munson,
Stranger Things 4.6

TABLE OF CONTENTS

1. The King of Partying?
2. Share One More Drink With Me
3. ...Or the King of Chaos?
4. Thanks for the Memories
5. American Nightmare
6. The Man Who Would Be King
7. The Fear of Falling Apart
8. Let the Good Times Roll
9. Laissez les Bons Temps Rouler
10. Dancing's Not a Crime
11. Crossroad Blues in the Crescent City
12. The Name of the Game
13. Creatures of the Night
14. All Magic Comes With a Price
15. Poor Unfortunate Soul
16. I've Got Friends on the Other Side
17. Family Affairs
18. I Think We're All Damned
19. Even When Your Hope is Gone
20. Two Minutes to Midnight
21. Gimme Shelter
22. End of the Road
23. At Death's Door
24. Pull Yourself Back to Creation
25. Survival of the Fittest

26. No Rest for the Wicked
27. Bloodlines
28. Before the Storm
29. Living Through It Was Just a Luxury
30. Storm Killer
31. Picking up the Pieces
32. The Strongest Form of Magic

About the Author

I. THE KING OF PARTYING?

(THE SIREN, THE GORGON, AND THE TRICKSTER)

The siren Calliope wasn't in a partying mood. However, she knew that she should at least pretend to be having fun, so she leaned into her best friend Nagaveni's ear and whispered, "Well, it looks like Dys rolled out the red carpet for us. Does that secure his place as the king of partying...? Or maybe as the king of chaos for his dramatic grand entrance?" She mischievously raised her eyebrow and smirked. Although she did question if Dysnomi, the trickster, had something bigger planned for his nightclub on its opening night.

"WELCOME... TO... TARTARUS!" Dysnomi announced to the crowd. His voice reverberated throughout the club, causing the crowd to cheer deafeningly loud.

Calliope always wondered how Dysnomi could make his voice sound so loud and commanding that it could be heard over the loud music and sizable crowd. *He's a trickster. Just don't even question it,* she thought.

Nagaveni rolled her eyes, but she was careful to avoid accidentally making eye contact with anyone. "A+ for the theatrics, but did he HAVE to draw so much attention over here? He couldn't have, like... I don't know, waited... Until I WASN'T standing right next to you?" The gorgon sighed and picked at her skin-tight dress' thin forest-green strap. She had never done well in crowded places, and the club was packed like a snake pit. At least, it felt that way to her. Her anxiety soared when she noticed all of the attention that she and Calliope were attracting. Strangers allowed their eyes to linger on the women's dresses, especially down their deep V-necks. Nagaveni was doing everything that she could think of to not notice, but Calliope seemed to be relishing in it. She figured that had to be due to Calliope's siren abilities. *Plus,* she thought. *Even I have to admit that the sequined orchid-purple looks amazing on Calli, and I'm glad we decided to buy matching dresses.*

"Hey... Try to relax," Calliope told Nagaveni. "No one knows who you are except your friends. Plus, you don't have to worry about keeping your 'little Jörmungandr babies' hidden. This Serpent Tamer necklace that I had Salem enchant for you is gonna work, no matter what. You can just... Be yourself tonight."

Calliope's words made Nagaveni feel a little better. She remembered when Calliope had first hooked the enchanted necklace onto her—the two snakes on the back of her head had hissed like crazy. Calliope had simply called them stubborn before nicknaming them *Julius Squeezer* and *Fangis Khan*. She laughed so hard, and that moment was when she knew that her roommate would ALSO be her best friend.

Calliope looked at the man who was standing directly across the club from her and Nagaveni. He stood near the crowded high-top bar. He was a tall, lean man. She had found him attractive since the day that she met him, with his shoulder-length champagne-blond hair, alabaster skin, and hazel-colored eyes that had small golden flakes inside of them.

Nagaveni looked at the man as well. She felt like she had known him all of her life, yet she knew that she had only met him a handful of times. *He just seems SO familiar,* she thought.

Dysnomi had been making drinks behind the bar when the Supernatural women first walked inside the club. However, when he noticed them, he had moved to stand in front of the bar, his arms outstretched like he was Jesus. His face formed an enigmatic smile as Calliope and Nagaveni crossed the only clear path through the dark, crowded floor. Purple, blue, and pink lights danced over their faces and bodies.

Dysnomi took a moment to fully appreciate Calliope, admiring her wild turquoise hair and the way that it fell in loose waves to her petite waist, like a breathtaking waterfall. He always felt a strange emotion whenever she was near. He soon found himself thinking, *It's like the siren calls me out to the sea.*

Dysnomi studied Calliope, noticing the way that her eyes matched her dress. He then noticed how the iris-purple color of her eyes started glowing from the amount of energy that she was absorbing. Her dress sparkled, reflecting the club's bouncing lights and commanding the crowd's attention. The thin fabric clung to her flawless cappuccino skin like the dress had been made specifically for her. His breath hitched in his throat as his eyes roamed over her round thighs and wide hips. His eyes then moved to the middle of her chest. Her skin-tight dress clung to her body so much that it would have made ANY man feel jealous of the contact.

Dysnomi became wrapped up in his lustful thoughts that he didn't notice when Calliope stopped in front of him. She just appeared there one moment, leaving him scrambling to gain some composure.

"You're a vision tonight, Dys. Well... Maybe just, like... An early 2000s goth girl's vision of the handsome Supernatural from her dreams," Calliope teased.

Dysnomi eagerly watched as Calliope's garnet-pink lips curled into the sexiest smirk that he had ever seen. Then, he lifted an eyebrow at her and laughed.

Calliope made a show of roaming her eyes over Dysnomi's body for once and he—being a good sport like always—held his arms out and slowly spun in place.

"I mean it, Dys," Calliope said, throwing her hands up. "You look like a DREAM." She made a small, wistful sigh, glancing up at Dysnomi's flushed face. Her heart skipped a beat the way that it did every time that she was close to him.

For the first time, Calliope thought that the *'ever-so-confident'* Dysnomi looked nervous. He gazed down at her, and for a second, she got lost in his eyes–his golden flakes seeming to hint at the mischief inside of him. Startled, she realized that she had telepathically sent him all of her thoughts and emotions. She was usually better at keeping those to herself.

"I almost forgot how soft your hair looks," Calliope whispered. She lifted her hand and lightly traced her thumb across Dysnomi's bottom lip, causing him to inhale sharply. She traced a line up his cheekbone, leaving the ghost of her touch tingling against his skin as she reached up to play with a fallen strand of his hair. "You have the most gorgeous blond hair... Every strand looks divine, like it was woven by *Rumpelstiltskin* himself... And it has the beauty of a dozen rays of sunlight that bounce off a puddle and create a rainbow," she whispered in his ear with a serene sigh.

'Well... Everyone here looks happy. I bet anger feels weird,' a mysterious female voice said, reverberating inside Calliope's mind.

When Calliope heard the strange female voice inside her mind, her body stiffened and she realized how sensually she had been talking to Dysnomi in front of Nagaveni. She thought, *I guess it's a good thing we're at a bar... It's the perfect place for awkward situations...*

Calliope stepped back and cleared her throat, internally cringing. She grabbed a shot of whiskey from the bar and tried to change the conversation, but she was useless in uncomfortable situations. "Hey, I mean... You should know by now that the only reason I'm here is to make sure you don't get ALL the attention. You already have a big head," she teased. "But, seriously, Dys... You DO look good."

"WHAT?!" Dysnomi yelled, jumping upright. He was uncharacteristically offended, but he stopped himself and adjusted his phthalo-green tie and smoothed his coal-black button-down shirt. "I look good? GOOD?! Calli, I'm one of the most attractive men ALIVE and we BOTH know it," he said confidently. He stepped forward and lowered his head to look down at Calliope, showing her his big, hazel puppy-dog eyes. There was a glint of roguish sparks inside of the hazel, his small golden flakes reminding her of lightning.

'Your choice... Yours alone, and it comes with SERIOUS consequences. The trickster knows, yet he's still wearing that DAMN smirk on his face,' a strange voice said inside of Calliope's mind. The voice was new. It was a deep male voice, unlike the first.

Who said that? Calliope thought.

Without warning, lightning stormed down from above the nightclub! It crashed through the roof of Tartarus with ease, aimed directly at Calliope. She caught a glimpse of a ginormous onyx-black bird seconds before an excruciating pain shot through her entire body... And her vision faded away.

2. SHARE ONE MORE DRINK WITH ME

(LAST CALL)

Opening her eyes, Calliope came back to reality on the balcony of the nightclub. One hand was resting on Dysnomi's arm while she spoke, but her words sounded foreign to her. She looked up at him with confusion before she removed her hand from his arm and stepped away from him.

"Hey! Don't even joke about that! You know Loki's my hero," Dysnomi said, smiling. "And you want me to live up to him? I mean, I would never leave a woman unsatisfied, but..." His voice became husky before trailing off when he noticed that Calliope was confused. He stepped forward and wrapped her in a big hug, his arms enveloping her small frame.

For a moment, Calliope allowed her head to rest against Dysnomi's firm chest, listening to his heartbeat—she heard it skip when he pulled her close. She relished the heat that radiated off of his chest to warm her cheek, and the feeling of his strong arms holding her. When she pulled away from his embrace, she took another moment to get a good look at him. She noticed tattoos covering both of his arms then. She was shocked for a half-second, wondering when he had the time to get tattooed; though, she knew that he could change his appearance using his trickster abilities. *Wait,* she thought. *So... He gave himself tattoos using his magic? He CAN do that, right? Yeah, I mean, if he could bend reality to his will, then I don't see why he couldn't do something that simple.*

"Uhh... Calli? Are you just gonna stare at my biceps all day, or are you gonna introduce me to your beautiful new friend over here?" Dysnomi asked.

Calliope jumped at the sound of Dysnomi's voice. She had not even realized that she had zoned out. Looking over his shoulder, she noticed Nagaveni standing behind him.

Dysnomi stood there with confidence, turning away from Nagaveni. He smirked at Calliope the moment that his eyes met hers.

Nagaveni was staring at the floor, blushing. She peeked underneath her long eyelashes at Dysnomi, only to catch him blowing her a kiss and winking at her. She blushed crimson-red and looked down again quickly, too shy to say anything to him.

"What?! Dys, you know who Nini is!" Calliope laughed, gliding over to Nagaveni gracefully. She draped an arm around Nagaveni's shoulders before speaking again. "However, I've got her wearing this concealment necklace, which we've been calling the Serpent Tamer, so the humans won't freak out. You know how humans are... They'd prefer to believe that Supernaturals don't exist," she finished with a hint of disgust in her voice and her lips slightly curled into a snarl.

"Nini?!" Dysnomi asked. He stood there looking amazed before regaining his composure. "Damn... I knew you were beautiful, but I can't believe I didn't even recognize you. The jet-black hair disguises you well." He paused to lift his eyebrow at Nagaveni. "And having a gorgeous woman like you here for Tartarus' opening night? I mean, your beauty alone will bring in half of Los Angeles. And Calli's siren song is gonna bring in the other half." With a theatrical flourish, he then conjured two purple and blue drinks into his hands. The drinks shimmered and sparkled, almost looking like a galaxy. "To a successful opening night?" He handed both of the Supernatural women a drink before conjuring another one for himself. "The alcohol's straight from the Fae Realm," he admitted, holding his drink toward the light and admiring it. "From a city called Ravenward. I just thought about what I wanted... Something that would make tonight special... And the drinks appeared. Honestly, I don't even know if it's true that you shouldn't answer any questions the Fae Folk ask you, but... I do know that I have a big mouth, and unfortunately..." He paused, patting down his pockets for dramatic effect. "I don't keep sugar on me just to throw it down to distract the Fae. I figured willing the drinks into existence would be better than traveling to the Fae Realm."

"What do you mean?" Nagaveni asked. "Throwing sugar down as a distraction?"

"Oh, the Fae have to stop whatever they're doing to count every single grain of sugar if it's spilled," Calliope answered. "They have to do that for salt as well."

"Every single grain?" Nagaveni asked, her mouth hanging open. Calliope nodded. "Wouldn't that take years?"

"Well, it depends on how much sugar or salt was spilled, I guess," Calliope said. "And how many Fae are around... But they live probably as long as you can, Nini. Years don't really feel like years to them." She shrugged then, turning to Dysnomi. "I'm disappointed in you, Dys. You really don't keep sugar in your pocket? You should be prepared for ANYTHING. ALL the time. ESPECIALLY when it comes to the Fae. Also.... couldn't you just... Conjure up some sugar if you needed it? Oh, well. Whatever. This drink looks like *Starry Night,*" she teased as she admired the swirling galaxy drink. *It does look fairly impressive,* she thought.

Nagaveni snorted, trying to hold back a laugh, and for the first time that night, she lifted her head. She looked confident despite having to keep her eyes averted to avoid accidentally turning anyone to stone. "I will try this drink you magicked up for us... IF you let me name it," she said to Dysnomi, staring at the drink like it was the greatest thing that she had ever seen.

"I don't know, Nini... Trusting a trickster seems like a pretty bad idea..." Calliope teased, trailing off with a sarcastic smile on her lips. Dysnomi contorted his face into an admittedly cute pout. She thought, *He's definitely practiced that pouty face before.*

"Come on, Calli..." Dysnomi said as he reached out and lifted Calliope's chin. He forced her to look up at him, already causing her to melt inside. In his peripheral vision, he watched as Nagaveni became wide-eyed. He and Nagaveni had not known each other long, so she must not have realized that he and Calliope were natural flirts, but it didn't mean that there was something between the two Supernaturals. *Although,* he thought. *It doesn't necessarily mean that there ISN"T something between us, either. Calliope's so gods-damn good at keeping up with me. She always has been, and I still can't figure out how the hell she does it.* He brushed his thumb over Calliope's chin, and asked her with a feigned sad voice, "You honestly don't trust me?"

Calliope smiled and stepped away from Dysnomi, not wanting to allow herself to feel anything more than friendship toward the trickster. She cleared her throat and averted her eyes. "Of course I trust you, Dys. Duh. I wouldn't be your friend if I didn't. It's not like I go around telling everyone who and... WHAT... I really am."

"Alright..." Dysnomi said with a suspicious tone. Then, he nodded at Nagaveni. "Hey new girl," he said. He crossed the floor of the balcony and leaned back against the side of one of the black-leather couches in the middle. "What'cha got for us?"

That damn smirk really does never leave his face, does it? Calliope thought. She could still see Dysnomi's smirk from the corner of her eye. She could also see Nagaveni smiling brighter as she sat in the chair next to Dysnomi. "Nini?" Calliope questioned, crossing the balcony to sit on the couch near Dysnomi and Nagaveni.

Nagaveni could see that Calliope also had a smirk on her face. It made her well-defined cheekbones stand out more. So much more, in fact, that when she crossed her legs, held her drink in one hand, and crossed that arm over her bare legs, Nagaveni couldn't help but to think that she looked like a supermodel. Nagaveni knew that she could look like a supermodel as well, if she wanted, but she had never gained that kind of confidence. She simply leaned back, stretching her legs before leaning forward again. Her emerald-green eyes were shining with excitement. "I propose a toast with our new liquid courage—and pray to all the gods that it's a good concoction so this won't be a satirical name—the Cosmic Paradise!" She lifted her glass, smiling.

"To the Cosmic Paradise! And to Tartarus' grand opening! You deserve this, Dys," Calliope said, lifting her drink into the middle with Nagaveni.

"To the Cosmic Paradise... And to Nini for finally loosening up a bit," Dysnomi said. He winked at Nagaveni then, just so he could watch her blush. "Also... To Calli, because I know your voice is gonna have everyone in this club begging you for more when you get on the stage." He met Calliope's eyes with a smile that set her on edge as he lifted his drink and tapped his glass against hers and Nagaveni's.

The three Supernaturals threw their heads back, chugging their galaxy-inspired drinks. Then, they all slammed their empty glasses onto the table in the middle.

Tartarus was entirely full by then. It had been a vast sea of humans and Supernaturals dancing and having fun in almost every space that the new LA nightclub had to offer.

"Hey, Calliope, someone just dropped off some kinda weird note for you...?" Dysnomi said, noticing the name that had been written on the outside of the note. He walked over to pick the paper up from where someone had left it at the balcony door.

When Calliope crossed over and accepted the paper from Dysnomi, she said, "Well... Let's read it then, shall we?" She waved Nagaveni over to her and Dysnomi, then read aloud,

"Word of advice: Viking parties get outrageous, so don't go to one if you aren't ready for things to get wild. We know you can handle it though, so go raise hell as an honorary Berserker. And get ready for your present, Calliope. She's dying to meet you."

"Well, that... Certainly...?" Calliope trailed off. She was extremely confused. Then, she heard something happening inside the club, and said, "Wait, it sounds like some commotion coming from the main room." She was about to ask either Dysnomi or Nagaveni to brave the crowds with her when sudden shouts and grunts came from across the floor toward the balcony, then soon followed by a loud bird screech.

"What the fuck?!" a random man in the club yelled. The man then turned and ran away. Calliope watched as people in the crowd were carelessly tossed to the side, but it was impossible for her to see what was shoving its way through them. The only thing that she could see was a humongous red and orange bird, which was flying overhead, aiming straight toward her, Nagaveni, and Dysnomi.

"Wait, do you two know ACTUAL Vikings?" Nagaveni asked, her mouth hanging open.

"Yeah, Dys has taken me to some pretty insane parties in the two years that I've known him. And you've only been here for... What? Three months now? You just wait—I'm sure we'll get into something together," Calliope answered.

When Calliope was finally able to check the area again, she inspected the humans who had been shoved aside. She noted that most of them appeared to be confused—like they hadn't actually seen anyone or anything move them. But it couldn't be who she thought it was... Could it?

3. ...OR THE KING OF CHAOS?

(THE HELLHOUND AND THE PHOENIX)

Calliope's mouth hung open and she turned to Dysnomi, asking, "Is that...?" She pointed to a corner, where a huge pitch-black mass was bounding toward them, crossing the dance floor with incredible speed. The giant figure was so dark that it made her think of a black hole. "My gods, it is her! I can't believe she's here!" she squealed. The siren continued rambling while preparing herself to catch what she knew was a giant beast running toward her. "You'll love her, Nini, I swear. I'm not too sure how *Hissy Elliot* and *Lady Hiss-A-Lot* will react though, so maybe keep the Serpent Tamer on." Calliope turned toward the balcony door and stretched her arms open.

Before Nagaveni could even ask what the siren had meant about her snakes, the most massive wolf ever seen jumped into Calliope's waiting arms. With its obsidian-black fur and scarlet-red eyes, the wolf was a menacing sight to behold, but it proved to be a gentle creature... After it knocked Calliope down on her ass and assaulted her with kisses.

Meanwhile, the red and orange bird, which turned out to be a phoenix, watched Calliope play with the wolf after landing on the back of a chair. The phoenix kept its head tilted to one side like it was curious as it watched.

Calliope picked herself up from the balcony floor with a laugh, scratching behind the wolf's ears before crossing the floor to greet the phoenix.

When Calliope pulled her hand away from the wolf's fur, Nagaveni noticed that it was slick with blood. There were small cuts on every part of Calliope that the siren had used to pet the wolf. "Calli, oh my gods, are you okay?" Nagaveni asked as she ran over to inspect Calliope's wounds. She noticed that the siren's smaller wounds had already started healing, and that gave her a bit of relief.

"What?" Calliope asked, looking at her hands. "Oh. Yeah. Nanuk is a hellhound. She's really friendly, but you gotta be willing to pay the price if you wanna pet her... And the price is... A thousand papercuts?" she said, laughing. "But that's kinda how everything goes in the Demon Realm." She shrugged. "I got Nanuk from an ex boyfriend before we broke up three years ago. It's a little bittersweet, but I wouldn't trade her for anything."

"Does it hurt to pet her?" Nagaveni asked.

"Nah, not really," Calliope answered. "I mean, it might hurt the way a scratch from a cat would hurt, or the same way that getting a ton of paper cuts at once would, but I think it's worth it. Plus, it's nothing I can't handle."

"Here Nini, gimme your hands. We can pet her together," Dysnomi said, stepping forward and offering his hands to Nagaveni. She hesitated, looking at Calliope for guidance. Calliope simply nodded, so Nagaveni placed her hands in Dysnomi's as Calliope turned her attention toward the phoenix.

Calliope sucked in a sharp breath as she approached the phoenix, unsure of what to say or do. *Phoenixes aren't supposed to exist anymore! ...But if the legend's true, they're highly intelligent,* she thought. The siren awkwardly attempted to bow, which was the most formal greeting that she could think of. Then, she stammered out, "Forgive me... I'm not sure how I'm supposed to greet a phoenix. No one's heard of one being alive for a long time... Most people believe you're extinct... I don't know if the legend's true, but if it is, I'm hoping that means you can understand me...?"

The phoenix only stared at Calliope with its head tilted. Its gaze studied the siren before the phoenix nodded its head at her—a sign of respect. Then, a heavenly female voice spoke inside of her mind. Calliope gasped and stared in awe. "Do not apologize, child. I would not expect you to know the ways of a world that no longer exists. You must have questions... I shall try my best to answer them... And to guide you on your journey forward, if I can," the phoenix said.

"Yes, I do have a few questions, actually..." Calliope said. "First, how did the berserkers even find you? And... Why did they send you to me?" Nagaveni and Dysnomi walked up beside her then, both Supernaturals giving her a questioning glance. Nanuk came over as well, bowing her head politely before wandering off. The siren prompted her friends to bow to the phoenix before introducing them. "Oh, but I don't think I got your name," she said to the phoenix.

Calliope's Supernatural friends gave her questioning glances again. Then, the phoenix's voice telepathically called out to all of them. "You may call me Wrath. To answer your question, the berserkers did not send me. I chose to come because I can feel that you have strong powers within you. You are not an ordinary siren—you have much more inside of you. First, the spirit of a phoenix inside of you called to me. She calls herself Ember, and she is very strong. She will appear at times when you are angry and when you need justice or want vengeance. As long as she resides in you, you will not be hurt by any flames. However, there is another voice inside of you, as well. The second voice to call to me is the spirit of a thunderbird named Lyn. I believe that one of the Norse gods has already tried to test her abilities."

"So that's why Thor struck me with lightning?! I just thought he was being a dick!" Calliope exclaimed. Thunder rumbled in the sky above her, prompting her to quickly look up and follow her previous sentence with, "Oh, shit. I'm sorry, Mr.Odinson! Please don't hit me again!"

"He has never been the best at explaining his processes," Wrath said with a laugh. "I can tell that Lyn is strong, though. Your connections with others... What you might call 'the sparks' that you feel between you and another—those are the feelings that make the lightning strong. Beware, however, as the lightning can be stronger if you are in pain... And it can become excruciating if you are not used to it. Moving forward, the last voice I hear is a siren—which is you, of course—and you have your telepathy, levitation, rapid healing, and sonic shriek. Your sonic shriek is your strongest defense. It can rival a banshee's screech in power. It also has the potential to level buildings, to reach pitches high enough to paralyze humans—and certain Supernaturals—momentarily. It can also be loud enough to blow out one's ears," Wrath added. "That kind of power should not be used unless necessary, but I understand that it can be hard to control. And with all of these abilities, they have the possibility of creating mayhem. The phoenix and the thunderbird spirits only show themselves to powerful Supernaturals. It is rare for a Supernatural to have one of these spirits inside of them. But to have both spirits? It has only been heard of one time before you... Which leads me to believe that your abilities are far beyond what you have discovered... Now, do not take this the wrong way, child, but do you know both of your parents? ...Are you certain of who they are?" the phoenix asked.

"My mother is a siren, like me, but I've never met my father. Mom wouldn't talk about him. She insisted it was because he wasn't 'worth' talking about," Calliope answered. "And I guess I never thought more about it. But... Why would these powers only appear NOW? I've been alive for

118 years and have never noticed them." Her eyebrows furrowed as she tried to understand.

"Perhaps you need to hear the spirits and to use the powers now more than you ever have before," Wrath offered in response.

"Maybe... Anyway, thank you, Wrath, for helping me understand all that," Calliope said as she shared a worried look with her friends.

"It was my pleasure, child. I would like to help you guide yourself through your new powers, if I can... Oh, but I do believe that there was still one question that you sought the answer to, was there not?" Wrath asked.

"Oh, was there? I, um..." Calliope said, stuttering as she tried to think. However, she couldn't remember what her last question had been... Not after Wrath had given her so much to think about.

"Oh! Yes, I remember now—you asked how I came to live alongside the berserkers," Wrath said. The phoenix's voice sounded like she was thinking back to a fond memory.

"Sorry, but what's a berserker...?" Nagaveni asked, raising her hand above her head like a schoolgirl.

"The Vikings we told you about," Dysnomi answered. "Unfortunately, I don't know much about them... Other than a handful of stories that THEY told us during their last party."

"In human history, they're remembered as being the strongest of Vikings. They're depicted as warriors who took drugs on the battlefield, stripped naked—with only a bearskin covering them—then charged head-first into the battle, cutting their enemies down with two-handed axes. But in reality? They're literally just werebears," Calliope said, laughing when she noticed Nagaveni's dropped jaw.

"That is correct," Wrath replied, sounding surprised. "It was a very long time ago, but I do remember that there was a man who was in trouble. He needed help. The berserkers did not like the man, however. Váli, the leader, did not believe that phoenixes existed, so he told the man, *'Bring me a phoenix and we will help you.'* Everyone laughed at the man, but he returned three days later with me in tow. Váli had no choice but to keep his word. I have been with them ever since," she said. Calliope heard the fondness of Wrath's memory in the phoenix's tone.

"And... THAT is why you don't jinx yourself," Nagaveni said jokingly. The whole group laughed then, including Wrath.

4. THANKS FOR THE MEMORIES

(DIRTY LITTLE SECRET)

A while later, after checking the time, the small group parted ways to enjoy the rest of their night.

Wrath was the first to leave the group, stretching her long wings and flapping them a few times before flying over the balcony railing and into the sky.

Only a few moments later, Nagaveni slipped back into the upper floor of Tartarus as quietly as a thief in the night, silently closing the balcony door behind her. She then wandered through the crowd, hoping to make a few new friends.

After talking with Dysnomi for what felt like forever, Calliope stood and stretched. She began to walk toward the door, swaying her hips as she slid her hand along the side of her neck. She then slowly traced a line down her bare cappuccino-colored skin at the opening of her dress' deep V-neck. It wasn't until Dysnomi was hooked on her every move that the siren realized what she had started. Feeling embarrassed, she made an abrupt turn and began walking toward the door, leaving him behind with nothing but a quick, nervous glance at him over her shoulder.

Dysnomi stared at Calliope's retreating form, longing to touch her. She may have only given him a quick glance as she walked toward the door, but he noticed the small way that her eyes lit up when she realized that he was staring at her. He had spent two years holding himself back, not wanting to ruin their friendship, but he couldn't stop himself at that moment. He grabbed her wrist, pulling her into him. He placed his hand against her cheek as he turned her to face him, and pressed a gentle, lingering kiss against her luscious full lips. "...Stay?" he asked her, sounding hopeful. "...Just for a while?" His voice was soft, sweet, and quiet. At that moment, he sounded vulnerable for what was possibly the first time since they met.

Instead of answering, Calliope simply reached up, placing a hand on the back of Dysnomi's head and twisting his hair through her fingers. Then, she pulled his head down until his lips met hers. They kissed slowly and sweetly at first, giving her the feeling of butterflies in her stomach.

Dysnomi slid his arm around Calliope's slim waist, pulling her into his taut chest. She let out a small gasp, the sound of which was swallowed with a deep, passionate kiss. He let his guard down then, which allowed his emotions to invade her mind. She felt how starved he had been for her, how badly he had been wanting her. She felt that he cared about her, as well... However, she also felt that he had accepted that he was going to have to let her go.

That's strange, Calliope thought.

Most of Dysnomi's emotions were not strong, so Calliope could not tell what a lot of them were. She could only fully make out a small feeling of guilt—*Or maybe it's regret?* she thought—along with a feeling of loss. Most of all, though, she felt his desire. It was intense, overtaking all of his other emotions... Like he needed her at that moment in order to feel alive.

Calliope kissed Dysnomi again, one hand still tangled in his hair while her other hand trailed a line down his chest with a manicured turquoise nail, soliciting a low, rumbling growl from deep in his throat.

Dysnomi grabbed Calliope's petite waist tighter with one hand. Then, he used his other hand to grab her face as he parted her lips with his tongue, deepening the kiss. It made her knees go weak then, so he held her up, supporting her weight.

Calliope felt her way down Dysnomi's shirt, working each of the buttons open, her intentions clear, before helping him slide the shirt to the floor. Then, she stepped back to admire his taut muscles. She flashed him a mischievous smile as she reached her hand out to touch him again, but Dysnomi grabbed her hand before she could, holding it away from his bare chest. He returned her playful smile, and before she knew what was happening, he had seized her by the waist and was walking her backward toward a small office behind the bar.

Once inside the office, Dysnomi kicked the door closed before slamming Calliope against it. She allowed herself to moan out his name when her entire body was suddenly aching for more. "Please, Dys," she whined, begging him to take her.

"Beg some more for me," Dysnomi said smugly. He pulled away from Calliope, but only far enough for him to flash her his usual cocky smirk.

"Dys... Please... I need you," Calliope whined, her tone raising slightly. Dysnomi responded immediately that time, roughly turning her around and slamming her chest-first into the door. He pinned her against it with her hands pressed down hard against the wood on either side of her head. He leaned down to kiss her neck as he fiddled with his belt buckle and the button on his jeans. He was listening to the way that she moaned for him, each sound of hers causing his hard length to throb against the back of her warm thighs. He quickly pulled her dress up to her waist, feeling like he was going to burst from simply needing so badly to feel her. He ran his hand across her perfectly round ass before giving one cheek a loud, stinging slap, groaning with desire as he watched it jiggle. Calliope cried out, sounding like she was feeling a mix of pain and pleasure. He pressed his body into hers then, teasing her with the tip of his member as she writhed between him and the door. He felt slightly amused at the sight when she begged him again, whimpering out, "Please, Dys. I need you... Oh, gods. I need you now..."

"You know, if you just wanted me to fuck you, you didn't need to work so hard for it. All those sexy outfits, the flirting, the teasing... I'd have eagerly obliged at any moment if you had just asked me, Calli," Dysnomi whispered into Calliope's ear, his breath tickling her neck and causing her to shiver in anticipation. He kissed a line down her neck, ending with a sharp, painful bite that made her cry out once again—louder. He took one hand and ran it down the curve of her back, making her shiver a second time. Then, he grabbed hold of her hip. His other hand was tangled in her hair, and he pulled on it. He felt a deep satisfaction inside himself when he heard how eager she was for more of him. He then thrust his throbbing member inside of her, finally achieving what he had been dreaming of doing to her since the first day that they met...

5. AMERICAN NIGHTMARE

(THE CAMBION AND THE THUNDERBIRD)

After driving Calliope into the door of that tiny office for almost an hour, Dysnomi finally broke away with one last, lingering kiss. He felt like he was certain that he would never get to see her again. She could remember the emotions that he had felt, which had flooded her mind earlier that day—the way that he cared about her, yet was content with letting her go...

He must know something that I don't... Calliope thought. *I just wish I knew what it was. It seems like he's trying really hard to keep it down.*

After the two Supernaturals smoothed their clothes and fixed their hair, Calliope leaned against the desk, trying to find something to say so she did not feel awkward.

But he's probably done this with plenty of women since I've known him, Calliope thought. *I mean, the human women alone fawn all over him and* his... 'magic tricks'. And there's no telling how many Supernaturals he's been with, either.

'Magic tricks... Those are the most disrespectful words for power as great as the one that he possesses,' a voice, which Calliope guessed was the phoenix, said inside her mind.

I know, Ember, but that's what the humans think his powers are—nothing but magic tricks, Calliope thought in response.

The only thing that came out of Calliope's parched mouth when she tried to speak to Dysnomi was, "We're... Friends. We can't..." Then, she looked away, feeling annoyed with herself. She glanced at him, then away again, hoping that he wouldn't notice. He did, though.

"I just want you to know, Calli... I've never used my powers on you. I mean... I wanted to," Dysnomi admitted. Then, he laughed, sounding like Calliope's friend again. "Believe me, I fucking wanted to. And it wasn't even about wanting to hook up with you. Though, I'd be a liar if I said I HAVEN'T wanted to do that since Day One. It was just... Well... I wanted you to like me, even if it was only a little bit. You seemed like you couldn't fucking stand me when we first met and it just made me want to impress you even more." He was pacing across the small room then, stopping to run a hand through his hair. Calliope could only think that she wanted to be the one running her hands through his hair and feeling his golden locks slipping between her fingers as easily as silk.

"You look so much like *Alucard* right now. The *Castlevania* version, obviously," Calliope said jokingly, managing to solicit a shallow laugh from Dysnomi. "I like it," she continued. "And, for the record, I DID like you when we first met. But what I really wanted was for you to stop trying so HARD to impress me. I just wanted you to get to know the real me, and I wanted to get to know the real you. Your abilities—as amazing as they are—have NEVER been what's impressed me, Dys. But YOU impress me because you're amazing. You're funny, cunning, and... Surprisingly caring for someone who's always pretending to be an asshole."

Dysnomi laughed and shook his head then. Just like that, he was back to just being Calliope's friend. He tilted his head to one side, giving her a long, scrutinizing look. "So... I look like the *Castlevania* version of *Alucard,* huh?" he asked. Calliope nodded in response. Dysnomi seemed to be debating with himself about something. He hesitated at first, but he then smirked, making up his mind. The air seemed to glimmer around him, the light dancing within it, rainbow colors blocking

Calliope's view... After a moment, however, she heard, "So... You have a thing for guys with long blond hair and pale skin?"

His voice sounds different, Calliope thought. She squinted her eyes, attempting to see what image Dysnomi was projecting. "...Whoa, that's amazing, Dys! It's the perfect *Alucard* mirage!" Calliope gasped. Then, she said, "And to answer your question, I'll just let you take a guess at who my favorite *Lord of the Rings* character is."

Dysnomi laughed and said, "I should've known. But, I'm glad you enjoy it. Unfortunately, we better get back in there." He nodded once toward the door, and after a moment of hesitation, he transformed into himself. He then led Calliope toward the door, flashing her his signature smirk. "Nanuk's gonna kill me for stealing you away for so long. For the record though, I am absolutely NOT sorry." He looked at her, smiling, and winked.

Calliope blushed and looked away, suddenly overcome with a feeling of guilt. "I... I don't wanna hurt you, Dys. I mean, you know what I am... You know I unintentionally make people like me, but if someone feels strong enough emotions around me, it sorta... Feeds me... Gives me energy... And... If I don't distance myself, I could accidentally absorb too much. I mean, that could leave someone catatonic, like a lobotomite... Or... It could leave them stripped of all emotion, like a sociopath... I'm not really sure if this sort of emotional manipulation even works on other Supernaturals, but if they do... I just... I don't wanna be responsible for anything happening to you," she said.

Dysnomi looked at Calliope when she said that, raising an eyebrow at her. Then, he threw his head back and howled with laughter.

"Are you really laughing at me?! Why is that even funny to you? Do you care that little about your own health?" Calliope asked.

"Calli... You have no idea how old I am... OR how powerful I've become over the years," Dysnomi said as he laughed again—harder—like Calliope was nothing more than a child who didn't understand anything about the world. "Oh, you poor, adorably sweet, young woman." She cut her eyes in his direction as a warning, but he, of course, ignored her. "I'm a trickster, Calli. You can't take ANYTHING from me. All of reality is MINE. I can create literally anything, and I can even CHANGE reality itself. You don't have anything to worry about. But, wait..." He gently grabbed her arm, showing her until they were both standing still. "I think it's the perfect moment to give you this," he said, holding a hand out in front of himself. A rainbow of lights swirled around his hand, curling around it like they each had a mind of their own. The lights were all turning over each other before twisting and bending, seemingly helping one another to create some kind of object.

"Looks like Dys rolled out the red carpet for us, securing his place as the king of partying...? Or as the king of chaos for his dramatic grand entrance?" Calliope heard her own voice echo inside of her mind, reminding her what she said about Dysnomi earlier that very night.

"Is that... A dagger?!" Calliope exclaimed. She took it from Dysnomi with gentle hands. It shone a glorious golden light and was warm to the touch. The hilt of the ornate dagger was obsidian-black with gold swirls all around it. "It's gorgeous, Dys," she said.

"It's a gift... For you," Dysnomi whispered, sounding sad. He pressed the dagger into Calliope's hands gently but firmly, closing her fingers around the hilt. "Let this Blade of Light protect you... *'my exuberant flower,'*" he said in a fake Transylvanian accent as he imitated *Dracula*. "You might need it."

Calliope mock-gasped, putting a hand over her mouth in an exaggerated display of shock before laughing, causing Dysnomi to laugh with her. Somehow, though, she still felt in her gut that there was something he was keeping from her. She did feel a bit safer holding the Blade of Light, however.

"Anyway, Nini must be worried sick by now," Dysnomi said, shaking his head. "I don't wanna make her wait on us uncomfortably, or make her more upset than the fight had to..." He stopped, shook his head like he was confused, then continued normally. "Besides, I know for a fact that there is not one more person who deserves to see your beautiful face before you appear on-stage."

At first, Calliope's eyes lit up with a playful gleam as they walked through the crowds of Tartarus together—practically having to shove people away—toward a booth in the far corner, where they could just barely make out Nagaveni. The gorgon was sitting with Nanuk, petting the hellhound behind the ears while nursing another drink.

"Okay, okay..." Calliope said light-heartedly. "BUT.. How dare you use *Dracula* like that." She half-laughed then. "He might be over-eccentric... and EXTREMELY theatrical like... *Phantom of the Opera* style... But getting absolutely fucking RAILED by a vampire...? On the CEILING...?! That was so much fun! Secondly..."

Dysnomi was still watching the club lights dancing inside of Calliope's eyes when she talked. He was transfixed by the way that her iris-purple eyes would shine when she was happy, almost seeming to glow. But he soon realized that she was no longer happy at all.

"...Wait," Calliope said, slowing her walking pace. She gave Dysnomi a suspicious glance. "Let's not pretend I didn't notice the way you worded that... Trickster."

Shit. She got me laughing and feeling comfortable just so she could get me to talk. Damn, she's good, Dysnomi thought, half-panicking. He composed himself, but he had been hoping before that Calliope would get out of there and go home before anything happened. He wasn't sure what was going to happen, but he knew of two people who were looking for her—one with bad intentions—and he had a sinking feeling that he might not see her again. "What do you mean... Siren?" he asked, trying to sound nonchalant.

"You said you would hate to keep Nini waiting... That you'd hate to make her more upset then *'the fight',* but we haven't even been in a fight, so why would she be upset about one?" Calliope asked.

Damn. She is good, Dysnomi thought.

"Okay, I feel like you owe me SOME answers. You said that you know for a fact that *'there is not one more person'* who deserves to see my *'beautiful face'* before I appear on-stage," Calliope said. Then, she cast Dysnomi a knowing look. "AND you created a dagger for me... This... Blade of Light." She pat her thigh, where she had strapped the dagger. "Dys, you're scaring me. Please... Tell me... If there's a person who does not deserve to see my face... Well..." She knew the answer before the question ever came out of her mouth. His face told her everything, and it hit her like a 100 pound weight.

Dysnomi's normally arrogant face faltered when he looked at Calliope again. His eyes were glistening, and his voice cracked when he said, "I've done all I can. I'm sorry, but you're on your own for this one."

Before Dysnomi could duck through the dense crowd, Calliope pulled him into her, wrapping him in a tight, miserable hug before releasing him, then watching as he disappeared into the sea of dancing people.

What the fuck am I supposed to do now? Calliope thought while trying to push her way through the dense crowd, attempting to remain calm. The more she tried to find an open space in the floor without using her powers, the more she got jostled around like a ragdoll. She could feel strong emotions rolling off of a man somewhere in the crowd—an incredibly angry man. She couldn't see who the angry man was, however, because it was too hard to pick out any singular person and their emotions under the club lights, especially when the crowds were that size.

'Just levitate above everyone and leave!' Ember yelled.

No... I can't do that... It would draw too much attention, Calliope thought.

Calliope was still attempting to push her way through the crowd when a drunk man suddenly stumbled and rammed into her from behind, causing her to lurch forward, careening to catch her balance. She didn't fall at first. But she then felt a sudden, sharp jab in her ribs. It felt like someone had elbowed her, but she didn't have time to look—she was getting pushed around by the throng of party people once again.

Calliope doubled over, clutching her side and trying not to show any fear. She pushed her way through a few more drunk human men, ripping her wrist away from one, who—she assumed—had been attempting to flirt. Then, she felt someone slam into her yet again, throwing her directly into the chest of another man who had been standing nearby.

"Oh! I'm so sorry!" Calliope cried out to the man, placing a hand against his chest and gently pushing herself off of him as he helped steady her, his hands holding onto her shoulders. She felt the angry man becoming momentarily jealous, though she still didn't know who, or where, the angry man was. The emotions of the man that she bumped into suddenly washed over her like a tsunami as she searched for the angry man in the crowd. There was a bit of anger, but not enough... There was also misery, regret, and a small, sudden bout of panic as he looked down at her.

Intrigued by all of the conflicting emotions that were coming from the man standing in front of Calliope, she craned her head up to get a good look at him. He was tall and tan with a chiseled jawline, high cheekbones, and broad shoulders. He glanced down at her in a panic, then looked away just as quickly when his ink-black eyes met her iris-purple ones. Then, guilt began eating away at him.

Wait, I know this guy... Calliope thought. She was still trying to think of HOW exactly she knew him, while still feeling his emotions. Before long, however, the other man's seething rage was close behind her, threatening to take over all of her senses.

'He's getting close!' the spirit of the thunderbird yelled.

I know, Lyn. It'll be okay, Calliope thought. But right after she said it, she realized exactly who the man standing in front of her was. *Oh no... This is Amadeo! He's a DEMON. Fuck, not the demons... Fuck my life. Well, I guess that's it. I'm dead.*

Impending doom hit Calliope at that moment, crashing down on her entire reality as she finally realized who the man behind her was. *Of course,* she thought. *The literal Prince of Demons—Asmodeus—has finally come to deal with me after three years. I mean, he's the one who hates me the most, so I guess it makes sense. Fuck.*

"What the fuck do you think you're doing?" Amadeo asked. He was attempting to sound calm while staring over Calliope's shoulder at Asmodeus.

"Please, Amadeo... Don't believe her lies. Just... Don't believe HER. I'm sorry, man... You're like a brother to me, but she's been fucking with my head! Everything just gets so... Fucking SCRAMBLED every time she's around! They SAID I need to take care of her! They SAID that she's a problem and that I'd feel normal again when she's gone!" Asmodeus' voice sounded uncomfortably close to Calliope, and it became uncomfortably closer with every step that she heard him take. The anger was radiating off of him in heat waves, filling her to her core with dread.

    A blunt object suddenly slammed into the back of Calliope's head, the force sending her stumbling forward on shaky legs as her vision blurred. At that moment, however, she was mainly worried about what would happen to Amadeo due to him attempting to stop Asmodeus. She only knew that he would have to fight for his life... *And it'll probably be Menoetius that he'll have to fight,* she thought. Menoetius was objectively the worst of all of the demons. He definitely did not fight fair. In fact, he was far more likely to have his friends jump someone if he suspected that he might lose a fight—although he seldom lost—and he would do anything to ensure that his fights always ended with the opponent's death.

    A searing, white-hot pain ignited in the back of Calliope's head and tore through her skull before moving down to her jaw. Lightning began shooting through her body as the pain became almost indescribable. It was so incredibly painful that she couldn't stop herself when she eventually let out an ear-piercing shriek. It was an invasive, harrowing sound, the ethereal scream used enough energy to exhaust her. She could barely even process what she was seeing when the pain took hold of her again. Everyone involved Tartarus was holding their ears and abandoning the club and the building itself was shaking, glasses of alcohol falling off of the shelves and shattering on the floor while pieces of the building crumbled around her... Amadeo fell to the floor after being struck by Asmodeus. His thick, shaggy spider-black hair... *Looks wet or... Bloody, maybe?* Calliope thought. Her conscious thoughts came in and out then. She was worrying about Amadeo, thinking that he shouldn't have stood up for her, thinking, *He's barely conscious, if not dead... There's blood coming out of his ears...*

    Sparks of lightning shot out of Calliope again, darting wildly around her head and flashing out through her eyes while she screamed—the bolts hitting randomly in a small area around her until they fizzled and died. She swayed on her heels, subconsciously taking a step forward as the phoenix spirit, Ember, sought vengeance against

Asmodeus. However, she was too exhausted and she fell on her knees next to Amadeo's unconscious form. She was too weak to fight the demon prince. Her screams slowly died on her lips and her pain overtook everything else.

There was a dreadful darkness creeping in through the edges of Calliope's vision and an ocean of exhaustion seeping into her muscles.

Just as the darkness began overwhelming Calliope, she noticed a flash of red and orange swooping in—fire flying in a high arc—before the phoenix, Wrath, landed on her lap, warming her and giving her extra strength to fight her overwhelming exhaustion. *Thank you, Wrath,* she thought.

Suddenly, the loudest thunderclap that Calliope had ever heard came booming from outside of Tartarus. It was deafening, shaking the entire club. She jerked up, surprised, then watched the terrified look on Asmodeus' face as the biggest onyx-black bird ever seen stormed inside—lightning zipping around its wings as it flew—and landed next to her, tilting its head and looking at her curiously.

"This is the thunderbird, Thora," Wrath told Calliope as her vision started to darken again. "She is a gift... From Thor."

6. THE MAN WHO WOULD BE KING

(THE POINT OF NO RETURN)

"Stay awake, Calliope. Come on. Push yourself up. Stay awake," Wrath encouraged, but Calliope still felt herself slipping away. The energy used by her sonic shriek, along with the energy that the lightning used, left her feeling exhausted. She felt helpless as she could only watch in defeat. She could see Asmodeus beginning to stand, casually using a napkin to wipe blood out of his ears.

Wrath spread her giant wings—spanning seven feet from the end of one to the end of the other—in front of Calliope protectively. Her wings ignited, creating a wall of fire between Calliope and Asmodeus.

To Calliope's surprise, however, Asmodeus leaned down, allowing the warmth to sweep over him and the lights to dance across his face. Then, he laughed, his cruel, mocking tone snapping her out of her trance.

"Really? Did you expect me to be afraid of a little fire? I am the Prince of Demons," Asmodeus explained, before ranting—half in English and half in Spanish. "Fire doesn't hurt me," he said. He then disappeared in the blink of an eye, reappearing behind Calliope and reaching around to grab her throat before she, Thora, or Wrath had time to react.

Asmodeus squeezed Calliope's throat, easily cutting off her airflow. He then jerked her up so they were face-to-face, levitating.

A show of dominance, maybe? Calliope thought.

The thunderbird, Thora, stepped forward then. The massive *'dinosaur'* made a low rumbling sound from deep inside of her chest, bellowing like an alligator and tapping one of her long, sharp kill-talons on the floor. Lightning began to dance off of her wings as thunder shook the nightclub.

Asmodeus jerked when a bolt of lightning hit him, traveling through both him and Calliope. He threw her into a wall and he teleported, moving away from the second bolt, which barely missed hitting Calliope as she fell to the floor.

Asmodeus teleported back to Calliope, grabbing her throat once more and sliding her up against the wall. "The lightning hurts you, too. Call them off," he commanded. She grunted her defiance, but her vision was fading and she struggled to breathe with his hand wrapped around her throat. "Call them off!" he yelled, pulling her toward him, then slamming her back into the wall hard enough that part of it crumbled down around her.

"The lightning... Doesn't hurt me... I'm strong... I can take it..." Calliope said between gasping breaths. Technically, that was a lie, but Asmodeus didn't know that and she didn't want to let him off easily.

"Call them both off now or I'll kill you," Asmodeus growled. "You say it doesn't hurt, but I've seen your pain... I will NOT repeat myself again, *puta pequeña...*[1] Call. Them. Off. Now."

Calliope was barely conscious, but she was able to clear her mind and focus enough for her to speak to her fierce feathered protectors telepathically. *Wrath... Thora... Thank you, but you've gotta go... This battle's mine,* she thought. *Thor warned me that my choices would have serious consequences. This must be what he meant. Go now.*

Thora looked at Calliope with her head tilted to one side, but her storm died down. Wrath nodded once, allowing her flames to turn to ash. Then, the birds flew out the same way that they

---

[1] "little whore..."

had come in, leaving her to deal with Asmodeus by herself.

Just as Calliope's vision began to fade completely... Just as true panic set in and her hands flew to her attacker's wrists—scratching viciously at them as she attempted to pry Asmodeus' strong hands away from her throat—he dropped her, letting her body crumple in a heap on the floor.

Calliope struggled internally when she looked up at Asmodeus then, thinking of how attracted to him she still was. Despite him beating her, she wanted nothing more than to kiss him. That disgusted her, but she also wondered if she could use it to help her situation.

Calliope barely managed to push herself into a sitting position, leaning heavily against the wall. Her legs were shaking violently from even the smallest movements.

Asmodeus squatted in front of Calliope and released a short, bitter laugh. Then, his gaze softened and he reached his big, hazelnut-colored hand out to stroke her cappuccino-colored skin at her cheek. He almost looked sorry for his abuse.

Calliope flinched away, terrified as Asmodeus' fingers brushed against her, and whimpered quietly. Asmodeus appeared hurt by that. She could feel how he hurt, along with another emotion, which she quickly realized was the way that he had been longing for her body, needing her... Unfortunately, she could also feel the way that he hated her for being his weakness.

In an instant, Asmodeus' lust for her was gone. It had been replaced with a deep rage that felt so terrifying, Calliope was afraid to look at him while he felt that way. Yet, she forced herself to peek up at his face from underneath her long lashes.

He's still so hot, Calliope thought. Asmodeus had long off-black hair, electric-blue eyes that almost seemed more unnatural than the nightmarish ink-black that they were when he was angry, and flawless hazelnut skin that was accentuated by his pouty lips, high cheekbones, and sharply arched eyebrows—one that had a thick scar cutting through it and down over his eyelid, ending right underneath his eye. *I remember that scar,* Calliope thought. *He had a party one night. Menoetius tried to hit on me, and he grabbed me and hurt me when I turned him down. Then, he tried to force himself on me. Asmodeus caught him, pulled him off me, and started beating him... But his half-brother pulled a knife on him.* She stared up at Asmodeus' eyes, remembering the way that he used to basically hypnotize her with his piercing stare and the way that she would get lost in the ocean waves on the inside of his eyes. She sat there, leaning against the wall, her whole body aching. She searched the storm inside of him for some kind of answer, watching in fear as his eyes began to darken...

Remembering Asmodeus' feelings for her, Calliope tried to take advantage of his emotions for a few moments, breathing in to try and heal herself. Anger didn't work very well for healing, however.

Calliope opened her mind and allowed Asmodeus to feel everything that she was feeling. She sent him the longing that she had felt for his presence in the years that they had been apart. She also sent him the terror, which was mixed with the excitement, of all the possibilities now that they were reunited... Suddenly, she closed her mind, cruelly blocking him out of it when her emotions became too painful for her.

Asmodeus jerked back like Calliope had slapped him when their mental connection was broken. He appeared to be sad at first, but his face soon contorted into a dark, murderous rage. As his mood changed, so did his eyes. They became darker and darker, until both were terrifyingly ink-black.

"Finally! The demon comes out to play," Calliope sang, then laughed. "Asmodeus wasn't even REALLY trying to hurt me, was he? He'll leave that to you. Well... I can't wait to see what YOU do, demon."

"I don't know who the FUCK you think you are, or what you fucking did to me, but I will not entertain your drama! ¡*Maldita perra!*"[2] Asmodeus hissed—though, the demon's voice was the one that came out—through his clenched jaw, a vicious snarl on his face. "I used to feel nothing for anyone. I was SMART and a damn good ruler. Then, you came along. I started... FEELING things. I CARED about you. I... LOVED... You. And the moment that you saw THIS side, you left me. You ruined everything!"

"You and your pathetic demons were hurting people I cared about, destroying their lives for fun. I couldn't be a part of that. And you know what? It fucking SUCKED! I wanted so much BETTER for you. Even with the knowledge that you're a cambion AND the LITERAL Prince of Demons, I cared about you so FUCKING much," Calliope argued. She forced a shaky arm up to

---

[2] "Fucking bitch!"

brush her fingers delicately along Asmodeus' hazelnut-colored skin. She caught him admiring the way that her small hand with her manicured turquoise nails looked as it glided along his chiseled jaw. She could feel his muscles tense underneath her. He was expecting her to slap him, or to do something else cruel—it's what he would do, after all... But she wouldn't. He shuddered at her touch, his desire flaring to life inside him once more.

  However, Asmodeus stopped himself, grabbing Calliope's hand and yanking it roughly away from him. He held it tight enough that she had no choice but to watch as her skin almost instantly began bruising underneath his fingers. She could feel her bones in her hand crunching as he squeezed even tighter. When he finally released her hand, it dropped to her side like a dead weight. She tried to lift it, but the pain was too much. She could lift it just far enough to see that it was bruised badly—dark shades of purple, blue, and black all over.

  Great, he broke it, Calliope pouted, her lip quivering... Although, she had already guessed that it was broken before looking at it. Then, Asmodeus leaned into her, one hand coming up to stroke her cheek while his other hand slid up from her knee until it rested on her plump, round thigh.

Calliope pulled in a shaky breath, both scared and excited by his touch. Asmodeus leaned in, his lips ghosting over hers as he moved the hand he had resting on the top of her though to the inside of it, stroking slow circles against her skin. His electric-blue eyes let her know that the demon was gone as he fixed his gaze on her delicate face. He took a bit of delight in the way that her expression contorted with her emotions as she tried to keep herself from giving in to him.

Calliope's legs trembled underneath Asmodeus' touch and she held her breath as his lips passed over hers again. Then, a tear fell from one of her eyes and she released her breath. She leaned away from his touch, then looked at him, struggling to find something to say.

When Calliope finally spoke, her voice wavered. "I... I'm sorry. It was... Amazing... Being with you," she said, stuttering. She watched as Asmodeus' face went from longing to confusion before settling on a stormy expression as he listened. "I never wanted to hurt you," she whispered. "I guess I never should've let myself get attached to you. I swear, it was supposed to only be a one night stand... But... You just kept inviting me over and one night turned into a wonderful relationship." Her eyes drooped as her energy officially ran out. "I didn't mean to hurt you, but I guess I did. I guess I turned you into..."

"Into what?" Asmodeus questioned, challenging Calliope. His voice was dripping with malice. "If I were you, I would choose my next words very carefully."

"Does it really even matter what I say, Deus?" Calliope asked. "You're gonna believe whatever you want regardless. You're so gods-damn stubborn and cruel sometimes! It has to be my fault... I'm a siren, after all... We're like parasites, living off other people, their emotions. And, look, I know you still have feelings for me, Deus. I can feel you fighting your demon half over this... I'm really sorry." She looked down with a guilty expression. Her face twisted with her emotions and she used her good hand to pull her broken one into her lap.

For a moment, Calliope forgot to keep her mental walls up and Asmodeus could feel her emotions changing with her facial expressions—from a tsunami of sadness to a fiery pit of anger that she was desperately trying to keep hidden. The only thing that feeling her emotions did was make him more attracted to her—especially when he felt her anger.

"Asmodeus... Prince of Demons: half-human, half-incubus... Both halves are always fighting each other. Sometimes... I swear... You're so... Gods-damn... Stupid!" Calliope suddenly screamed at Asmodeus, spitting the words out at him like venom.

Asmodeus reeled back, looking at Calliope like she was a stranger as his eyes flickered between ink-black and electric-blue. Her words invoked the anger inside of him, though, and before he could even think, his eyes turned ink-black again and stayed like that, the demon pulled back a fist, and he punched her. Her head snapped to one side from the force of his punch and blood dripped out of her mouth immediately.

Calliope turned to look at Asmodeus, but she was smiling in a way that he had never seen. She laughed, letting blood fall out of her mouth... "Just fucking kill me already... I know you, Deus. I know all your desires. I can feel your lust, your pain, your anger... Go ahead and have whatever fun you want with me... But please... Just hurry up and fucking kill me when you're done."

"Shut up!" Asmodeus yelled in the demonic voice as he hit Calliope again, slicing open her cheek. He hated his demon half for reacting that way, but he couldn't control it. *"¡Cállate!*[3] This... Is not you," he said. "I don't know what's going on with you or why you're intentionally trying to anger me, but I'm not wasting any more time on these games. Your little friends are probably already on their way back here to help you... I was going to go easy on you, but you're pissing me off, so I've just decided... *Voy a joder disfrutando de esto. Perra."*[4]

Calliope took a breath, calming herself. "I think I may have turned you into someone who's cold-hearted and closed off. You used to be so fun and happy, even if you did bad things every now and then... I think I might be the reason that you changed... I... Must have taken all your affection, leaving you with nothing. I'm so sorry," she said. She was struggling to stay awake. As her eyes closed, however, she heard Asmodeus laughing, causing her to force her eyes open.

"You think YOU turned me into a monster? Oh, give me a break. You were always so perfect..." Asmodeus said the word *'perfect'* with much disdain in his voice. "You were just so nice to everyone. The other demons wondered what it

---
[3] "Shut up!"
[4] "I'm going to fucking enjoy this. Bitch."

would take to break you, and I guess now we know..." The demon half of Asmodeus laughed harder.

As Calliope's vision darkened again, she heard Amadeo stirring awake in the middle of the destroyed dance floor. Asmodeus made a small, sort-of satisfied noise in his throat, which sent a shiver of dread down her spine. "Our mutual friend is waking up, it seems... Hey, do you remember when Amadeo introduced you to me? He had already asked me to break you. He wanted to watch. He thought it was hilarious to watch women break... And I was the best at it. That's why he even introduced us to begin with. He and the other demons begged me to destroy you in EVERY possible way. And I welcomed the challenge with others, but when it came to you..." He trailed off, looking dejected for a moment, his eyes flickering to blue as he fought his demon half for control.

Calliope felt Asmodeus' longing for her, the way that he hated both her and Amadeo—wanting them both dead—and the way that he wanted her out of his life for good, while also wanting to keep her for himself.

"There was a time when every demon here wanted you... There was a time when every man here BEGGED me to let them *'take turns'* with you.

I mean, a beautiful siren stuck in a mansion full of demons? You could only IMAGINE the things they would've done to you," Asmodeus said, the anger in his voice rising. "And your little friend, Amadeo? He begged me more often than anyone else. He was convinced that if he could just have you to himself, somehow you would fall in love with him. I mean, it was pathetic—his weird little fantasy. It was DISGUSTING, even by a demon's standards. I wasn't gonna let that happen. Besides, I loved having you all to myself. No one ever tried to challenge me for you, other than Menoetius, of course... And seeing him on top of you that night... The way he was forcing you down, the way you struggled, the way he BEAT you for it... Your whole body was bruised, Calli, yet you continued to FIGHT... I remember hearing you screaming at him, telling him that you were mine..."

'He sounds so sad,' the thunderbird spirit said inside Calliope's head.

Yes, Lyn, he does. I hate seeing him like this, Calliope thought.

"What have you done to me, Calli?" Asmodeus asked. "I never cared about anyone enough to ever stop these fuckers from doing the awful things they wanted to do. The only rule was that we didn't break contracts. Then you came along and I couldn't let the kind of shit they did happen anymore," he said, brushing his fingers over Calliope's cheek. "I told myself it was only because I didn't want to share you with anyone, but honestly... I was scared of what would happen to you... I was scared of what they would DO to you. I wanted to protect you, but I guess it doesn't matter now... I... Have no idea how I'm supposed to kill you..."

Calliope jerked away from Asmodeus, managing to open her eyes long enough to give him a hateful look—one that she knew would hurt him. "You wanted to protect me? Is that what you told yourself when you got rid of all my friends? And my brother? Tell me, Asmodeus... Were you ALWAYS such a monster? I tried so hard to be careful around you, but if I had known what you were truly capable of, I never would've even TOUCHED someone as repulsive—"

Asmodeus grabbed Calliope's throat with one hand, lifting her off of the floor. She didn't struggle though. She just smirked at him and spit her blood in his face. Angry, the demon took control and hit her as hard as he could, knocking her out and letting her body fall limply to the floor.

How is there so much blood? Asmodeus thought when he looked down at Calliope. He dropped to the floor gracefully to check on her. *Her forehead got cracked on the floor... ¡Maldito idiota!*[5] He cursed his demon half for getting carried away. He then knelt before her and scooped her into his strong arms, bridal-style. *If I knew that things would end up this way, I would've carried her like this when she was mine... I would've made more of an effort...* he thought.

'It's too late now.' the demon half of Asmodeus laughed, and he screamed at it to shut up.

Asmodeus walked out of Tartarus with Calliope lying unconscious in his arms. Then, he called someone else to grab Amadeo. In the alley near the exit, he spotted scarlet eyes shining at him inside of a darkness so vast that it was impossible for him to even see into it. *Nanuk...* he thought. He looked toward the giant hellhound, which he had given to Calliope as a birthday present when they were together three years earlier. He whispered to the wolf, "Go home..."

The hellhound whined like a puppy—a sound that hellhounds never made—and nudged Calliope's arm, which had fallen to the side. Nanuk was careful not to touch her horribly bruised and swollen hand. She stirred like she was waking up.

---

[5] "Fucking idiot!"

However, when pain shot through her again, she made a small, strangled cry and blood bubbled out from between her abnormally pale lips, and fell back into her trauma-induced sleep.

7. THE FEAR OF FALLING APART

(LET LOVE GUIDE YOU)

When Calliope regained consciousness, she found herself sprawled out on a luxurious L-shaped couch. She scanned the length of the extravagant living room that she was in, finding Asmodeus on the other side, pacing furiously. She didn't think that she had ever seen him so angry. His face was contorted into what appeared to Calliope to be a homicidal rage. He seemed more terrifying to her at that moment than he ever had.

'He looks like a fucking psychopath,' the spirit of the phoenix said to Calliope.

I know, Ember. He's terrifying. But he wasn't always like this, Calliope thought in response. *I don't know what happened.* Dread set in soon after, when she realized that eventually, Asmodeus was going to kill her. She knew that he could do so easily if he had a bronze dagger in his possession. *That must be why I'm at the mansion,* she thought.

Calliope's forehead hurt and when she felt it, her hand came away slick with blood. Using a tremendous amount of effort, she donned a brave face and forced her aching muscles to push her body into a sitting position against the back of the couch.

Calliope was looking down at her hands absent-mindedly when a shadow was suddenly looming over her. Asmodeus was staring down at her, his form so large and threatening compared to her. She could feel the intense anger radiating off of him. As he stood over her and looked down at her small, weak form, his anger began mixing with a feeling of lust. To Calliope, it felt like the cambion's lust was winning, which made her feel afraid and excited simultaneously. As much as the siren had always wanted another night with him, that wasn't exactly what she had in mind when she thought about it.

Asmodeus leaned forward and placed both of his hands on the back of the couch—one on each side of Calliope, trapping her between him and the couch. He leaned over her—his face tantalizingly close—and fiercely stared into her eyes.

For a few moments, Asmodeus didn't move, which soon caused even the spirit of the thunderbird, Lyn, to squirm, becoming more uncomfortable. However, the spirit of the phoenix, Ember, was only getting angry, and had to say it.

When Calliope opened her mouth to repeat what Ember had told her to, Asmodeus pounced on her like a predator, growling and grabbing her by her petite waist. He pressed his lips against hers and squeezed her waist harder in his calloused hands until he heard her whimper. Her sounds were driving him insane, and every time he felt her surprise, pleasure, and pain at once, it seemed to make him practically feral with lust.

Asmodeus' kisses were passionate and unyielding, clouding Calliope's mind. She focused her attention on the feeling of his lips pressed against hers, his tongue roaming along her bottom lip before pushing her soft lips open, forcing its way between them to find her tongue. As his tongue danced with hers, swirling around her mouth hungrily, she quickly lost her senses—as did he. She felt him letting his walls down, a tidal wave of emotions crashing out of him.

Calliope gave in to Asmodeus, losing herself in his arms. She couldn't stop herself from moaning passionately, which he swallowed the sound of when he deepened the kiss. *...I missed this,* he thought telepathically to Calliope. *Missed your perfect little body,* he added. She moaned loudly, arching into him as desire coursed through her. Her broken hand lay completely useless on her lap, but she didn't even notice. She used her good hand to reach for his long off-black hair. She grabbed a fistful of it, pulling him down on top of her.

Asmodeus noticed how Calliope winced when his body pressed into hers, jostling her broken hand. He pulled away, gently took her hand, then held it to the side as he lay her down on the couch. He kissed down her jaw to her neck, relishing the sound that she let out—a needy, insistent moan. He found himself staring at her lips as she moaned, watching the way that her mouth would stay open in a perfect *'O'* shape.

Calliope's lip quivered with her need for him. It appeared so inviting that Asmodeus couldn't stop himself from roughly pressing his lips against hers once more. One of his hands tightened around her hip, deeply bruising the siren in a matter of seconds. His other hand tightened around her wrist, causing an involuntary tear to slide from her eye as pain ran through her broken hand. He began roughly grinding his body into hers, driving her deeper and deeper into the couch cushions as his lust controlled him.

'...Just fuck her already!' Asmodeus' demon half screamed inside his mind.

Calliope could feel Asmodeus' thick length throbbing insistently—almost violently—against her inner thighs and she moaned loudly. Whimpering in his ear, she begged him, saying, "Please... Oh, gods, I've missed you, Deus... Oh, please take me."

Asmodeus groaned into Calliope's mouth as he kissed her again, releasing her to hurriedly remove his jeans. When he was free of pants, he ran his hands up her soft round thighs, sliding her bloody and torn dress up to her waist. She writhed impatiently beneath him, rocking her hips forward to grind against his length. He let out a low groan, then grabbed both of her wrists roughly as she rubbed against him a second time. He forcefully held her wrists down with one hand, placing his other hand on her hip. Using the hand that he had placed on her hip, he pinned her against the couch, not allowing her to move as he shoved almost his entire length inside of her. She screamed in pain and pleasure from the sudden sensation. He groaned at her tightness, forcing his length even deeper—as deep as his thick, long member could go inside of her.

Calliope moaned for Asmodeus and he squeezed her wrists tightly in response, causing her to whimper from the pain. He used one hand to hold her hip—grabbing at it harder—and thrust himself into her tight wetness as hard as he could. *You feel so... Gods-damn... Good,* he told her telepathically as he thrust his length into her, moving faster. He was unrelenting in his forceful, rough penetration, bruising her body more and more as he roughly drove himself into her tight, wet opening, slamming his thick length as deep as he could every time. The Supernaturals were both so caught up in that moment together that they seemed to completely forget that they were on the living room couch, where anyone could have witnessed their actions.

When Asmodeus finished, slamming into Calliope's tight opening one last time, he had to pause and catch his breath before pulling his pants back on and hoisting Calliope up into his arms. The siren weakly wrapped her legs around his waist and her arms around his neck, her movements lazy after the way the cambion had used her—his intense lust for her head kept him going all night. She noticed him walk past a few demon men in the hallway, who she had never seen and who quickly averted their eyes. She started to ask about them—wondering if they were new demons—but he picked her up from his waist and threw her unceremoniously over his broad shoulder, causing her to land harshly. She shut her mouth—pressing her lips together in a thin line—not wanting to piss him off. She could feel his mood shifting, turning sour. He began walking up the stairs with her, his face set in a determined expression. She knew what was going to happen to her once he got her wherever he was headed.

The cambion that Calliope had once loved had his fun with her throughout the night... *But now,* she thought. *Now it's time for him to get rid of me... Permanently, because I'm his weakness and the demon half thinks that his weaknesses must be purged.* Though she tried not to let it happen, her lip quivered, betraying the calm that she was trying to exude. *It really sucks being a Supernatural created by lust,* she thought.

They reached the top of the stairs then, causing Calliope to let out a low, guttural moan of pain when Asmodeus bounced to readjust her. She landed on his shoulder with a force equivalent to getting punched in the gut.

"Oh, shut up," Asmodeus commanded. His tone had become cold, uncaring... Cruel.

"Fuck... You," Calliope whispered defiantly in Asmodeus' ear. He growled and grabbed a handful of her turquoise hair, pulling on it—hard.

Her bad hand fell off of his shoulder, going limp by her side.

Calliope whimpered quietly in Asmodeus' ear and he whispered a warning to her. He hissed, "Don't fucking test me. *Te van a matar, niña.*"[6]

"You're younger than me," Calliope replied. Asmodeus sighed and slammed her down hard, releasing her hair.

Calliope then noticed all of the demons that were standing in the hallway. *They must have gathered to watch the fight,* she thought. *Amadeo had to fight because he stood against Prince Asmodeus. If he won, he got to keep his life... If he lost... He died. Unless... Unless Asmodeus pardoned him,* she thought.

'But he wouldn't,' Lyn reminded Calliope gently.

No, Lyn. You're right... He wouldn't, Calliope agreed sadly.

Calliope kept a mental note of how many demons were lining the hallway, each standing outside of their bedrooms. Some were staring solemnly at her broken hand hanging limply by her side. Some looked disgusted with Asmodeus while others looked at him like he was the greatest man they'd ever met. Two female demons, who Calliope

---

[6] "You're going to get yourself killed, little girl."

recognized as Lilith and Abaddon, caught her eye and nodded toward their rooms, offering her a hiding space. From all of the different expressions, it seemed that not all of the demons agreed with Asmodeus' reign... *Some are looking at him like they're gonna kill him... Like they're sizing him up. Then, there's... Oh,* she thought, pausing to take in the demon who was walking toward them. Asmodeus quickly set her on her feet beside him, pulling her close, his arm wrapped around her small waist.

"Have you come to claim the prize from your victory?!" the man yelled to Asmodeus. *He looks familiar...* Calliope thought. Then, she recognized him as Asmodeus' younger half-brother, Menoetius. He had blood on his hands and clothes, splattered all over him... *He must have been the demon Amadeo had to fight,* she thought.

"Oh, Calliope... You know, I've always found you very beautiful. It's a shame that Asmodeus got to you first. I would've had SO much fun with you..." Menoetius said as his ink-black eyes roamed up and down Calliope's body. She could feel the psychopathic pleasure that he felt when he looked at her broken hand, her bloodied face, and her bruised throat...

Menoetius made Calliope uncomfortable and she began squirming against Asmodeus' grasp. Desperately wanting to leave, her eyes found Lilith and Abaddon, who both appeared horrified and shook their heads at her sadly. It was clear that they couldn't help her—at least, not while the psychopath was around. Asmodeus wrapped his arm around her waist possessively, digging his nails into her side.

Calliope looked up again, just in time to see Amadeo coming up the stairs. He had a hellhound puppy on a leash and the adorable young hellpup was hyper. *That adorable little runt must have been his prize for winning his fight,* she thought. Amadeo quickly resigned himself to cradling the hellpuppy in his bloody arms, near his chest. He glanced over his shoulder at Calliope and she could tell from the severity of his wounds that he had been jumped by multiple demons, not given a fair fight. *Well... At least he's not dead,* she thought.

'I guess that means he won, then?' Lyn asked inside Calliope's mind.

He did, Lyn, but he got lucky. He might not be so lucky if they decide to jump him again out of spite, Calliope thought to the spirit.

"I feel like you must be going soft, brother. Or maybe the siren's beauty is blinding you? Give her to me... I can't be swayed by her looks, no matter how attractive she is. And if you do give her to me, I can promise you..." Menoetius said, flashing a psychotic grin. "She won't look NEARLY as beautiful by the time I'm finished with her. I know that she's trying to act tough, but let's not forget that it didn't take me very long to break her the last time I got my hands on her. In fact... I seem to remember her wrist snapping quite easily when I pinned her down by it. Come on, brother. Let's see if she can hold out against me any longer this time."

Asmodeus' words came out quietly in response, with a deep, seething hatred in his tone. "Shut... The fuck... Up," he commanded his half-brother. His tone caused Calliope to jerk with fear involuntarily. His body stiffened and she could feel his anger rising as she buried her face into his side, scared. He always needed to appear in charge when he was around his younger half-brother. He let a deep growl rumble down from his throat, sending shivers down her spine. Then, he tightened his arm around her waist until her chest was pressed so tightly against him that she could barely breathe. His free hand moved around to grip the back of her thick, round thigh, digging his sharp nails into it. She was trying her best to focus only on her breathing rather than the pain she was experiencing or Menoetius' psychotic satisfaction from watching his older half-brother take his anger out on her.

Calliope squirmed against Asmodeus' hand when she couldn't ignore how uncomfortable she was. He immediately responded to her... What his demon half would call... *'Disobedience'...* By pushing his nails into her side, through her dress. He pressed them in as hard as he could, and the marks that he created on her skin started bleeding. She could feel his other hand—which had stayed against the back of her thigh—do the same. His nails punctured her delicate, soft cappuccino-colored skin deeply. An unexpected jolt of pleasure coursed through her body as her blood began flowing freely down her thigh from the wounds.

Calliope tried as hard as she could to keep her breathing steady. She didn't want to make Asmodeus seem like he wasn't in control of her and everything else while they were around his psychotic brother. However, her lips quivered and she couldn't prevent the small, breathless moan from escaping. He inhaled sharply at the sound, and she immediately felt his lust stirring underneath his anger once more.

Suddenly, Menoetius snatched Calliope away by her arm, causing extremely deep scratches where Asmodeus had been holding onto her, blood running freely from each wound. He was holding her arm so tightly above the elbow that her skin began bruising a raisin-purple almost immediately. She tried to pull away from him, but he only tightened his iron grip, causing her to wince from the pain. With his free hand, he pinched her chin with his index finger and thumb, lifting her face to meet his.

For the first time, Calliope noticed how much Menoetius resembled his older half-brother. He and Asmodeus were both handsome. They both had the same shade of flawless hazelnut skin and the same chiseled facial features. The main difference in the brother's appearance was that Asmodeus had unnatural electric-blue eyes unless he was angry, while Menoetius had ONLY the deep ink-black eyes of a demon.

"Oh, there it is... That fear in your eyes," Menoetius said. "I've missed that... I wonder how long it'll take for you to go from begging me to stop hurting you... To you begging me to finally kill you." His hand slid from Calliope's chin down to her throat, then began to roam lower. With one sharp fingernail, he slowly sliced down her mostly-exposed chest, effectively making the pain last longer. Her upper lip curled in pain, but she refused to make a single noise, instead meeting his eyes with a defiant glare the entire time. "Curious... I thought you'd be shaking with fear by now. Oh, but this will make breaking you even more fun. Let's see what makes you tick." Menoetius' hand slid from the fresh cut in the middle of her chest down to her hip, grabbing it roughly and pulling her into him. His other hand finally released her arm in favor of grabbing the back of her neck, twisting his fingers into her hair, and pulling it as hard as he could in order to make her cry out. He had never felt so attracted to anyone before, and he had also never had anyone defy him as much as she did. It infuriated him.

What infuriates me more, though, Menoetius thought. *Is that Asmodeus—the man who's SUPPOSED to be our PRINCE—won't even allow me to break the fucking bitch. He won't allow me to take her, even knowing that I'd be the best option if he wants to break the little slut!* Then, he thought, *My brother may still claim that he wants to do it himself, but he's WEAK when it comes to her. He already let the little whore seduce him once. If I could just have MY way with her, maybe my brother would finally harden into a REAL leader. And if not... Then maybe I should be the one leading.*

"So, you wanna have FUN with me?" Calliope asked, making her voice sound silky and seductive. "Why don't you let me show you how to have fun?" She lifted a hand to Menoetius' face then, cupping his cheek. He eyed her with a suspicious look, but she could feel him leaning into her gentle touch regardless. She smiled at him invitingly and watched his eyes as he glanced down to her full lips and back up. He smirked and leaned into her then, kissing her lips deeply.

As Menoetius distracted himself by kissing her, Calliope soon pulled away. Then, she leaned her head back before slamming it forward as hard as she could, headbutting him in his nose and breaking it. He stumbled backward from the force of the blow, his hands flying up to cover his broken nose. A few of the demons stepped forward to help him, but even more stood back and attempted—very unsuccessfully—not to laugh.

Asmodeus quickly grabbed Calliope and picked her up. He then turned away from his younger brother, stomping into his bedroom—the extravagant master bedroom—and slamming the door behind him. He walked to the center of the room with her... Then, he dropped her!

Calliope let out a panicked gasp and instinctively threw her arms up to protect her head. To her astonishment, however, she landed on Asmodeus' soft, comfortable bed rather than the floor. She took a moment to gaze out at his bedroom then. She had always loved the lavish four-post bed in the center, which sat on top of a raised platform. Half of the room had been turned into a study—complete with bookshelves, a computer desk, and a mountain of paperwork. The other half of the room was much different, with a minibar that was full of expensive alcohol, a massive television that was mounted on the wall, and an expensive gaming setup that looked like it didn't get used very often.

Was he just playing with me, then? Calliope thought. *I mean, why even bother laying me on his bed if he's just planning on hurting me anyway?* She sighed and forced herself to just enjoy whatever moments she could, embracing the feeling of the soft comforter caressing her exposed skin... Which she had just realized was extremely cold. She wore nothing more than the ruined, torn up dress from the night before, which had barely covered her body to begin with. She smiled and closed her eyes, attempting to stop the pleasant moan that suddenly began rumbling up her throat.

Asmodeus' head snapped around to look at Calliope when he heard the soft noise come out of her mouth. Sitting on the edge of his bed, he quickly turned his head away from the sight of her mostly-exposed body, hanging it slightly and looking exhausted.

'Heavy is the head that wears the crown... It must be hard for him—pretending to be cruel constantly... But, he wants to prove that he deserves his position,' Lyn said inside Calliope's mind.

It IS hard on him, Calliope replied. *He somehow looks even more exhausted every time I see him.*

Calliope cautiously opened her mind to Asmodeus' emotions, where she felt his anger and lust fighting for control. As if he knew that she was feeling everything that he did, he slid backward, leaving his hands lingering tantalizingly close to her. "What did you do to me...?" he asked, his emotions surging. He looked up at her with dark, sad eyes that reminded her of a thunderstorm. "And WHY did you have to piss off my brother? He was already still angry at both of us because I didn't let him take you the last time."

"What do you mean...? I don't know what I've done to you, Deus. I thought... That I was making you colder," Calliope responded. "But after the way we hooked up... And how you saved me from Menoetius..." She trailed off, trying to pick her words carefully so she wouldn't anger Asmodeus again. She slowly opened her mind to him and allowed him to understand better by showing him all of her emotions. She opened her mind just enough for him to understand where each of her emotions originated from—fear from his violent rage, comfort from the blanket and its warmth, and sadness for her brother... Who Asmodeus had dragged into the Demon Realm because Raiden didn't approve of him. She was left in the dark, not knowing what had happened to her brother for months. When she eventually found out, she was sadly informed that it was too late to save him, so... She broke up with Asmodeus and left. Looking at Asmodeus' brooding expression and his arm muscles—which flexed in response to her emotions—she then felt how much she had longed to be with him again.

    Calliope felt a deep sadness inside Asmodeus, followed by shock when he realized that she was really still into him. He moved closer to her until they were laying side-by-side, but didn't break the uncomfortable silence. He simply grabbed her hand and held it in his as he stared at the ceiling.

After a long silence, when Calliope couldn't stand it anymore, she heard Asmodeus' voice inside her mind. He sent her a thought telepathically, sounding nervous. *I've really missed you... So much,* he said.

Calliope turned to face Asmodeus, admiring his chiseled jawline and the way that he looked... *Like he was designed by the gods themselves,* she thought. "I've missed you, too," she whispered in his ear. Painfully, she pulled up her broken hand so she could drape her arm around his waist, nuzzling her face into his neck and kissing him there.

Asmodeus put one hand on Calliope's arm, slowly running it up and down her soft skin and making her feel like there was electricity running through her entire body. "I'm so sorry about your hand," he choked out. "And for letting Menoetius hurt you." He slid his other arm underneath her then, so that her head was resting on top of his chest.

Calliope planted a gentle kiss on Asmodeus' lips. "Hey, it's fine, Deus. I'm just shocked that I haven't started healing yet. I don't know what could be slowing my healing ability," she said.

Asmodeus brushed his fingers along Calliope's cheek, careful not to touch the deep cut across it. "I really shouldn't still care about you, Calli..." he whispered. His voice sounded pained. "I'm supposed to want you dead..."

"I understand, Deus. I'm not gonna fight you or run away... I don't have it in me anymore. So I'll just wait for... Whatever you decide to do with me, I guess," Calliope responded.

"Hell... If you were anyone else, I'd have fucking killed you already! But you're not someone else... And every time someone asks me what I want to do with you or if I'm looking forward to killing you... All I can think is that if you die, I'll never get to see you again," Asmodeus said sadly before removing himself from Calliope's arms and sitting on the edge of the bed.

It was silent for a few minutes. Calliope's breath was coming out shaky—she was terrified of saying the wrong thing. "It's okay, Deus... But... What ARE you planning to do with me? Are you just gonna deny what we had between us? Or... Can we at least agree that..." She sat up and reached out while talking, taking Asmodeus' hand in hers.

Asmodeus jerked away from Calliope immediately. He pulled his hand upwards and back, then slammed it down, delivering a vicious backhand slap across her face. She cried out, her hands flying up to try soothing her stinging skin while tears began to fall from her eyes and blood began flowing out of her mouth.

What happened? What did I do wrong this time? Please, Deus... Whatever I did, I'm sorry... I'm so sorry, Calliope cried, telepathically talking to Asmodeus. Her face was stinging from his brutal slap, her tears continued falling, and her ears were ringing loudly—making it difficult for her to hear.

When Calliope's words filled Asmodeus' mind, he angrily punched himself in the temple before turning his vengeful gaze on her. His eyes had turned ink-black and curved barn-red horns began growing from his head. When he spoke again, the voice no longer belonged to him. She realized that he wasn't in control at that moment—the demon had taken over completely. "How dare you?!" the ethereal demonic voice shrieked. "Stay out of my head, *puta!*[7] Don't ever fucking touch me! I only fucked you because I needed a release. That's all you are to me and all you'll ever be. Don't presume to know me," he said. She had to remind herself that it wasn't him—it was the demon.

Asmodeus' demon half could come out on its own sometimes—mostly when he was feeling too conflicted. It didn't take full control most of the

---

[7] "whore!"

time, so Calliope could only assume that Asmodeus was having a breakdown. Essentially, though, the demon was the Supernatural's equivalent of a split personality.

"I'm sorry, Deus, I didn't mean to mess with your head," Calliope said. "I wish I could fix it, but I don't think I can, so... I understand. Do whatever you need to." She looked Asmodeus in the eye when she spoke, hoping that he was watching inside, even if his demon half wouldn't let him regain control... But his fist came flying into her jaw then, sending her crashing into the wall.

Calliope pulled herself up with a grunt and looked up at Asmodeus' handsome face. He appeared angrier than she had ever seen him. He was really hurting and it made the demon want to hurt her so that she would understand how he was feeling.

Asmodeus' face softened when he looked down at Calliope. The demon could only think about how beautiful she was when she was lying broken and beaten in front of him. It was exactly what his demon had always wanted—it knew that it would break her eventually. Seeing her with bruises and blood all over, with Asmodeus' handprint making its own deep blue and purple bruise on her cheek, the demon thought to him, *'I just love seeing the little whore get exactly what she deserves.'* The demon felt equally angry and aroused, but Asmodeus prevented it from acting on its arousal. He tried to prevent it from acting on its anger as well, but he was only strong enough at that moment to deal with one issue.

"Asmodeus, I know that you're feeling conflicted," Calliope said. "And I know that you're hurting... I'm sorry. Maybe I did that to you—caused this pain... If you need to hurt me, it's okay... You can. I won't pretend I'm not terrified, but I'm not gonna fight you. Everything will be okay." Blood poured out of her mouth when she spoke and it was clear that she was having a difficult time breathing, yet she was only thinking of Asmodeus... What he needed or wanted... Hoping that he was okay.

Asmodeus thought, *She still loves me...?*

The demon responded, *'No! She only loves the HUMAN part of you! She could never accept BOTH of us and you know it! She'd never accept you for who you ARE!'*

"Fuck you!" Asmodeus yelled out loud to his demon half, once again punching himself in the temple.

Calliope watched in horror as Asmodeus waged war on himself. She stayed sitting against the wall, afraid to make a noise or move and risk upsetting the demon again.

However, the demon turned on Calliope again anyway, furious at her for causing so many conflicting emotions. "And I don't need your fucking permission!" the demonic voice yelled out. The sound was deep and penetrating, reverberating inside her mind as she sat trembling against the wall. She had never been scared of Asmodeus. At least, not like that. "I am the Prince of Demons! I don't need anything from you! Don't you fucking get it? I was only using you the whole time we were together, *tu puta perra ingenua!*[8] I was kissing you, taking you on romantic dates, fucking you... Seeming to be the perfect boyfriend. Did you honestly think it was a coincidence that ALL your friends disappeared? And your brother? Though, you did figure out what happened to him eventually. After all of that, I was still planning to lead you on longer. I was going to give you the time of your life, the best memories you could ever ask for, and ride you harder than you've ever been ridden. Then, right when you thought you were fine, I was going to tell you everything just to see the look on your face when you realized that you had been fucking the person who destroyed your

---

[8] "you fucking naive bitch!"

life. You are so fucking STUPID! You should hate me, but here you are, all over me instead. You're pathetic... *Pobre, inocente, confiando...*"[9]

The demon's voice began to sound strained as Asmodeus' sorrow-filled voice found its way out to say, *"Hermosa..."*[10]

Then, the demon took control again, yelling *"¡Increíblemente estúpida pequeña perra!"*[11] The demon spit those words at Calliope, causing her to flinch back, pressing her body into the wall.

When Asmodeus stepped toward Calliope, the demon said, "I should've just given you to Menoetius. At least he would be having fun with you... I'm just doing what I have to." She cowered, hiding her face between her knees, feeling too afraid to even look at him.

Whether Calliope looked at Asmodeus or not made no difference to the demon, though. He started brutally beating her, over and over... She was terrified that if she looked up at him, he'd kill her. That was when Calliope realized that the demon was going to kill her anyway. It pulled out a bronze dagger then, and she immediately understood why she had not been healing.

---

[9] "Poor, innocent, trusting..."
[10] "Beautiful..."
[11] "Incredibly stupid little bitch!"

After a moment of hesitation—while getting brutally beaten—Calliope decided, *Fuck it. I can do this! Ember... Lyn... Blood of fire and thunder... Please give me strength.* Asmodeus punched her again and she finally stood up, staring at him. His eyes were dark, but he stopped hitting her. Soon after, his eyes began to lighten and his horns disappeared.

Calliope didn't know if she could even help Asmodeus, but she knew that she needed to try. If she didn't, his demon was going to kill her. So, she sighed, holding her hand out to him. She maintained eye contact, trying not to show her fear. "Let me help you Deus... please?"

After a few agonizing minutes, Asmodeus reached out a shaky hand and took Calliope's. He lowered the dagger, then put it away, and he quickly and quietly guided her out of the mansion. He was talking, mostly to himself, on the way out. He whispered, *"Ella nunca te va a perdonar... No volverá a confiar en ti."*[2]

The pair soon made it to the garage, where Asmodeus stored his motorcycle. He gave Calliope a helmet before putting the second one on himself. "I'd hate for you to survive all this just to die in an auto accident," he said, a half-hearted attempt at a joke.

---

[12] "She will never forgive you... Never trust you again."

Calliope laughed. "Unless the road is a human who can resist my siren song or that bronze dagger of yours, I'll live... Even if I'm not healing at the moment," she replied.

"I hurt you pretty badly. I... I thought the demon was gonna kill you," Asmodeus told Calliope. His voice wavered at the idea that he could have killed her.

"Honestly... I thought so, too," Calliope whispered. Then, she hopped onto Asmodeus' motorcycle behind him, holding onto him with her good hand. She ground her teeth together due to the pain that shot through her elbow as she did. She tucked her broken hand protectively in her lap, keeping it there as they rode. He dropped her off at her shared apartment before leaving to pick up some things for her. He may not have had a plan, but he didn't want to leave her alone all night. He wanted to stick around to take care of her.

"Nini!" Calliope yelled as she walked through her front door. She ran to her roommate, hugging Nagaveni fiercely. Then, Nagaveni tended to her wounds as she explained every event that took place. She mentioned every detail that she could remember—Dysnomi knowing that something was going to happen, Asmodeus losing himself to his demon, and how she helped

Asmodeus regain control. "...Anyway, after tonight, I think I've had enough adventures. I don't even know when I'll start healing... Or IF I'll start healing like I'm supposed to," she said.

Nagaveni started pacing while thinking of ways to help. "Oh!" she exclaimed as an idea hit her. "You should call Salem! She's gotta have something that can help, right?"

"Nini, you're a genius!" Calliope said as she jumped off her bed and pulled her phone out, calling Salem. A giant black mass prowled into her room then, scarlet eyes shining in the darkness. She sat down again, patting a spot next to her on the bed. Nanuk whined, her head hanging low, then gently climbed up and lay down. Calliope sat on the bed, absent-mindedly petting Nanuk for a half-hour, until Salem barged into her room.

Salem's pale skin appeared flushed. The vanilla color of her skin caused her freckles to stand out, and caused her long, ginger hair to appear a brighter shade of orange. Her black leather jacket and the dark colors of her usual punk attire also contrasted sharply with her skin tone. "I brought everything I had that could help you!" she said in a rush. "So, you got a Blade of Light from Dys, right? Well—" she continued, pulling out a red and black marbled dagger. "This is called Hell's Scream. It's basically the complete opposite. Oh, and this," she said, pulling out a necklace with a silver heart one the end, a shiny ruby in the middle. "Is the Heart's Desire. It can redirect some of your siren abilities, including your passive emotional manipulation." She then pulled out one last thing: a plain gold ring that had an inscription around the band. "This last one's the Hand of Restoration. You should put it on now. You need it."

Calliope slipped the ring on and her smaller wounds began healing immediately. "Thank you, Salem. You really are the best witch in Los Angeles," she said, hugging Salem.

"Anything for my favorite customer. And hey—these are on me. You just worry about finding whoever's decided to fuck with you. Good luck, Calli," Salem said.

Asmodeus returned with supplies and a bouquet of flowers as Salem left. He eyed her suspiciously. She just grinned and gave him a silly two-finger salute with a wink before ducking out of the door.

"You're so sweet," Calliope said when Asmodeus gave her the flowers.

"I have a lot to apologize for... I don't deserve to have you in my life," Asmodeus whispered, looking at the floor.

Calliope laughed and touched Asmodeus' cheek. "Well... I WANT you in my life," she said when he finally met her gaze. "EVERY part of you... Asshole demon part included, assuming that part can learn to use his words sometimes."

"He's gonna try," Asmodeus said with a small smile. "But I've gotta admit something to you... Someone left me a note that told me where you were going to be. It also said a lot of things about you... Like... It said you were laughing at me... That you think I'm a joke. It talked about your brother and I guess it really fucked with my head. Then, with my demon half and Menoetius both telling me what to do, I guess I just acted on my raw anger. Amadeo tried to reason with me. He tried to convince me that you dumping me three years ago and me letting you live didn't make me look weak. He tried to tell me that I could still be a good leader," he said, looking down at the floor. "I'm so sorry that I didn't listen. But... Someone CLEARLY wants you dead, Calli. Or... At the very least... Severely injured. I think we need to find out who... And why."

8. LET THE GOOD TIMES ROLL

(INTO THE BAYOU)

Calliope leaned forward on the balcony's railing at Tartarus. It had been a week since she and Asmodeus decided to try to find whoever wanted her dead when they finally discovered a lead.

Calliope's arms were draped elegantly over the railing, one hand holding Tartarus' signature drink—the Cosmic Paradise. She tapped one of her nails against her glass absent-mindedly before lifting it to her lips for another drink.

Calliope's hair fell in luxurious waves down to her waist, a few of the strands falling loose near the front. The turquoise waves easily complemented the lavender of the formal gown that Nagaveni had picked out specifically for her to wear that night. The dress was a slightly lighter shade of purple than her iris eyes, with skinny straps at the shoulders and a V neck. "It's the perfect mix of sexy and classy," Nagaveni had said about it. She agreed, but said that she would only wear it if Nagaveni would wear a matching one.

The bass was pumping loudly from the club's first floor—which was fairly standard—but the music that was playing upstairs was more reserved. The only people who were on the upper floor were Calliope's friends and other Supernaturals. She loved the second floor being exclusive, and she knew that Nagaveni had also adored the idea when Dysnomi first mentioned it. Supernaturals could be themselves there, thanks to Dysnomi's powers. Under the enchantment that Dysnomi put on Tartarus and the area surrounding it, the humans on the first floor would see any Supernaturals there as other humans.

'It must be really nice to have powers that can change reality,' Lyn said inside Calliope's mind.

It definitely sounds nice, Calliope replied to Lyn. She then sighed and took another sip of her drink. Suddenly, a pair of alabaster hands came around from behind her, covering her eyes.

"Guess who?" a husky voice whispered in Calliope's ear.

"Dysnomi, if you don't get your hands off me, I will sing you to your doom," Calliope announced, her voice laced with sarcasm. She didn't mean it, especially since she learned that her siren abilities didn't affect other Supernaturals. Yet, as she said the words, her hand moved to her neck on instinct. She then remembered that she hadn't worn the enchanted Heart's Desire necklace because Nagaveni had convinced her that she wouldn't need it. To prove her point, Nagaveni had only worn the enchanted Serpent Tamer necklace to stay disguised before arriving. Nagaveni's 'little Jörmungandr babies' had been roaming free on her head the rest of the night.

"I'm doomed regardless, Calli. I mean, I'm a trickster. I'm pretty sure tricksters don't get into any version of heaven," Dysnomi replied, removing his hands. "I missed you. I haven't been able to stop thinking about the time we spent together... Before everything went to shit. It was... Perfect." He leaned against the railing and tilted his head back, feeling the breeze with his hair hanging behind him. He looked at Calliope with his deep hazel eyes, light gleaming within the golden flakes—or, the mischief sprinkles, as she used to call them.

Calliope finished her drink, then walked to the bar for another. Dysnomi followed behind her cautiously.

The bartender that night was a cute anthousai—flower nymph, as they were commonly called—who Calliope had never met. The nymph had baby-pink skin, straight hot-pink hair, and delicate pointed ears. Her name tag had *'Nasrin'* written on it. She slid one of the galaxy-inspired drinks across the bar to Calliope, and their fingers brushed against each other's when Calliope accepted it. She blushed, then held up a hand to stop Calliope from trying to pay for it.

"Oh! Thank you, goddess," Calliope said to the minor deity with a wink. She then placed the money on the bar top anyway. She always paid for her drinks, despite Dysnomi telling his entire staff that drinks for his friends were on the house. Nasrin looked away from her, blushing.

Calliope sauntered over to the seating area in the middle while Dysnomi continued to follow her like a lost hellpuppy. "Can we just talk, Calli? Please?" he begged, sitting next to her on the couch. He began to reach out to her, but decided against touching her. He didn't want her to hate him more than he felt like she already did.

"What is there to talk about, Dys?" Calliope asked with a sigh, using her nickname for him for the first time in over a week. "That night... It was a mistake."

"I'm sorry, Calli," Dysnomi whispered. His voice sounded pained, and Calliope shied away from him instinctively. "And I'll continue to be sorry... But I couldn't tell you something was going to happen. I'm not allowed to interfere with stuff like that... Things that... Are supposed to happen. Plus, I didn't know exactly what was gonna happen. I just had a feeling that it was something bad. The best thing I could even think to do for you was to give you hints and conjure the Blade of Light."

Calliope sighed and stared down at her glass, which was shaking in her bruised hand. She had worn the Hand of Restoration ring since Salem gave it to her, yet her hand remained a glorious eggplant-purple. Her bones had healed, but the bruise remained—as did the bruise above her elbow on the opposite arm. "I'm not mad at you, Dys," she whispered. "I'm just hurt. I mean, look at me," she added, laughing bitterly. She gestured toward her body to prove her point. "And I couldn't even think about using the dagger... No matter what Deus did, I couldn't even imagine hurting him."

Dysnomi let his eyes roam over Calliope's body, first noticing her tired eyes. He also noticed that she had tried to cover her bruised face with makeup. It did work for the bruises, but he could still see the cut across her cheek where Asmodeus slapped her and the gash on her forehead where it had been cracked open on the floor of Tartarus. Further down, on her neck, there was a deep bluish-purple bruise where she had been choked. She insisted that her throat didn't hurt when she spoke and that it wasn't swollen, but the bruise never changed. There was also a thin, long cut down the middle of her chest from Menoetius slicing her open with his fingernail, and Dysnomi knew that she was self-conscious about it. There were also bruises on one of her hands as well as her arm. Beyond that, she had many other battle wounds across her body; though, he couldn't see most of them through the long dress that she was wearing. Any part of her the demonic prince touched is bruised. *Wait... Not demonic,* he thought. *Cambionic? Half-demonic?* He was so angry about everything after seeing how beat up she was. He was angry at Asmodeus, hated Asmodeus for what Asmodeus had done to her. He was also angry at Menoetius for touching her—in fact, he hated Menoetius even more than he hated Asmodeus. He was angry at himself as well, for not helping her. No matter how many times he tried to convince himself that he couldn't interfere, it sounded like bullshit to him every time that he looked at her battered body.

"...You're still beautiful," Dysnomi assured Calliope. She snorted, dismissing his comment. Then, she finished her drink, placing the empty glass on the table. "I mean it," he insisted. "I know you think I say that to every woman. Hell, I know I've lived up to that reputation. But I feel so different when I'm around you... And I'm ashamed of myself for allowing something so awful to happen to you. I'm sorry for leaving you to fight alone. Your scream..." He paused, shuddering. "Most of the humans ended up in the hospital with busted eardrums. Your scream was more powerful than that, though. It also broke through the Serpent Tamer's enchantment. The snakes woke up after that and became hostile. I had to enchant the humans who saw Nini as I was helping her out... Nanuk cleared a path for us." He paused again, looking at her thoughtfully. "...I could feel the pain you were in when you screamed. It was like nothing I'd ever felt... Like, I could feel it in my soul that you were calling out for help. I should've come back for you. I'm so sorry I didn't, Calli." He slid closer to her and laid his arm around her shoulders. She trembled, scared at first—the way that she had been for a week. After a moment, however, she relaxed into his hold, leaning her head against his shoulder.

"I'm sorry for how I've been acting, Dys," Calliope whispered. "I know you tried to help me, tried to give me a fighting chance."

"It wasn't enough," Dysnomi growled, clenching his jaw. "I should've done more."

Calliope placed her palm against Dysnomi's chest. He laid his hand on top of hers, holding it gently as she leaned up to kiss his cheek. He was shocked for a moment, but he soon let out a content sigh against the side of her face.

Calliope moved her hand to the back of Dysnomi's head then. She twisted his hair between her fingers and gently pulled his head down, pressing her lips against his. He held onto her waist, pulling her into him.

"Hey, Calli, where are you? Everyone's—Oh!" A shocked squeal caused Calliope and Dysnomi to jump apart, feeling embarrassed for getting caught up in the moment. "Sorry! I didn't mean to interrupt!" Nagaveni blurted, looking away as her snakes hissed softly.

Calliope blushed, then turned to face Nagaveni. She noticed that Nagaveni was indeed wearing the dress that she picked out—the twin to her own dress except Nagaveni's dress was a chartreuse-green instead of lavender. Better than Nagaveni wearing it, though, was seeing how confident Nagaveni looked in it. Nagaveni had always looked like a supermodel. *But,* Calliope thought, *It's nice to see her at least walking with the confidence of one.* "Sorry, Nini. Everything's amazing, but I'm really enjoying the peacefulness out here," she admitted.

"That's okay. I totally get it," Nagaveni replied. "How about... I round everyone up? We can just drink and talk out here instead?"

"That actually sounds amazing. I'd like that," Calliope answered. "Dys and I can grab drinks for everyone. Besides, it's about time Deus gets to try the Cosmic Paradise." She stood and walked over to Nagaveni, lightly touching the gorgon's arm. Some of the snakes hissed, but she only laughed while petting one, and said, "I almost forgot how jealous *Snake Gyllenhaal* here gets when I'm too close... But... Anyway, I just wanted to say thank you for setting this whole party up. You and Dys have transformed Tartarus."

"I almost forgot about the nicknames you give them," Nagaveni said, petting one of her snakes and laughing. "It feels like it's been forever since you've done it. But seriously, it's nothing, Calli. We all need a place where we can be ourselves. We shouldn't have to live our whole lives pretending to be human."

Dysnomi walked up behind Calliope and placed a hand on her waist, causing her to jump.

"Shit, I'm sorry, Calli. I don't mean to keep scaring you," he said, pulling his hand away.

"I know. It's okay, Dys. How about we go get those drinks now while Nini rounds everyone up?" Calliope asked.

"Sounds perfect," Dysnomi replied, though Calliope could tell that something was bothering him. She assumed that it was because Asmodeus was there. Everyone else had forgiven Asmodeus. Not him, though. He was still angry.

"You know, Deus really isn't that bad. You should at least give him a chance," Calliope told Dysnomi.

Dysnomi's whole body tensed at the mention of Asmodeus. He clenched his fists and set his jaw before saying, "Look at what he did to you, Calli. Look at what he allowed his brother to do to you. I might be pissed at myself for letting this happen, but I'm even more pissed at him for doing it. I have no excuse for my part in all this. Trust me, I know... I knew something was going to happen and I didn't stop it. But he has no excuse, either."

"Part of this is on me... I just ended up pissing off the demon half of him," Calliope said. "I'm fine, Dys. Besides, he was manipulated into doing that. It wasn't his fault."

"Yeah? And what about when he fucked you? Was he manipulated into that, too?" Dysnomi asked.

"No, of course not," Calliope answered as they reached the bar. Nasrin got to work on making their drinks, and she explained. "But there's a lot of history between us and it's hard for us to be close to one another and NOT want each other. There's also the fact that he's half-incubus and I'm half-siren... We're both Supernaturals made from lust."

"That's not a good excuse, Calli," Dysnomi said. "He assaulted you."

"No, he didn't, Dys. I wanted it," Calliope insisted. "And Deus is trying really hard. You know, he doesn't have to keep making so much effort to be here helping me—especially when half the demons now think he's going *'soft'.* He now has to worry about being overthrown. If Menoetius were the Prince of Demons, it would be so much worse than you could imagine. If he ever tried that, I'd be the first person he'd come after, just to hurt Deus. And the things that he'd do to me..." She shuddered when she said that, a choked sob escaping her lips. It was like she already knew exactly what he would do.

Horrified, Dysnomi realized that Calliope had to have seen or felt what Menoetius wanted to do. *Maybe he sent her his thoughts? It seems like something the bastard would do,* he thought. Then, he sighed, saying, "Okay, fair point, Calli. I just don't wanna see you get hurt again."

At that moment, Nasrin came back with the drinks. Calliope handed her the money and blew a kiss at her, causing her to blush once again. Calliope and Dysnomi took the drinks, then walked toward the balcony door so they could pass the drinks out to everyone as they arrived.

The first person through the door was Salem. Calliope noticed that Salem had her normally-wild hair curled and secured in a formal updo. She was wearing a flowing black dress with off the shoulder mesh sleeves. On her neck was a black choker, which had a ruby on its front. Her freckles contrasted against her vanilla skin and her forest-green eyes were shining in the lights.

"Wow, you look amazing!" Calliope exclaimed, handing Salem a drink.

"Aww, thank you! I can't go with you, unfortunately, but you know I'm only a text away if you need any magical help. And I'll be taking care of your apartment while you're gone. Nini asked me to. Will you need me to feed your familiars or are they going with you?" Salem asked.

"Familiars?" Calliope asked, confused. After a moment, however, she thought, *Oh! Familiars are what witches call pets. They believe animals choose their owners.* "No, thank you," she said. "Wrath and Thora kinda just do their own thing unless they think I need them and Nanuk might need some food left out for her, but I doubt you'll see much of her. She kinda... Dissolves into a mass of shadows when she doesn't wanna be social."

"She does WHAT?!" Salem exclaimed.

"Yeah... Hellhounds can do some REALLY weird things," Calliope said, laughing.

"...Huh. Well, that's good to know," Salem said, laughing along before walking to the seating area.

A few minutes later, Nagaveni appeared, accepting a drink from Dysnomi and promising Calliope that Asmodeus would be right behind her.

Exactly as promised, Asmodeus appeared seconds after Nagaveni walked away. He was wearing a midnight-black suit with a barn-red tie and Calliope thought that it looked perfect on him. As he accepted a drink from her, he pulled a bouquet of colorful daisies from behind his back and gave them to her.

"These are beautiful, Deus. Thank you," Calliope said, accepting the flowers. "But... You're coming with us, right? I mean, you didn't need to get me anything."

"Yeah, I'm coming with you. I've put Amadeo in charge of operations while I'm gone, so I'm sure everything will be fine. He's good at looking over the contracts, and he can definitely hold his own in a fight," Asmodeus replied. The way that Calliope looked at him when he spoke made his heart skip a beat. His demon half became uncomfortable, however—it didn't like the *lovey stuff*. Though, technically, his demon half was still a part of him. So, in a way, it was he who felt uncomfortable. He had never felt that way about any man or woman before. It was a strange feeling to him. Yet, it also felt right. He felt like a better person when she was around, like he could be more than just the Prince of Demons.

Dysnomi snorted and rolled his eyes, breaking up their moment. "Yeah, trust your whole operation to a random demon. There totally won't be any usurpers that'll rise and go after Calli to do gods-know-what solely to hurt you," he said, his words coming out in a venomous hiss. His face twisted with anger as he looked between Asmodeus and Calliope. He didn't understand why she had ever dated Asmodeus, much less why she still cared so much about Asmodeus. Asmodeus is a literal demon, but she acts like she can fix him... *Okay, Asmodeus is a cambion, technically,* he thought, correcting himself. *But who really cares?* He'd never felt so much resentment before. He had never let himself get attached to anyone the way that he'd let himself get attached to Calliope. He despised the feeling he had while looking between the siren and the cambion. It made him angry at himself for ever getting involved.

"Dys!" Calliope hissed. She specifically asked him to give Asmodeus a chance. She didn't understand why it was so hard for him or why he was so pissed at Asmodeus. He knew that something was going to happen and he allowed it to happen. However, as upset with him as she was, she was mostly upset with herself for allowing everything to go too far. She knew that it was going to be a mistake to sleep with him, but that night had been intense. *I should've known better though,* she thought. *Now I'm stuck here with two Supernaturals who I've slept with. They are not gonna even TRY to get along.*

"What? It's the truth, Calli!" Dysnomi exclaimed, raising his voice. Calliope's lip quivered and her eyes got watery, making him immediately feel guilty and lower his voice again. "You told me about his brother... The way he looked at you like you were a piece of meat, the way he talked to you and said he'd have *so much fun with you*, the way he hurt you... Calli... I saw your face when you said that whatever he'd do would be worse than anything Asmodeus did. Either he sent you his thoughts or you accidentally heard them... And now demon-boy here's about to leave Los Angeles. Is he gonna just hope someone else can keep his brother from doing whatever the fuck he wants?" he questioned.

"I'm well-aware that my brother's dangerous," Asmodeus said. "And I have no intention of letting anything happen to Calli. I wouldn't let him hurt her again." He turned to look at Calliope, his electric-blue eyes shining. "I know that when the demon took over, I said some cruel things. I'm sorry for saying I should've given you to him. I never would've done that... And I hope you know that... But it was awful to say. I'm also sorry that I didn't stop him. He likes hurting... Everyone. And maybe I did, too... At one point. I'm trying to be better, though. I want more for the demons. I want them to see that I can be a good leader and they can be great at what they do without being cruel... Whether it's making contracts, collecting them for review, deciding which afterlife everyone goes to, or training the hounds," he said.

"Really? You didn't seem opposed to something happening to her last week," Dysnomi said with a sneer. "In fact, it kinda seemed like you wanted something to happen to her. I mean, unless I'm wrong about where she got all these wounds? And if I'm wrong about that, I guess I'm also wrong about how she flinches anytime someone moves too fast around her. It ALMOST seems like a psychopathic ex of hers abducted her, sexually assaulted her, and tried to fucking kill her!"

Asmodeus' eyes turned ink-black as he stepped toward Dysnomi. Calliope laid a hand on his bicep, feeling his muscles tense as she pulled him back.

'Not even five minutes of them being in the same room together and they're already trying to kill each other. That's just fucking great,' Ember said inside Calliope's mind.

I know, Ember. It's a complete disaster, Calliope replied. She looked at Dysnomi and said, "That's enough. Everyone else is giving Deus a chance. You're the only one being difficult. But Deus is here now and you're gonna have to get used to it. Let me make something clear to you, though, since you don't seem to get it. He may have hurt me, but he did not fucking assault me," she said, shaking her head. "Did you miss the part where I said that I wanted it? And... You know, Dys, you could've helped me, but you didn't. You're not exactly innocent in all of this. You knew something was gonna happen, but you didn't even TRY to stop it. I've forgiven you both... And for right now... I just need you to be civil." Asmodeus nodded and turned away, but before he could leave, she drew him back with a question. "Wait... I'm curious. You mentioned that the demons decide which afterlife people go to? So, does that mean there are layers of hell? Like in *Dante's Inferno?*"

Asmodeus laughed loudly. "No, no," he said. "Nothing like that. It's just that there are separate hells for different religions. Since all the pagan gods and all versions of *'paradise'* are real, we made all versions of *'eternal damnation'* real as well. Oh, the *'big G'* that modern religions believe in? He doesn't exist. The people who believe in those religions just reincarnate and hopefully never remember their past life. Though, if they do, it won't matter much since everyone will just think that they're crazy. The REALLY bad people get reincarnated into something less sentient... Like a fish."

"So every religion is right? Other than the major ones, I mean," Calliope questioned.

"That's correct," Asmodeus replied.

"That's so cool!" Calliope laughed. "But... Wait, what about Supernaturals? Like... What about me?"

"Supernaturals go to Purgatory," Asmodeus explained. "Well, that's the name you'd know it by. Because you're not human, your soul can't be judged as a human's, so you'll go to Purgatory. That's where I'll go as well. And every animal goes there. But it's not bad like some religions would make you believe. Think of it like this... It's basically Earth 2.0."

"Oh... That doesn't sound bad," Calliope said.

"It's definitely not. To me, it always sounded like... Well... Heaven," Asmodeus said, smiling. "But I'm gonna go take a seat now. I'll be waiting for you." He kissed Calliope on the cheek before walking away.

Dysnomi huffed like a pouting child when Asmodeus left, then looked at the floor. He mumbled, "Even if you wanted it... He abducted you, Calli. The power that he held over you made it assault, whether you agree or not... It wasn't right."

"Dys..." Calliope whispered. "If I had been alone in a room with him under any other circumstance, I still would've done it. It may not seem right to you, but I wanted him. Hell, I NEEDED him. I don't expect you to understand, but... It's always felt like my soul is aching to be with his. It's so hard to control myself around him. I know we hooked up and I told you we can't do it again... And I'm sorry that I hurt you... But he didn't assault me. It was wanted and reciprocated. I need you to understand. I realize it hurts, Dys, but please don't be upset with him. I'm the one who hurt you."

Rather than saying anything, Dysnomi just looked at the floor and nodded. At first, was trying so hard not to scream, but when he walked off, he had to hold back a rueful smile as he thought about how ironic it was that the first person he had caught real feelings for loved someone else.

Salem and Nagaveni had taken seats on the front couch, Dysnomi was in a chair, and Asmodeus was on the back couch. Calliope sat next to Asmodeus, laying her hand on his knee when she noticed his nervous expression. It was the first time that he was hanging out with all of her friends. He had been around Nagaveni a few times in the past week, but he had never been around all of them at once. *While Calliope assured me they've forgiven me, it seems that at least the trickster has some hard feelings,* he thought.

"Alright, so..." Calliope said, pulling Asmodeus from his thoughts. "I was contacted by someone online. They might have a lead on whoever wants me dead. Personally, I think it's worth checking out since we don't have any other leads. We're leaving for New Orleans tomorrow morning. But first... I would like to propose a toast... To tracking down whoever this fucker is and figuring out why they want me dead."

"Alright! Here's to... The Cosmic Paradise for bringing all of us back together," Nagaveni said. "And to Calli for playing the diplomat tonight. She's able to keep us civil and fun." Calliope snorted in response.

"To the Cosmic Paradise... And to all of you for being so supportive of me this year. I love making all kinds of wonderful magical objects for you and I hope I can continue to be your go-to *'witch bitch'* for many years," Salem joked.

"My turn next," Dysnomi announced. He leaned forward with his drink, looking at Calliope with a smirk. "To the Cosmic Paradise... And to Calli for coming back here in one piece. I already knew that you're a hell of a lover, but as it turns out, you're a hell of a fighter, too." He smiled and winked at her. "I'm so proud of you for being able to face that terrifying situation and come back to me." He blew a kiss in her direction, ignoring Asmodeus' death glare.

Calliope gave Dysnomi a shocked look while Asmodeus' eyes darkened. Asmodeus reached his arm around her waist then, pulling her into him. He made eye contact as with Dysnomi while he did, smirking. He was so caught up in proving that Dysnomi couldn't have her that he didn't notice the way that her body tensed, or how her hand started shaking as she desperately tried to calm her breathing.

Dysnomi started to stand—wanting to protect Calliope—when Nagaveni touched his bicep. Her snakes hissed and she shook her head no, causing him to let out a frustrated sigh as he ran his hands through his hair.

"I guess that makes it my turn," Asmodeus mumbled. "To the Cosmic Paradise, although I've never tried it." He smiled at Calliope and she nodded at him, encouraging him to continue. "And to Calli for believing in me, seeing the best in me, and doing everything to bring that out of me." His eyes were shining, looking at her like he was going to cry. "I'm so sorry for everything. I really don't understand how you can forgive me... I'll never be able to."

Calliope smiled at Asmodeus, her expression soft and caring. "I guess that leaves it up to me to close it out," she said, laughing. "To the Cosmic Paradise—the best damn drink I've ever had—and to all of you for being the best friends I've ever had. You've been there for me through everything. I just want you to know that I couldn't do any of this without you." She laid her head on Asmodeus' strong, muscular shoulder and he drew her closer to him to kiss the top of her head. She smiled and relaxed into his touch, wishing that she could forget how she had jerked away from it the week before. She watched Dysnomi clench his fist, clearly pissed at Asmodeus for touching her. "...And to you, Deus, for helping me get out alive," she whispered, craning her head up to look at him.

Before Asmodeus could respond to tell Calliope that he didn't do anything but hurt her, she leaned forward, kissing him on his lips. He hesitated, then pulled her closer to him and deepened the kiss with one arm around her waist while his free hand placed his drink on the table before cupping the back of her head.

Dysnomi watched them from his seat with disgust and anger. Nagaveni reached over and squeezed his knee, calming him. However, the contact caused her snakes to hiss angrily.

Dysnomi lightly brushed his thumb over Nagaveni's knuckles and smiled at her. There were times when he thought that he could have really liked her if he had met her first. *Then again,* he thought. *I'm not really the relationship type. Something tells me she is.* He cleared his throat, causing Calliope and Asmodeus to finally break apart.

"Sorry," Calliope said, laughing breathlessly.

"I'm not," Asmodeus growled in Calliope's ear, making her shiver.

"Anyway..." Calliope said as she sighed. "To the Cosmic Paradise—straight from the Fae Realm and Dys' brilliant mind!"

"And to Nini for naming it!" Dysnomi added.

"AND..." Nagaveni continued. "To our little vacation in New Orleans!"

Most of Calliope's friends laughed, but Asmodeus just said, "You all realize this isn't a vacation, right? We need to figure out who was fucking with Calli and why. They used my anger against me. I could have killed her."

"Hey..." Calliope whispered, placing a hand on Asmodeus' knee. "It's okay. They know it's not a vacation, but sometimes it helps... To keep things light." She hugged him and he returned it, taking a shaky breath and nuzzling his face into her hair.

"I know. I'm sorry, Calli. I'm just worried," Asmodeus replied.

Calliope nodded and finished her drink. Her friends smiled and did the same, taking her lead when she stood and offered Asmodeus a hand. "Do you wanna dance with me and forget about everything else tonight?" she asked.

Asmodeus smiled at Calliope as he accepted her hand. "I'd love to dance with you, *mi hermosa chica,*"[13] he responded.

Calliope pulled Asmodeus toward the door, the rest of her friends following them. In the upper level of Tartarus, many different Supernaturals were still on the dance floor, having fun. She pulled him close to her in the sea of people and they danced—along with the rest of her friends—for what felt like forever.

When they all finally were tired enough to go home and sleep, it was during the dark, early hours of the morning. Asmodeus kissed Calliope as softly as he could before they parted ways. He was constantly holding himself back, terrified of hurting her again. He watched as a car pulled up for her and Nagaveni. Then, waited until he

---

[13] "my beautiful girl,"

couldn't see the car anymore before finally calling his own and going home.

9. LAISSEZ LES BON TEMPS ROULER

(AIN'T IT FUN)

An almost four hour flight the next day came unceremoniously to an end, its journey landing everyone aboard the plane at the Louis Armstrong International Airport in New Orleans, Louisiana. Soon after touching down, the group of Supernaturals were grabbing their luggage, then calling a car to take them to the hotel, which Calliope had booked the night before. When they arrived, Calliope checked everyone in, then dragged her suitcase up to her suite with the others doing the same.

After settling in, Calliope changed into a pair of tight, distressed skinny jeans and a tight black crop top. An area of exposed cappuccino skin allowed her to show off her gleaming diamond-studded navel piercing. Her tattoo of a mermaid tail was also visible—it followed along the side of her left hip bone and ended at her lower back, where coral and other colorful sea plants burst from the waistline of the tail. She then styled thick Viking braids along both sides of her head, letting them hang loosely down her shoulders and her back with the rest of her hair until it reached her waist. She pulled on high-heeled black ankle boots—complete with laces up their fronts and a silver buckle at the sides—before replacing the black half-inch tunnels in her earlobes with a set of golden tunnels. The tunnels also had golden pentagrams that dangled from the ends.

    The Hand of Restoration sat on Calliope's finger, though she didn't believe that it was working. *I hope I'm wrong, of course,* she thought. *But it doesn't seem to be helping anymore.* Her hand and elbow both had deep bruises on them and her chest was sporting the cut down the middle, which had been sliced open by Menoetius. She checked her face in the mirror, gently touching the scarring red line across her cheek—the one place that seemed to be healing, even if it was only a little—and the jagged gash along her forehead, which ran into her hairline. She sighed, feeling sad, then jumped when she heard a sharp knocking on the door to her room. She took a moment to compose herself, then hurried over to answer the door, where she found Nagaveni standing on the other side.

"Whoa, you look gorgeous!" Nagaveni exclaimed.

"You must be talking about yourself, 'cause look at you!" Calliope replied, whistling at Nagaveni.

Nagaveni blushed and dismissed the compliment, but Calliope had been serious. Nagaveni had changed into a pair of black skinny jeans and a tight hot-pink shirt with long sleeves and she had tucked the shirt into the waist of her jeans. Her enchanted Serpent Tamer necklace was hanging around her neck as usual, meaning her snakes had been put to sleep. In their place, only long jet-black hair could be seen flowing over her shoulders... All the way down to her waist. She was wearing a pair of three-inch hot-pink heels, and a pair of linear diamond drop earrings dangled from her ears.

"Are you ready to go? I think the guys are already waiting for us in the lobby," Nagaveni said. She sounded excited, her emerald eyes sparkling as if to prove it.

"Yeah, I'm ready. The person meeting us shouldn't be at the bar until the sun goes down, so we've got plenty of time to kill. We might as well get a drink or two while we're waiting," Calliope said. She grabbed the key to her suite before hurrying out. shutting the door behind her and following her best friend into the lobby.

When Calliope and Nagaveni made it downstairs, they noticed Dysnomi and Asmodeus. The Supernatural men were standing across from each other in the hotel lobby and pointedly ignoring one another.

Dysnomi whistled when he noticed the two women, then commented, "Damn, look at you two. You both look amazing!" He looked at Nagaveni with a mysterious gleam in his eyes, then turned his gaze to Calliope. He let his eyes roam down her body, then back up. A smirk was playing on his face, making him look arrogant, which was pretty typical for him.

Nagaveni blushed and looked at the floor while Calliope returned Dysnomi's gaze, fully taking in the sight of him.

'Wow, he's looking as good as always,' Lyn said to Calliope.

Yes, he is, Calliope replied, tearing her eyes away from Dysnomi.

Dysnomi was wearing a black tank top and a pair of jeans, along with black combat boots. His shoulder-length champagne-blond hair was perfectly disheveled, flipped over to one side.

It looks like he just woke up, Asmodeus joked telepathically to Calliope.

He's perfected the look of not caring, Calliope replied, jokingly.

Dysnomi's black and gray tattoos lined both of his arms from his shoulders to his wrists and made the rest of his alabaster skin look as light as porcelain. He was wearing plain gold chains on his wrists and around his neck; he even had one hanging from the side of his jeans, connecting from one belt loop to another.

Calliope met Dysnomi's eyes, watching the golden flakes shine mischievously inside of them. "You're not looking so bad yourself, you know," she said with a sly smile. "I love what you did with your hair."

Dysnomi smiled and ran his hands through his hair, messing it up even more. "Oh, yeah? You like that, huh?" he asked, teasing.

Asmodeus shot a hard look at Dysnomi, his eyes turning dark for a moment before he finally broke his glare to look at Calliope in awe. "You look so beautiful," he said, breathlessly. "I just gotta tell you, I've dealt with so many contracts involving beautiful women—from models and actresses to dancers and singers—and none of them could ever even HOPE to attain the beauty that you possess."

He looked her up and down, and she could see in his striking electric-blue eyes how badly he wanted her. "...I didn't know that you ever got a tattoo," he mentioned then, shocked. "It fits you, though. I mean, the tail, the sea plants, and all the beautiful colors... *¡Me encanta!*[14] It certainly looks amazing on you. Though, so does everything else."

"Oh, you didn't know about her tattoo? I'm surprised... I thought you were intimate with her," Dysnomi said with a sneer, the disgust evident in his voice. "You must have noticed it." He shrugged before continuing. "Then again, it must be so fucking hard to control yourself around beautiful women like Calli, especially when it goes against your... Nature..." He curled his lip up like he was snarling. "To control yourself at all. I'm sure you just weren't paying attention to the little details."

Calliope watched Asmodeus as his eyes turned ink-black. He took a step toward Dysnomi, angry at Dysnomi for telling him that he probably couldn't control himself because it wasn't *'in his nature'* to do so.

Deus looks like a god with his flawless skin and his silky black hair, Calliope thought. *And his blue eyes when he's got his demon half under control.*

---

[14] "I love it!"

Asmodeus' hair was flipped to one side. He was wearing a blood-red long-sleeve shirt that he'd left halfway unbuttoned, leaving his taut chest muscles and abs exposed for Calliope—further cementing his godlike appearance in her mind—and a pair of black skinny jeans, which had a hole in one of the knees. He was also wearing a black pair of *Vans* shoes. He had a thick chain hanging around his neck, along with a thin necklace which hung down lower and held a steel horned demon skull between his pecs. "What exactly are you implying, trickster?" he asked. His voice cut through the air, sounding ethereal and demonic. For once, however, Calliope didn't feel like it was penetrating through her very soul... Not at first, anyway.

Dysnomi did not back down from Asmodeus' challenge. Instead, he mimicked Asmodeus' actions, taking a step forward before using his magic to project an image of himself in an attempt to appear more threatening. "You fucking heard me, demon," he replied, using his magic to make his voice surround them, blocking out all other sounds. "You're a piece of shit. Coming here now to try helping? Really? You're the one who fucking broke her in the first place! I can't even move too fast near her now without her jumping! Do you feel no shame for what you've done? No remorse? Look at her! She's not even healing like she's supposed to! She has a fucking scar now! You had to have that damn dagger, and because of it, the damage can't be fixed! And even if she hadn't returned your advances that night, you would have just used her anyway before you fucking beat her to death!"

"Stop it, both of you!" Calliope yelled. "We're in public! What if someone sees you?"

Calliope reached out, trying to grab one of the men to make them stop fighting. Asmodeus lifted himself into the air before she could touch him, coming eye-to-eye with Dysnomi's projection. His body caught fire then, thick black smoke rising from the flames.

At the same time, Dysnomi used his magic to lift a type of translucent-blue barrier between them to keep her from interfering. The air shimmered around the magical wall as he waved her off.

Calliope and Nagaveni looked around the lobby, ensuring that no humans were witness to the utter catastrophe. The women shared an exasperated look—Nagaveni shaking her head with embarrassment, and Calliope mumbling, "These fucking children."

"You're really gonna judge me like you aren't just as bad?" Asmodeus asked in his demonic voice as his horns appeared from his head. "Didn't you fuck her the same night that I appeared, assuming it would be the last night you'd ever see her? You did that, but you refused to warn her that something was going to happen."

Calliope's body stiffened. She grabbed her arm, digging her nails into it so hard that she punctured it, blood spilling out over her cappuccino skin. However, she was too upset to notice. She felt sick when she was hit with the realization that she had been used by both of them. She thought to Lyn, *Dysnomi just wanted someone to hook up with, and Asmodeus just needed someone to use as a punching bag. And I thought they were my friends.*

'They are, Calliope,' Lyn replied. *'They both clearly care about you. They're just too angry right now to realize that they're hurting you.'*

Nagaveni stood next to Calliope. She was frozen in shock while watching Asmodeus and Dysnomi with one of her hands held over her mouth. Her fingers were covering most of her face, but she didn't even seem to notice. "Please, stop..." she cried, but her voice was too quiet at the time for the two feuding men to even notice.

"Yeah, okay? I just wanted to know what it would feel like! I wanted to know what could have been between us! I had this sinking feeling that something was gonna happen and that I'd never get a chance like that again. But you know what? I was wrong, and I should have fucking stopped you," Dysnomi replied. He snapped his fingers and a scene from that night began to play in front of the group like it was a movie. They all watched, unsure of what they should feel. He pointed toward the scene and said, "Look at the way she walked and how her hand roamed over her body. Now, look at the way she glanced back at me. I was not going to let her tease me like that and then leave me. It was so fucking obvious that she wanted me. All I had to do was make a move." They all watched the scene as Calliope started to walk away. Then, they watched as he grabbed her wrist, pulled her toward him, and planted a kiss on her lips—lingering there a moment before asking her, *'...Stay. Just for a while?'*

"You're just as awful as me, then," Asmodeus told Dysnomi. "You wanted her. No–you needed her... The same way I did. The only difference between you and me... Is that I'm willing to admit that when I felt like I had power over her, I only cared about what I could do. Meanwhile, you—even after watching yourself grab her and pull her back—will continue to claim that there was more to your decision than you simply wanting to fuck her before you missed your chance."

Calliope couldn't take it anymore. Everything that Asmodeus and Dysnomi said hurt her, and she was at her breaking point. Tears filled her eyes as she levitated over the magical barrier that was between her and the two hateful men. "Do you both only see me as a body? As nothing more than a tool to satisfy you? I know that I'm essentially the personification of lust... I really can't help that. And I thought you'd understand that, Deus, since that's essentially what you are, but in the form of a cambion. Yet, I've never treated you that way... Or even talked about you that way. I thought you—and maybe even you, Dys—would recognize that I could be so much more than that... I'm sorry if I haven't proven any more worth to you than that..."

With that, Calliope landed on the floor of the hotel lobby, tears streaming down her face. Asmodeus and Dysnomi both dropped their magical effects, the two men feeling guilty. They began to walk toward her—wanting to apologize—but she didn't allow them to. She just wiped away tears that were running down her face and stormed out of the door of the hotel. She wanted nothing more in that moment than to get away.

Nagaveni gave both Asmodeus and Dysnomi an angry glare before she raced out after Calliope. She wanted to scold the men, but she knew that it would have to wait because her best friend needed her more than anything at that moment. She looked back to see that both men were following behind her cautiously as she walked out into the streets of New Orleans.

"Wait," Nagaveni said, stopping Asmodeus and Dysnomi by putting her hand up. "You need to make sure that no humans witnessed your little display, so check around. And Dys... If anybody saw that, you're gonna need to enchant them." Dysnomi nodded, then turned to go back inside. She nodded back at him and Asmodeus before running off to figure out where Calliope went.

10. DANCING'S NOT A CRIME

(THE WEREWOLF, THE ELF, THE HUNTER, AND THE ONE LEFT BEHIND)

By the time Nagaveni caught up with Calliope, she found the siren inside the bar they were supposed to meet at after dark. Dysnomi and Asmodeus walked in behind the gorgon, just in time to hear her exclaim, "Whoa, what is Calli doing up there?"

Dysnomi and Asmodeus looked at where Nagaveni was pointing. They saw Calliope front-and-center on a raised stage across the room. She was singing a sad, sweet melody while leaning against a beautiful grand piano, which was being played by a tall, muscular man with mocha skin, shaggy dark copper-brown hair that fell down past his shoulders, and bright golden-yellow eyes that reminded them all of a wolf's. He was wearing an expensive black suit with a gold button-up shirt underneath it. A few buttons remained open, revealing a hairy, muscular chest.

He was smiling at Calliope as he played, but he didn't seem to be completely enamored with her like the crowd of humans were. Instead, the man seemed to just be playful with her, like he was flirting rather than falling in love under her spell.

"What the hell is she doing? I thought we were supposed to lay low when we got here," Dysnomi said. Nagaveni thought he sounded annoyed... And slightly jealous.

"And that's coming from the guy who just used his magic to place giant projections in the middle of a hotel lobby," replied Nagaveni, rolling her eyes at him playfully.

Dysnomi simply shrugged and said, "Fair point, Nini."

"On another note, look—" said Asmodeus, pointing at Calliope. "Her bruises are finally healing."

Nagaveni and Dysnomi looked closely. They did see that the deep bruises Calliope had were almost completely healed, while the gash on her forehead had become nothing more than a faint scar. They couldn't see the one on her chest because of the top that she was wearing, but considering the way that the other wounds healed, they were almost certain that it was also nothing more than a scar. "I hope it didn't freak any of the humans out to watch her heal some pretty OBVIOUS wounds right before their eyes," Nagaveni said, rubbing at her temples. *My friends are stressing me out today,* she thought, sighing. *Why do they all insist on giving me a migraine?*

When Calliope and the man playing the piano finished, the bewitched audience gave them a loud round of applause and begged Calliope for more. "I'm so sorry everyone, but I really need a break," she announced, fanning herself with her hand dramatically. "You've all been an amazing audience, though. Please give a round of applause to my new friend on the piano, Amarok! I never could've done this without him." She grabbed the burly man's hand then, and they bowed together.

When Calliope and Amarok stood up, Nagaveni noticed for the first time exactly how big Amarok truly was. *He has to be at least six feet, eight inches tall,* she guessed. *That's insane!* She walked to the front to greet Calliope as the siren climbed off of the stage. As she walked, she whispered to herself, "That is a giant man."

"Hey!" Calliope exclaimed when Nagaveni got close, throwing her arms around Nagaveni's neck.

"Oh! Hi!" Nagaveni said. She was surprised, but she returned Calliope's hug. When they broke apart, she looked up at the man who was standing next to Calliope, Amarok. She was in complete awe of the man. She thought, He looks like a professional bodybuilder. "I can see that you've made a new friend here at the... Wait, what is this place called again?" she asked.

"The Tipsy Piano," Amarok answered. His voice was deep and commanded attention. When he laughed, Nagaveni could feel the vibrations that rumbled from his chest. "I... May or may not have had something to do with the name," he said. He shrugged, then laughed again.

"Oh! That reminds me! The owner named a new drink after me!" Calliope said, bouncing with joy. "C'mon, you gotta try it, Nini! You all definitely need to catch up with me anyway." She laughed, grabbing Nagaveni by the hand. She grabbed Amarok with her other hand while smiling at him, and dragged them both to the bar. Dysnomi and Asmodeus followed behind the three of them, feeling awkward.

As soon as Calliope sat at the bar, the bartender—a slender man who had flawless ebony skin, chest-length jet-black dreadlocks with silver and gold pieces decorating them, and a silver hoop piercing in his bottom lip—slid a turquoise-colored drink toward her. She giggled as she accepted it and asked him, "Can I please get one for my friends as well? They'd love to try this drink you named after me."

"Anything for you, cher," the bartender said with a wink, already working on making the other drinks.

"You're the absolute best, Zeph," Calliope said with another small giggle. Nagaveni could tell that Calliope had already had quite a few drinks and she wondered if she should cut Calliope off. However, she didn't want to be too overbearing.

The bartender finished making their drinks, then slid each drink across the bar to each person. "Thanks, brah. These are great," Amarok said, picking his drink up in his massive hand. "But you already know I like all the drinks you create."

Calliope raised her glass in the middle of the group and said, "I would like to make a toast to the beautiful city of New Orleans, to my amazingly cool new friends..." She paused to wink at Amarok. "And to this awesome drink that Zeph's created for our enjoyment. May I proudly present to all of you... The Siren's Lament," she finished, smiling.

"Calli!" Dysnomi hissed at Calliope. "Why the hell would you tell these people that you're—"

Before Dysnomi could finish his sentence, Calliope raised a hand, stopping him. "Relax, Dys," she said, rolling her eyes. "Amarok over here's a fucking werewolf." She shrugged, patting Amarok affectionately on his arm. She acted like her friends were all supposed to know that the man who she had just met was a werewolf.

"Whoa, you're really a werewolf?" Nagaveni asked, in awe of Amarok.

"Yeah, I am," Amarok replied, laughing.

"Well, I guess that explains how massive you are," Nagaveni commented. Then, she shook her head as she blushed with embarrassment. "Oh, I just meant... Well... It's just that... You're like, the tallest person I've ever seen. I... Well, I was just amazed."

"You should definitely see me in my wolf form then," Amarok said, laughing. "I'm easily eight and a half feet tall as a wolf."

"Okay, but Calli," Asmodeus said, cutting in. "What about the bartender? You also told him what you are."

Calliope waved a hand and rolled her eyes, dismissing Asmodeus' comment. "Oh my gods, Deus, chill out. Zeph's an elf."

Zephyr heard them and joined in their conversation, saying, "I figured mon cher wasn't human when I noticed the Hand of Restoration on her finger. Those rings are not easy to come across. That inscription—" He pointed to the writing around the ring. "Is what gives the ring its magical abilities. And it changes to say something different for each and every person who wears the ring."

That information intrigued Calliope. She sat a little straighter on the barstool and asked Zephyr, "Can you tell me what it says while I'm wearing it? I can't read Álfarin, unfortunately."

Zephyr took Calliope's hand, inspecting the ring that was sitting on her finger. He turned her hand over as he read the Álfarin runes that were etched into the side of the gold ring. "It says..." he started. Then, he paused, making a 'hmm' sound like he was confused.

"What is it?" Calliope asked Zephyr, worried. "Is it something bad?"

"No, no, nothing like that," Zephyr replied. "It simply says, *'et pourtant je souris'.* Hm. I've never heard this phrase before." He read the Álvarin runes that were etched into Calliope's ring out loud in French, giving a sound to them for her.

"Umm... Could you please translate that into English for me?" Calliope questioned with a slight laugh and a curious raise of her eyebrow.

"Yes, of course, cher. It simply says, *'...And yet, I smile.'* But I'm sorry to say that I can't provide you with any insight about what that might mean," Zephyr responded.

Calliope smiled, telling Zephyr, "Not to worry, Zeph. I know exactly what it means. Would you like to know?"

"Of course, cher. I've never heard that phrase before," Zephyr replied, curiously.

"Okay, so it's from a TV show, *The Walking Dead*. Basically, the phrase just means that despite all the bad things in our lives—despite everything that's knocked us down over and over again—we never gave up hope and we never stopped trying to see the light at the end of the tunnel," Calliope answered. "It means that no matter how dark or bleak the world may seem, I'll always smile because I know that at least I'm still alive and well."

"I like that," Zephyr said, smiling.

Just as Calliope finished her drink and started feeling a nice buzz, a slow romantic song began to play over the bar's surround-sound speakers. She grinned, swaying her hips side-to-side in rhythm with the music as she stood. With a sly smile toward Amarok, she held her hand out to him and asked, "I'm not exactly dressed for this occasion... But... Nevertheless, would you like to dance with me?"

Amarok flashed Calliope a wolfish grin, then bowed deeply, answering, "I would be more than honored to dance with you, beautiful." He took her small hand in his giant one—enveloping it—then led her to the middle of the floor.

Calliope allowed Amarok to lead her around the floor, between the booths and the bar, gliding with more grace than she had ever known anyone to have. Calliope's left hand was placed delicately on Amarok's broad shoulder during their dance, while Amarok's right hand was placed on Calliope's hip. At least, it was meant to be placed on her hip, but his hands were so large that his fingers wrapped around to the small dip in the middle of her lower back.

Amarok slid his hand up Calliope's side and over her arm, finding her hand that was placed on his shoulder. He pulled her hand away from him with a tenderness that she had rarely felt. He paced backward, holding her away from him gently. Then, he led her into an elegant spin, which ended with her pressed forcefully into his strong chest.

Calliope could hear Nagaveni gasp with excitement and clap for her, but she was so distracted by Amarok that the sound seemed far away. The only thing that kept her grounded in reality was Asmodeus; his feelings of jealousy were invading her mind while she danced.

Calm yourself, Calliope thought to Asmodeus. *Please. It's only a dance. I'm allowed to dance, aren't I?*

Of course you are, Calli. I'm sorry. I'm trying not to be jealous, I really am, but it's just so hard, came Asmodeus' reply inside Calliope's mind.

When the song was ending, Amarok wrapped one of his arms around Calliope's waist and tilted her back, dipping her down far enough that her hair almost touched the bar's floor. She clung to him, relishing the feeling of him holding her to his body tightly. A lone strand of hair fell from behind Amarok's ear, landing on Calliope's cheekbone. She let out a slight gasp from the feeling of his incredibly soft hair caressing her skin. His golden-yellow eyes looked down at her succulent garnet-pink lips before eventually moving up to meet her gaze. She could feel a deep desire inside of him—one that he worked hard to control.

It almost feels... Animalistic? Calliope thought. *I wonder if that's from his wolf.* Before she could ask Amarok about it, however, he pulled her up, paced a few steps away from her, and ran his hand sheepishly through his shaggy dark copper hair. His hair went down past his shoulders, and she found herself thinking, *It definitely reminds me of a wolf.*

Amarok let out a breathless laugh and asked Calliope, "You really are somethin' special, you know that? So, um, what are you doing here in NOLA, anyway? It's not Carnival season yet."

The pair made their way over to the bar as Amarok asked Calliope that. When they sat down—after Zephyr slid another drink into Calliope's hand with a wink—she answered. "You're right, it's not Mardi Gras season, unfortunately," she said. "I'm here on some personal business. You see, someone tried to get me killed, and I fully intend to find out who.

"Why would someone ever try to kill you?" Amarok asked Calliope.

"We honestly don't know," Dysnomi answered before Calliope could.

"That's what we need to find out," said Asmodeus. "But I know no matter who it is, they're damn sure gonna be hearing from me. They fucking manipulated me and it almost worked.

"Are you saying you almost killed her?" Amarok asked Asmodeus.

Smoke began rising from Asmodeus' clenched fists, which he had resting in his lap. "I fuckin' hate myself for that. I can't even fuckin' believe I let anyone manipulate me like that," he said through gritted teeth.

Calliope took her hands and placed them over Asmodeus', extinguishing the flames before any of the humans in the bar could see what was happening. "It'll be okay, Deus. You'll see," she told him.

"I really hope you're right, *mi amor*.[15] I just want you to be safe... Even though I wasn't able to keep you safe from myself," Asmodeus said.

"You can't keep beating yourself up over that," Nagaveni said, leaning toward Asmodeus and laying a hand on his arm.

"Why not?" Dysnomi asked Nagaveni with that arrogant smirk of his and a nonchalant shrug of his shoulders. "I mean, he did try to kill her. Maybe he SHOULD feel bad. Calli's an amazing person. I've never even heard her say a bad word about anyone. Why should it be on us to absolve him of his guilt, anyway? She didn't even get to heal properly thanks to that damn dagger of his," he finished.

Nagaveni chimed in with a response to Dysnomi merely seconds before Calliope could. She told him, "Hush, Dys. You had a chance to help

---

[15] "my love."

Calli, but you chose not to. So, I really don't want to hear a single word from you about it." She jabbed him in the chest with her forefinger as she paused. Then, she gave him and Asmodeus both a hard look. "I expect both of you to stop this nonsense now. You both have caused Calliope enough stress for an entire lifetime. Give her a break for once, please. She has so much on her mind right now. She doesn't need you two fighting and making everything in her life worse," she said, scolding them in her best mom voice.

Asmodeus hung his head in shame while Dysnomi looked away, biting his lip with a guilty expression. It almost made Nagaveni want to cry. She didn't like having to be rude or overbearing.

Thank you, Calliope sent Nagaveni telepathically. *I really hate seeing them like this.*

You're welcome, Nagaveni thought in response. *They'll get over it, I'm sure. It'll probably just take them a little while.*

Calliope was getting antsy, wanting to check the time. She thought that it must have been time for her to meet the woman who had messaged her—someone with the handle *'LivingDeadGirl'* on a chat forum—though she hadn't seen anyone yet.

Right before Calliope could grab her phone, however, the door to the bar swung open and someone rushed inside. It was a young woman who had long and curly cobalt-blue hair, azure-blue eyes, and a skin tone that Calliope could only describe as looking dead. It was iron-gray and there were many charcoal-gray scars all over.

Why does that woman's skin look that way? Calliope wondered. *Is it some kind of disease? Is it contagious? Ugh, that poor woman,* she thought. *The poor woman clearly tried her best to mask what her skin looks like.* The woman was wearing a black-leather jacket over a plain black t-shirt and jeans, with black combat boots and a pair of black-leather biker gloves on her hands. The woman's bangs covered her forehead and her gorgeous cobalt-blue hair was a really good distraction from the iron-gray that was coloring her face. Though, Calliope noticed a few people were staring at the woman regardless.

That must be LivingDeadGirl, Calliope thought, sending that telepathically to all of her friends. Then, she thought, *We should all be prepared for anything. We don't really know anything about this woman.*

We've got your back, Calli, Nagaveni thought in response.

You know we've always got you, Dysnomi thought to her.

Asmodeus sent a thought to Calliope then, telepathically asking her, *So are we feeling suspicious of this woman or no?*

Calliope answered him, thinking, *I don't really know, but I definitely can't just trust a stranger.*

Then, the woman hurried over to Calliope, touching her arm lightly and telling her, "Dere's somethin' big followin' me. Come see wit me. I gotta deal wit it 'fore anyone here sees da damn ting."

Calliope nodded and looked at her friends, trusting that they'd follow her. *'LivingDeadGirl'* hurried toward the small bar's side door, pulling out a silver dagger as she walked. Calliope followed closely behind the woman, pulling the Hell's Scream dagger from the side of her ankle boot. Her friends followed closely behind her—including Amarok, which surprised her since she had only met him that day.

The side door swung open to reveal the alley outside. The whole group walked out cautiously, checking every single inch of the alley.

"So, where is this damn thing that's been following you?" Dysnomi asked the woman, giving her a skeptical look.

"Ya can't see 'less ya lookin' right at it, but I dunno why. I've neva seen one of... Whatever da fuck dis ting's gotta be," said *'LivingDeadGirl'.* She scanned the alley, waiting and ready with her silver dagger. "Dere it is!" she screamed, pointing her finger toward the far end of the alleyway.

It was a complete dead end—*And it's so fucking dark,* Calliope thought—making it hard to see anything at all... *Which is probably amazing for the damn shadow creature,* she thought.

Calliope defensively pulled the Hell's Scream dagger up in front of her. As her eyes adjusted to the vast darkness, she finally realized that although she hadn't seen anything in the shadows of the alley at first, she definitely did then.

What Calliope saw shocked her for a moment, leaving her completely speechless. *It almost looks like... Some kind of massive shadow creature,* she guessed. *It's easily around four and a half or five feet tall, but it may be even taller.* The shadow creature turned toward them abruptly. Whatever the Supernatural creature was, it had their group in its line of sight. It began running at them as fast as it seemed to be able to go.

II. CROSSROAD BLUES IN THE CRESCENT CITY

(BAD MOON RISING)

A giant shadowy figure was bounding toward the group of Supernaturals with impossible speed, and everyone was preparing themselves for a fight. Calliope planted her feet on the ground firmly and held the Hell's Scream dagger in front of herself protectively. The woman who she only knew as *'LivingDeadGirl'* did the same with her silver dagger, pulling it up in front of herself.

Dysnomi held his hands up, letting warm, golden light dance around them. Nagaveni had her eyes planted firmly on the shadows, Asmodeus' hands ignited with fire, and Amarok stood in a fighting stance—although he was hoping that he wouldn't have to turn into the wolf while he was outside in the open.

The shadow figure got closer... And closer... And closer. Everyone in the group had anxiety through the roof. Then, as the creature approached, scarlet eyes appeared inside of the black abyss of shadows.

"Wait!" Calliope yelled out when she saw the eyes. She dropped the Hell's Scream, then braced herself for the impact that she knew was coming. Everyone dropped their fighting stances except Amarok and the unknown woman.

"Stand down!" Asmodeus commanded the two.

"You crazy?! Dis ting's been followin' me all day, an' we're fixin' to get mauled by it!" the woman yelled at Asmodeus.

"Stand. Down," Asmodeus commanded again. Well, that time, the demon commanded her using its creepy, ethereal voice. Flames continued rising off of Asmodeus' body. They began at his hands, then traveled up his arms to his shoulders. "STAND DOWN!" the demon commanded louder. "I will not tell you again."

"Please!" Calliope begged, a choked sob coming out from between her lips. Amarok hesitated, looking at her for guidance. "Please," she begged him, her eyes watering. "She won't hurt you."

Amarok saw the sincerity in Calliope's eyes, so he hesitantly nodded at the unnamed woman. It was a signal for her to stand down, and for her to trust him. The woman sighed, but she put away her silver dagger regardless.

The dark shadows took on the form of a massive wolf moments before it leapt into Calliope's chest, knocking her onto the ground. Amarok protectively took a step toward her. The woman with cobalt hair just yelled, "Holy shit! What da fuck is dat ting?!"

Calliope pushed the huge wolf off of her, laughing. "Okay, okay. Easy now, girl," she said. Nanuk whined and sat back on her haunches while Amarok pulled Calliope up. He only used one hand to set her upright on her feet. She turned to Nanuk and asked, "What are you even doing here?" The hellhound whined and pawed at her feet when she asked, "Did you miss us?" She pat Nanuk on the head, which cut small, thin slices into her hand.

"You sweet little girl, come here," Nagaveni said in a baby voice as she walked over to pet Nanuk with outstretched arms.

Calliope pulled her hand away, wiping her blood onto a tissue, which Nagaveni had pulled from her purse. Her blood had spilled a bit as her cuts healed rapidly, leaving almost no trace of ever having them. She turned toward Amarok and the woman who she didn't know the name of before introducing, "This is Nanuk. She belongs to me. She's a hellhound. Nanuk," she said, turning toward the wolf. "This is my new friend, Amarok."

She held her hand out toward Amarok while she introduced him, and Nanuk moved forward cautiously, sniffing his hand.

Amarok waited patiently until Nanuk allowed him to pet her. When he pulled his hand away, he looked at the wounds—which were all over his hand—before saying, "Damn. Even werewolf hair isn't that fine... And here I was thinking that ours was the sharpest fur there is." As he spoke, Calliope noticed that his scratches were already healing.

"And this is..." Calliope began to introduce, gesturing to the woman known as *'LivingDeadGirl'.* She looked at the woman with a raised eyebrow.

"Oh... Name's Xena," the woman said, holding her hand out cautiously. Nanuk sniffed her hand once, then huffed at her and walked away to sit by Calliope's side once more.

"I am so sorry about that," Nagaveni apologized. "Nanuk's probably just upset about you almost attacking her."

Calliope mock-gasped and exclaimed, "Nanuk!" in a scolding, motherly, tone. "She didn't know who—or what—you were. You were just following her... You scared her because she didn't know what you were, baby." Nanuk put her head down, whining.

"Mais, it's awrite," Xena said. "Don't worry, I'm used to random creatures followin' me 'round here. It's kinda parta my job."

Calliope noticed that Xena talked with a thick Creole accent. *She's probably lived here her whole life,* she thought.

"Oh?" Dysnomi questioned, standing straighter.

"What do you do?" Asmodeus asked Xena.

"I hunt feral Supernaturals... Either Supernaturals dat were born feral an' can't be trusted to eva live 'round people, or Supernaturals dat start harmin' folks later in deir life an' became feral. Officially, I'm jusa fuckin' mercenary..." Xena said, trailing off. She brought her voice down to a whisper before admitting, "Unofficially, though, I get paid by da fuckin' government."

"So, does that mean you hunt... Things like us?" Nagaveni asked, training her eyes on Xena's ear so she could avoid looking into Xena's eyes. She didn't want to turn Xena to stone, but humans always became uncomfortable if she didn't look at them in their eyes. That was her way of working around that problem.

"Us?" Xena repeated, confused.

'Nagaveni just looks like a human at the moment,' Lyn said inside Calliope's mind.

Yeah, she forgets about that sometimes, Calliope told Lyn in response.

"Oh!" Nagaveni exclaimed. She looked around, ensuring that there weren't any prying human eyes. Then, she slipped the Serpent Tamer off and handed it to Calliope. She turned in a slow circle as the snakes atop her head woke from their slumber. When the snakes caught Nanuk's scent, however, they hissed like crazy.

"Okay... I definitely wasn't expectin' dat," Xena said. Her jaw was open in disbelief. She took a step backward, instinctively putting more distance between her and Nagaveni's angry snakes.

"Alright, let's put this necklace back on you before your snakes get too pissed off," Calliope told Nagaveni, walking back to her side with the Serpent Tamer. Two of the stubborn snakes in the back of Nagaveni's head were hissing the way that they always did. Then, one of the snakes attempted to strike at her. She dodged it with ease and joked to Nagaveni, "I see *Hiss Hemsworth* and *Reese Slitherspoon* are as joyful as ever."

Nagaveni laughed as Calliope finally clasped the back of the necklace together, once again putting the snakes to sleep and creating the illusion of long jet-black hair flowing down to her waist.

Xena leaned back against the cool brick wall in the alley and let out a long breath, calming herself. Then, she admitted, "Okay, so, I've hunted humanoid Supernaturals before. But only when they started killin' humans first. So far, dat's really only included some rogue vampires and werewolves."

"Bastian had it coming, though," Amarok said, defending Xena.

"Mais, ya really tink so? Wanna try tellin' dat to dose other big mutts?" Xena asked Amarok.

"Hey..." Amarok growled in a warning to Xena. Then, he sighed and answered, "You know I would if they would even bother to listen to me. But I'm not part of the pack, so my opinion doesn't matter to them."

Xena waved Amarok's comments off, unconcerned. She continued, saying, "Regardless, I only had to kill a handful of sentient Supernaturals. I mean, da occasional werewolf or vampire, a harpy, an' a witch... Once. Dat one was... Awful." She sighed, looking defeated.

"But witches are human," Nagaveni whined, her voice cracking. "I don't understand..." Her lip quivered and her eyes began to water. Dysnomi laid an arm around her shoulders and pulled her into his side, whispering comforting words into her ear as her tears fell. He held out his hand for her and in his palm, golden lights swirled around before a green stuffed snake appeared. The stuffed animal had a bow tied around it underneath its head, and there was a small bag of chocolates tied to the bow.

"If dere'd been any other way, I neva woulda killed her," Xena said as she sighed. "But she was killin' folks for money. She offed six people by da time dey called me. An' she wasn't gone stop. She said dat Hecate—da Greek goddess of da crossroads, witchcraft, an' da Underworld—called on her to do important work. She claimed it was her job to send people to da Underworld for Hecate, an' dat she *'might as well make some money while doin' it'.* She claimed she was only acceptin' jobs for people dat deserved death. But dat's da ting—da *'deservin'* people weren't nothin' more den slight annoyances. Ya can't just decide dat someone deserves to die when ya don't even have all da facts. Da damn witch had gone to da crossroads, performed a ritual, an' made some kinda deal with someone she said Hecate had sent her to strengthen her magic. Den, she abused her new power," Xena finished.

"Wait, she made a crossroads deal?" Asmodeus asked.

"Dat's what she told me, anyway," Xena answered.

"Is that important?" Calliope asked Asmodeus, turning to look at him.

Asmodeus let out a slight scoff with a raised eyebrow, looking amused. "I promise you, Xena, whoever the witch made that deal with was definitely not sent by Hecate," he said. "That had to be a demon. They're the only ones that even make crossroad deals anymore. I mean, other than Papa Lébat, but he conducts most of his business inside the city, and he wouldn't claim to be sent by Hecate. So, I can promise you that your little witch didn't even make it to the Underworld. At least, not the way she was hoping to. If she made a deal with a demon, she probably gave up her soul. See, souls are given to us more often than anything else because everyone thinks that souls aren't real... No matter HOW many times we try to tell them otherwise," he mentioned, rolling his eyes. "So, she's gotta be in whatever version of hell she believed in... Or locked away in the Demon Realm."

Nagaveni wiped her eyes while hugging her new stuffed snake. Then, she said in a small voice, "Well... I guess it sounds like what you did was for the best."

"It had to be done. No other way 'round it," Xena said. "Anyway, most Supernaturals dat I hunt're just tings like wraiths, revenants, ghosts—tings dat can't live in a society like y'all. I mean, dey're usually fine if dey're out in da wild somewhere, but occasionally, one makes its way to da city, an' it has a field day wit da residents. I'm da one dey call in to put an end to da violence."

"Alright, I can see how that's an important job," said Calliope. "Especially around here... But, what does that have to do with us?"

"Well, like I said, I'm officially a mercenary, so I take da occasional job from whoeva's willin' to pay me, provided dat whateva I'm killin' actually needa be killed. If it's sometin' intelligent like a vampire, werewolf, or whateva, I always try to find another way to handle da situation first. I know you may not like my job, but I promise I only kill when it's absolutely necessary." Xena sighed and ran a gloved hand through her hair. She seemed frustrated—though mostly at herself—and she seemed like she didn't want to admit what she was about to. "So, a stranga contacted me on da chat forum dat I found ya on. I neva saw deir face an' I neva met 'em in person. Hell, dey weren't even gonna pay me in person. Dey were just gonna leave da cash somewhere safe for me to pick up—half when I accepted da job an' da other half when I sent 'em proof da job was done."

"Okay, not to be rude, but... What exactly is your point?" Calliope asked. "Where are you going with this?" She leaned down, scratching Nanuk behind the ears and feeling the familiar sensation of a hundred papercuts opening up at once. Her cuts healed as soon as she pulled her hand away, though. The enormous wolf then stood and stretched, letting out an enormous yawn and padding away, dissolving into the shadows.

"Mais, I would neva be able to get used to dat," Xena said. She laughed as she stared into the shadows where Nanuk had disappeared. "Anyway, I'm tellin' ya dis 'cause da job dat dey wanted me to complete was killin' ya. Now, I wouldn't normally accept a job dat's across da country... But I gotta admit, I honestly considered it when dey told me how much dey were gonna pay me."

"Does that mean you're here to kill me?" Calliope asked.

"Please," Xena said, laughing again. "If I wanted ya dead, I woulda killed ya already. I do my research. I have to make sure it's well-deserved 'fore just murderin' anyone," Xena replied with a scoff. "Needless to say, though, you're nada threat to da public. Although, I did notice dat you had beaucoups of friends mysteriously disappear a few years back."

"Oh, about that... Um," Calliope started to say. She was wringing her hands together and trying to figure out what to tell Xena.

"But den I noticed dat it only happened while you was datin' a certain demon," Xena said. She shot Asmodeus a look, but as he opened his mouth to reply, she held a hand up and said, "Save it. I really don't care what'cha do in LA. But dis—" She gestured to the streets of New Orleans. "Is my home. So keep ya nose clean while you're here."

"Y-yeah... Of-of course," Asmodeus stuttered out. Calliope didn't think that she had ever seen him that nervous, or ever heard him stutter like that.

Xena turned back to Calliope, rolling her eyes and saying, "I didn't find out much 'bout da person who tried to hire me, but I know dey didn't want ya to come here. Like, at all."

"Here as in... The Tipsy Piano?" Calliope questioned. "Or like, New Orleans?" She raised an eyebrow. "Oh, and Deus is a cambion. He's half-incubus and half-human."

"New Orleans," Xena answered, ignoring the comment about Asmodeus. "I figure dat means dere was sometin' here dey didn't want ya to find.

Which also means dat dis is da best place dat you could be."

"So instead of killing me, you... What? Brought me here to use me as bait?" Calliope asked.

"Um, I was actually jus' thinkin' dat if you're here and dey don't want ya to be here, it'll probably make your search for dem beaucoups easier. Though..." Xena paused and held one finger out, thinking. "Bein' bait really ain't such a bad idea..."

"Oh, hell no. We are not offerin' Calliope up as bait," Amarok protested, stepping forward. "Xena, you know I respect you and the work you do. You've always been alright with me. But we're not about to just offer her up when we don't even know who we're up against. Let's at least search for whatever this person doesn't want her to find first."

"Mais, whadeva, if dat's what y'all wanna do," Xena said as she shrugged. "Not much more dat we can do tonight, though, so who wanna drink?"

Everyone agreed, perking up as they walked back inside the bar. Nagaveni was still rooted to Dysnomi's side while Xena caught up with Asmodeus to bombard him with questions about hellhounds and all the different hells, trying to learn as much as she could.

Amarok put his hand against the small of Calliope's back, covering it and warming her bare skin in the place that her crop top didn't cover. She hadn't even realized that she was cold until she felt his warm hand against her lower back.

12. THE NAME OF THE GAME

(DRINKING GAMES/A PARTY ON BOURBON STREET)

Zephyr was wearing a welcome smile on his delicate facial features when everyone made it inside of the bar. He also had drinks already waiting for them on top of the bar.

"Zeph, I swear, you are the absolute best," Calliope groaned, taking the seat closest to him, then clinking her glass against his. "So, you're drinking with us now?" Her eyes lit up with amusement and joy as she looked around, noticing that there was no one left inside of the small bar other than her and her friends.

"Of course I'm drinkin', cher. You would, too, after a long day of servin' and bein' nice to the *connards*[16] that come in here." Zephyr gulped down a shot of whiskey, slamming his glass on the counter. Nagaveni giggled at him from where she

---

[16] "assholes"

was sitting next to Dysnomi, prompting him to ask her, "What's so funny, ma chérie?"

Nagaveni replied, "You just look so... Elegant and put-together. It's not every day I get to see someone so regal-looking slam down a shot like that."

"Really, chérie? Hmm... Would you like to make a bet with me?" Zephyr asked Nagaveni with a gleam of mischief in his eyes.

"A-a bet?" Nagaveni questioned, looking down and blushing slightly as she picked at the seam of her shirt.

"Yes, of course. C'mon, it'll be fun. Whoever finishes five shots first wins the bet. The loser has to..." Zephyr said, trailing off as he became lost deep inside of his thoughts.

"Hmmm... If you lose, you have to give me the recipe for the Siren's Lament so I can get the bartenders at Dys' club in LA to make them," Nagaveni said as she looked up and smiled.

"Fair enough," Zephyr replied. "And if you lose, you have to show me your snakes. I would very much like to see the real you."

Nagaveni smiled. "How did you know about my snakes?" she asked. Zephyr nodded toward Calliope. Nagaveni rolled her eyes playfully, then said, "Alright, deal."

Calliope had Zephyr pour out some shots for herself and Amarok as well. "I'm not letting them have all the fun here," she joked. "So... You in, big guy?" She raised an eyebrow, challenging him.

"Bring it on, little girl," Amarok replied, giving Calliope a wolfish grin.

Xena, Asmodeus, and Dysnomi all grabbed their drinks and gathered around to watch the competition while cheering and joking with one another. Calliope thought, *It's really nice to see the guys getting along for once.*

'It has to be the magic of NOLA,' Lyn said to Calliope sarcastically.

Yeah, that's gotta be it. This just feels so weird, Calliope replied to Lyn, jokingly. She smiled at Amarok then as she slammed down her first and her second shots back-to-back. She picked up her third and threw it back as well, but by the time that she set the glass on top of the bar, she noticed that he was already finished with all of his drinks. "What?!" she questioned. "How did you even do that?!"

Amarok only shrugged. "It takes a lot to get werewolves drunk," he said. "Eventually, you learn to drink super-fast so you can actually feel anything from it."

"Well, it doesn't take much for me," Calliope said, shaking her head and giggling. She tilted her head backward, drinking her last two shots back-to-back. Then, she heard an excited squeal from Nagaveni and turned to see the gorgon raising her arms in triumph.

"AND THE WINNER IS... NAGAVENI!" Dysnomi announced, using the same loud, commanding voice that he had used on the opening night of Tartarus in LA. It was encompassing, blocking out every other sound.

It's like his voice is Gandalf and all the other sounds are the Balrog, Calliope thought, laughing to herself.

Zephyr sighed dramatically—almost like he was upset—but his eyes twinkled with a hint of amusement. "Okay, okay. I know when to quit," he said. Pulling out a piece of paper, he wrote down the recipe for the Siren's Lament and slid it across the bar to Nagaveni.

Nagaveni giggled and tucked it away inside of her purse. Then, she said, "I know you didn't win, but I think I still want to show you the real me."

"You serious, cher?" Zephyr asked, his face lighting up with joy and his chocolate-brown eyes shining in the light.

"Yeah. I think you're really cool, so I'd love to introduce you to my little Jörmungandr babies," Nagaveni replied. Then, she unhooked the Serpent Tamer as Zephyr watched, amazed by the magic and by how realistic the illusion had been. When the snakes on the top of her head moved around, hissing softly, he gasped in awe of them. "These are my little Jörmungandr babies. They don't really have names, but Calli kinda makes some up for them," she said.

"Yeah," Calliope chimed in. "Like, these two," she said, pointing to two snakes that were near the front, "This one is *Monty Python,* and this one is *Darth Viper."*

Zephyr laughed before telling Nagaveni, "They're beautiful, ma belle." Nagaveni looked away, blushing. When she finally peeked up again, Zephyr reached over and took her hand. "Thank you for showing me the real you. You're even more beautiful as your true self."

Nagaveni blushed again, and whispered, "Thank you," before holding the Serpent Tamer up to her neck and letting Dysnomi clasp it shut for her.

Zephyr then sighed, saying, "Unfortunately, I really need to close up and get going. I've got a lot to do tomorrow."

"No worries, brah, we'll get outta your way," Amarok told Zephyr, standing up. Amarok and Zephyr slapped their hands together in a type of farewell, then everyone stood up, heading for the door.

"You know..." Dysnomi started. "Just because we're leaving here doesn't mean that we have to go back to the hotel just yet."

"What do you mean?" Nagaveni asked.

"Well, New Orleans is known for its nightlife, right? So, why don't we go check it out?" Dysnomi suggested.

"There's an amazing place on Bourbon Street if y'all wanna check it out," Amarok stated, holding the door open for the group. "It's crowded, but it's worth it."

"You know I'm down for it," Calliope said with a smile as Amarok once again placed his warm hand against her lower back, leading her toward Bourbon Street. She shivered involuntarily and he moved to wrap his arm around her waist, keeping her warm.

Dysnomi had his arm around Nagaveni in the same manner while she held the stuffed snake that he had created for her against her chest.

They all continued walking along streets that were rich with history—Amarok and Xena stopping the group now and then to point out a historical or a cultural landmark—and they eventually came up to a loud, crowded club called Elysium.

Walking inside, Calliope took a moment to view the scene before her as she began seeking out the bar. There was loud music playing from a DJ, who was performing on an enormous stage at the far end of the club. There were also many people on the floor who were dancing, talking, and drinking. It was almost overwhelming—even rivaling the clubs that she would hang out at in Los Angeles. "This is amazing," she exclaimed. "It doesn't even look this big on the outside."

"That's the great thing about NOLA, Calli. Nothing is ever as it seems," Amarok said, walking up behind her. Then, he gave her a drink.

"Well, then... Here's to the Crescent City. I hope that it never changes," Calliope said, raising her glass in the air before drinking the burning liquid inside.

"To the Crescent City!" Calliope's friends repeated, following her lead. She even heard a few random people around her group toast to it and drink with them, which she thought was awesome. Before long, however, her group split apart—everyone either dancing or checking out different sections of the club.

Calliope could see Nagaveni dancing and laughing with Dysnomi, and she thought, *They look so cute together.*

Calliope then danced with Amarok, laughing when he twirled her around. The twirl ended with her back pressed firmly against his chest. He had his arms wrapped around her from behind, and she could feel his hot breath on the back of her neck as she swayed her hips against him in perfect rhythm with the loud music.

"Oh... You're killin' me, Calli," Amarok growled in Calliope's ear. His hands tightened painfully at her waist, causing her to whimper. To her, his growl sounded more like an animal than it did a man. She spun around to face him and found that his golden-yellow eyes were glowing as he stared down hungrily at her luscious, full lips.

"What..." Calliope started to ask, but before she could finish, Amarok's lips came crashing down into hers. His kiss was demanding and relentless. It left them both gasping for air when it eventually ended. She didn't notice until that moment that he had even picked her up, holding her tightly in his strong arms. She smiled and tapped him twice on the arm playfully. He set her back down onto her feet, grinning at her wolfishly.

The moment that Calliope's feet hit the club's floor, she felt anger and jealousy rising inside Asmodeus, who was approaching her and Amarok with Xena in tow. The cambion shook his head then, walking off to grab Dysnomi and Nagaveni. *I can't believe she fucking kissed him,* he thought angrily. *I know we're not together, but I thought we fucking had something.*

'*I fucking told you! She doesn't love you!*' Asmodeus' demon half screamed at him inside his head as he found Dysnomi and Nagaveni. He ignored it and led them back to the group.

"What's going on, Deus?" Calliope asked when Asmodeus returned.

"Xena needs to tell you something. I just figured everyone should hear it," Asmodeus said in response as he sighed.

Calliope could feel that Asmodeus was pretty upset with her, and she realized that he must have seen her and Amarok kiss. However, she reminded herself to focus on what Xena had to say and reminded herself that she could deal with him later. So, she turned to face the drunk hunter.

"So…" Xena started. She was wasted and it clearly showed. "I remembered sometin' dat might be important when I was drinkin' with Deus."

"Okay, what is it?" Calliope questioned. The entire group watched Xena with bated breath, wondering what she was going to say.

Finally, swaying on her feet and leaning on Asmodeus for support, Xena spoke again. "I forgot 'bout dis part before, but da person who tried to hire me mentioned dat you real powerful, 'specially with fire magic an' lightnin' magic. An' dey said dat's on topa your siren abilities like telepathy, levitation, an' da 'sonic shriek', whatever da hell dat is. Dey said…" She gasped and her eyes widened as she remembered. She attempted to walk toward Calliope, but she stumbled. Asmodeus caught her, helping her walk the last few steps like he had been doing that entire night. "Dey said ya dad might be a god, of sorts. A Loa," she said.

Calliope began to laugh. "A god?!" she asked. "Are you serious?"

"I mean… I dunno, but dey seemed pretty serious 'bout it," Xena replied, leaning on Asmodeus to stay upright. "Dey said dat you're da daughter of Shango. He was some… Yoruban king, but he's now known as da spirit of fire an' lightnin'.

He's... He's pretty well-known in da voodoo community."

"Oh, great. First, my mom made herself known to the New Orleans voodoo community, and now I find out that my dad's known around here, too," Calliope said.

"Wait, your mom?" Asmodeus questioned.

"Yeah. Around here, she's known as La Siréne," Calliope answered.

13. CREATURES OF THE NIGHT

(THE BIG BAD WOLF)

Hours passed before the group finally decided to leave and get some rest for the night. Xena stumbled on her way out of Elysium, then giggled when Asmodeus caught her. "Mais, I'm s-sorry," she said.

"It's all good," Asmodeus answered. "Hey, why don't you let me walk you home? You don't really seem like you're in any condition to walk by yourself." He glanced at Calliope, wondering if she would get jealous. However, he only succeeded in making his own jealousy rise when he noticed that Calliope was cozying up next to Amarok in front of him.

"Oh. Sure... Yeah," Xena replied.

"Mind if I walk you back to your hotel?" Amarok asked Calliope at the same moment.

"I would love that," Calliope answered as Amarok wrapped one of his arms around her.

A few steps ahead of Calliope and Amarok, Nagaveni yawned. "I'm so tired," she said. "I haven't stayed out all night like that in ages."

Dysnomi laughed and said, "You need to live a little, Nini. It's the weekend and we're in New Orleans. I don't know about everyone else, but I'm gonna be out all night every night."

As the group walked up to the front of the hotel, Calliope craned her head upwards to look at Amarok. She asked him, "So... I'm kinda curious... Do you have an actual wolf spirit inside you? Like, is it a separate entity from you? The phoenix and the thunderbird spirits inside me are both separate, and when I use their powers, it feels more like they're controlling me... Almost like they can just take over my body whenever they need to."

Amarok looked down at Calliope as they walked toward her room. "Yeah, that's exactly it. The wolf is separate from me. The wolf can take over and change me if I'm really angry or if I need to fight, but it can also take over without changing me," he said. "The wolf is a very simple creature, though, so I don't let him out very often. All the wolf cares about is hunting, fighting, and... Fucking." He looked down at her with hunger in his eyes. Then, he caught himself, shook his head, and said, "Excuse my language, darling." They reached the door to her hotel room and stopped directly outside of it. He said, "Lucky... You get to lay in bed now. I still gotta go home. I live on the outskirts of the city—I needed space to let the wolf run free."

"Well..." Calliope bit her bottom lip, thinking while Amarok sucked in a harsh breath, staring down at her seductive lips. "If you want to, you can stay with me... At least, for tonight," she offered.

"I'd love to..." Amarok started, but he trailed off mid-sentence, looking distraught.

"But...?" Calliope prodded Amarok, a small part of her feeling disappointed.

"But..." Amarok said, sighing. "It was hard enough to control the wolf when I kissed you in the club, even with the number of people that were around us. Calli, I can't promise you that I'll be able to control the wolf if I get you alone." He looked at the floor, appearing nervous and almost scared of himself.

"I guess that makes it a good thing that I don't want you to control it," Calliope replied as she smirked and opened the door to her hotel room.

In one swift movement, Amarok picked Calliope up with one muscular arm under her round ass and walked her into her hotel suite, slamming the door behind him. One of the last things that she heard from the hallway was Nagaveni cheering, "Get it, Calli!" before howling like a wolf.

Then, Calliope heard Dysnomi saying, "Nini... Shush," as he helped Nagaveni into her room. He then whispered to himself, "How the hell did I end up being the responsible one tonight?"

Everything was pushed out of Calliope's mind after that as Amarok threw her onto the bed. He ripped her crop top off of her like he was a savage animal, then tossed the destroyed fabric across the hotel room. He then moved down to her jeans and began jerking them down off of her, kissing his way down her stomach and thighs as he did.

Amarok eventually pulled his own clothes off. Then, he pounced on Calliope like he was a predator and she was his prey, growling into her ear, "You are so fucking beautiful... I'm going to ravish you."

"Yes, please..." Calliope whimpered with a quivering lip. Her eyes widened at the sight of Amarok, taking in his massive size as she grabbed hold of his giant arms, preparing herself. He thrust his huge member inside of her then, soliciting an excited moan from her as she realized that he had to be the biggest man that she had ever been with. His actions were forceful and wild, but they were also filled with passion. "Yes," she whimpered. "Harder... Please." She threw her head back with pleasure as he enveloped her petite body in his massive arms. "Oh... Gods!" she cried out. He dug his nails into her sides then, causing her to scream, "Oh, yes, Amarok!"

Calliope dug her sharp nails into Amarok's back as he thrust into her even harder. He let a growl rumble from his throat to her ear, sounding like a feral animal. "You feel... So... Damn... Good," he said. His words came out during his growl, making him sound more like a wolf than a man.

Calliope pulled back to look at Amarok, noticing that his golden-yellow eyes looked inhuman and that his canine teeth had grown much longer and sharper than normal. *The wolf's coming out,* she thought.

Amarok could see the concern on Calliope's face, so he reassured her by saying, "Don't worry, Calli. I've got it under control... Even though being with you does make it very, very difficult." He growled again, then whispered, "God, the things I wanna do to you..."

Amarok's grip on Calliope tightened, then he scratched down her back hard enough to draw blood. She whimpered in response before kissing him. Then, she scratched her nails down his back and moaned into him, "I like you exactly the way you are. Ravish me, Amarok. Gods, you make me feel amazing."

Amarok grinned, leaving kisses and bite marks down Calliope's neck, slamming his massive length into her harder every time that she scratched him, until they eventually both finished—her screaming his name and whimpering and him growling hungrily in her ear.

When Amarok and Calliope finally caught their breath, they both got ready for bed. After a while, they fell asleep together. Calliope momentarily forgot all of her troubles as she lay there wrapped safely inside of his arms.

14. ALL MAGIC COMES WITH A PRICE

(LA SIRÉNE AND THE BANSHEE)

"So... You're telling me that you have gray skin because a curse was put on you?" Calliope asked Xena the next day. They were sitting together at the bar inside The Tipsy Piano, drinking while they waited for Asmodeus to appear.

"It's not so much a curse as it is a... Sorta magical disease. Dere's no fixin' it," Xena replied. "One day it'll kill me an' dere ain't nothin' anyone can do 'bout it. Da only ting I've found so far dat even helps is an ointment made 'specially for me dat keeps da... Magical necrosis at bay."

"Oh, that sounds awful," Nagaveni said sadly.

"Have you ever had a trickster try to make it go away?" Dysnomi asked.

"Nah, but you're more den welcome to try," Xena replied.

"Alright, let's do this," Dysnomi said, clapping his hands together. He finished his drink, stood, and walked over to Xena. He held his hands out toward her, letting swirling mists of golden light wash over them both before the warm light curled around Xena's skin, enveloping her inside a bright cloud. He seemed to struggle, straining with his magic. His face began to turn red and he grunted like he was in pain.

"Dys..." Nagaveni said as she laid a hand on Dysnomi's shoulder. "Don't hurt yourself, please."

"The magic used to do this—" Dysnomi replied in a strained voice. "It's really fuckin' strong." He let out a pained grunt and was forced to let his magic fade, leaving Xena looking exactly the same. "I'm sorry, Xena. I thought I could fix it, but I guess I can't."

"Mais, it's awrite," Xena replied.

The door to the bar swung open then, and in walked Asmodeus. He glanced at Amarok, who was playing the piano on the raised stage. He sneered at Amarok as he said, "I bet YOU had a fun night."

"What's that supposed to mean?" Amarok asked Asmodeus curiously.

"Oh, nothing," Asmodeus replied, his eyes beginning to turn darker. "Just that I know how fun sleeping with a siren can be. As does Dysnomi. Evidently, it's pretty easy to get a siren to take you to bed."

"What the fuck, Deus?" Calliope asked, annoyed.

"Don't you dare fucking talk to me!" Asmodeus' demon voice was the one that yelled at Calliope then, and his horns slowly stuck out of his head. "I don't want to hear anything from *la puta*.[17] As a matter of fact, I don't want to hear anything from *el chucho*[18] over there, either."

"What the fuck did you just call me?" Amarok asked as he stood. Calliope noticed that his teeth and nails grew longer and sharper, and his golden-yellow eyes started glowing.

"Hey!" Zephyr called out to Asmodeus and Amarok. "Y'all are not doin' this in my bar. Either cut the *merde...*[19] Or leave."

"Whatever," Asmodeus said, shrugging before turning away and crossing his arms as his horns retreated. "So, what are we doing today, Nini?" he asked, his eyes slowly changing from ink-black to electric-blue, though his voice already sounded normal again.

"Calliope's gonna stay here and contact her mom," Nagaveni said, standing and smoothing out her form-fitting strawberry-pink plaid mini skirt.

---

[17] "the whore."
[18] "the mutt"
[19] "shit..."

Asmodeus noticed that Nagaveni and Calliope had coordinated their outfits—as usual—and were wearing the same skirt. He also noticed, though, that they were wearing different tops and shoes with the skirts. While Nagaveni was wearing a loose white crop top and a pair of white open-toed heels, Calliope was wearing a long-sleeve strawberry-pink off-the-shoulder shirt, a matching strawberry-pink cloth choker around her neck, and a pair of high-heel black knee-high boots. Nagaveni's version of the outfit was soft and sweet, while Calliope's version was very commanding and seductive.

"Xena and I are gonna go ask around and see what else we can find out about Shango," Nagaveni continued.

"You're welcome to join us if ya wanna," Xena offered as she stood up and stretched.

"Yeah, that... Um, that sounds great," Asmodeus said, sparing a guilty look at Calliope before looking down at the floor. He then followed Xena and Nagaveni silently.

Asmodeus glanced over his shoulder at Calliope as he walked out of the front door, thinking to her, *Mi amor,*[20] *I would like to apologize. I promise you I'll get better. You don't owe me*

---

[20] "My love,"

anything; I know that. I should never have called you any names. Espero que me puedas perdonar.[21]

That really fucking hurt, Deus. I understand that you can't control what your demon half says, but it still hurts me. I think I just need some space, Calliope telepathically sent Asmodeus in response.

When Xena, Nagaveni, and Asmodeus had left, Calliope waved Dysnomi and Amarok over to her spot at the bar. She pulled out a compact mirror, which had brightly-colored scales on the outside of it. *Those are mermaid scales... If I had to guess,* Dysnomi thought. *...Or siren scales, I suppose.*

Calliope tilted her head to one side, surprised that she could even hear one of Dysnomi's thoughts. He was usually careful about who he allowed to hear his thoughts. She shook her head and said, "That's actually exactly right, Dys." He and Amarok both gave her a confused look. "These are siren scales," she explained. "Before we leave home—if we choose to leave home—every female in the family adds one of her scales to it. The men don't because the men don't have siren powers. I mean, they have life spans as long as the rest of us and they can breathe underwater, but they don't get anything else. Anyway," she continued. "We can use the magic

---

[21] "I hope you can forgive me."

inside the scales to contact each other, no matter where we are in the entire world. Watch," she said, opening the compact and looking into the mirror. She took a deep breath and said, "Show me La Siréne."

A rhino-gray fog swirled within the small mirror. After a few seconds, a beautiful woman appeared on the other end. The woman looked almost exactly like Calliope, though she appeared to be older. The woman seemed to be underwater, making it difficult to hear what she was saying when she opened her mouth. Then, the woman broke the surface and climbed onto a rock, flipping her tail up. When the woman finally spoke again, it was in a language that only Calliope seemed able to understand.

"What the hell kinda language is that?" Amarok asked.

"I believe that's Yemoja—the language of the sirens," Zephyr replied. "I didn't know they even still spoke it."

After a long conversation with her mother, Calliope rubbed her temples and sighed, closing the compact mirror and putting it away. "Well," she said, turning to face the men. "It turns out that Shango actually is my father. But I still have no idea who would want me dead because of that."

"Well, it's a start, at least," Amarok replied.

"Don't worry, cher. We'll figure it out," Zephyr said as he slid a drink toward her.

"Yeah, and if we don't, the worst-case scenario is that we'll just have to fight off some assassins every now and then," Dysnomi joked.

"The problem with that is they'll eventually find an assassin who's more powerful than me," Calliope replied.

"Yes, but will they be able to find one more powerful than a Supernatural who can literally change reality with a snap of a finger?" Dysnomi asked Calliope with an arrogant smirk on his face.

"True," Calliope replied, rolling her eyes. She then joked, "So, I guess that means you're my personal security detail from now on?"

"If it comes down to it? Hell, yeah," Dysnomi said. "I'm not sitting on the sidelines anymore. You're my friend, Calli. I'm gonna fight for you. Consequences be damned."

"Thank you, Dys," Calliope said, laying her hand on his arm. "Oh, yeah. My mother told me to tell ALL of you—" She looked pointedly at the three men who were standing around the bar as she spoke. "That you are ALL very handsome. She reminded me, like... Five times... To tell you."

"Your mother seems very nice," Zephyr remarked. "I could only understand a small bit of what she was saying, but she seems to care about you and worry about you a lot."

"You can speak Yemoja?" Calliope exclaimed, her face beaming with excitement.

"Only small words and phrases, cher. It's not a very common language," Zephyr replied.

"Ah, that is true," Calliope agreed. She finished her drink, then turned to look at Dysnomi and Amarok. "Well, boys... It looks like we've got some time to kill while we're waiting on the others to get back. How should we pass the time?"

"I think I'm gonna go over to the piano. I've got a new song I wanna try," Amarok said. "You're welcome to join me if you'd like."

"Of course," Calliope replied, taking Amarok's hand and walking with him to the piano, which was sitting on top of the raised stage.

Zephyr and Dysnomi remained at the bar to talk while they listened to Amarok play the piano and Calliope sing. When the song ended, Zephyr and Dysnomi both clapped and cheered for them.

Zephyr said, "Beautiful, cher. Just beautiful."

Dysnomi teased Amarok, saying, "Nice tunes, wolf-man."

"Yeah, you wish you could play like that," Amarok retorted, laughing.

Then, Amarok hopped off the stage and held his hand out for Calliope. She accepted his hand, allowing him to help her off of the stage. They had to be careful so her skirt didn't get pushed up. She smoothed her skirt when she landed on the floor, then repositioned the sleeves of her shoulder-less top, ensuring that it didn't slip down and become indecent.

'I sense dread—'

'Danger—'

'Something terrible is coming.'

'Do not venture into the shadows.'

'The shadows—'

'There is evil within.'

Ember and Lyn talked over each other inside of Calliope's mind as they attempted to warn her about... Something. However, their voices sounded all jumbled together inside her mind. She could not figure out exactly what the two spirits were upset about. As she attempted to decipher their meaning, a bolt of lightning zapped through her skull, tapering off around her eyes. It hissed less than a second before dying out altogether. She gasped, her hands flying up to cover her mouth.

Her body felt unwieldy, causing her knees to weaken before failing altogether.

Amarok caught Calliope when her knees gave out, holding her upright. He asked her what was happening, but she didn't seem to hear him. Her eyes were glazed over and when she tried to tell him what happened, the words would not come out of her mouth. She could only make small groaning noises instead.

"It's alright," Amarok said, scooping Calliope into his arms bridal-style. "It's okay. You can come back now. You're safe." He rubbed her cheek softly as she came back to her senses.

"What happened to her?" Dysnomi inquired, helping Amarok set Calliope onto a seat inside a booth.

"I don't know. She was fine for a minute. And then, there was lightning coming out of her eyes and she was like this," Amarok answered worriedly.

"I'll get something for her head," Zephyr said.

As Zephyr turned to walk away, Calliope yelled after him, panicking. "Wait!" she cried. "Don't go into the shadows... Don't... Please..."

Before Zephyr could even ask Calliope what she meant by that or why he shouldn't go into the shadows, an ear-splitting, otherworldly shriek resonated all around the group of Supernaturals. It caused everyone inside the bar to fall to their knees.

"What the fuck was that?!" Amarok shouted when the scream ended.

"No..." Calliope whispered to herself, feeling sick. "That..." she said, answering Amarok and almost hyperventilating from the panic that she was feeling. "Was a banshee."

"Okay... Calm down... It's alright," Amarok replied. "It may have sounded close, but that doesn't mean it's here for you, right?"

"No... You don't understand," Calliope cried as tears streamed in rivers down her face. "There are only two reasons you would ever hear a banshee's sonic shriek: if you were going to witness a death... Or if YOU are going to die."

15. POOR UNFORTUNATE SOUL

(THE SHADOW WOMAN)

A little over an hour later, Calliope, Dysnomi, Amarok, and Zephyr were all drinking at the bar while they waited for the rest of the group to come back with the supplies that they needed to summon Shango. It took Calliope a while, but she had eventually gotten herself calmed down. She mostly had the alcohol to thank for that.

Calliope was feeling a buzz, and she assumed that the guys were as well. Amarok returned to playing the piano while she swayed to the music. Meanwhile, Zephyr became involved in a heated debate with Dysnomi over which trickster god or goddess they thought was the coolest.

"Obviously, it's Loki," Dysnomi argued. "I mean, look at how many modern pieces of media he's been depicted in. His name is known everywhere. That's legendary."

"I mean, Loki's cool and all, but it was the goddess Eris who caused the battle of Troy... And she did it all with a single golden apple—the apple of discord," Zephyr responded.

"Oh, wow, an apple," Dysnomi said sarcastically while rolling his eyes. "Loki has a giant snake, a *'fuck-off'* sized giant wolf, and an eight-legged horse for children. And he's the MOTHER of the horse!"

"We all know that Loki's a freak. That doesn't exactly make him special," Zephyr joked. "Eris had the balls to throw the apple of discord into a room that had three other goddesses in it, then to tell them it belonged to the prettiest goddess. Do you know how brave you have to be to do something like that to Athena, Aphrodite, and Hera? Brah, it even caused Zeus to put his foot in his mouth. He tried to get a human to settle the debate instead of getting involved himself. It takes a lot of balls to knowingly annoy the king of the gods."

Calliope was going to join in their debate when the bar's side door was busted down unexpectedly, making her jump. The force used on the door was so violent that it ended up fracturing the door's wooden frame into tiny pieces.

Calliope was momentarily frightened, but the three men inside the bar jumped up and were immediately prepared for a fight. A creeping sort of darkness came flowing into the bar in waves. Tendrils of dark shadows moved in, and they almost seemed to be alive. Behind the shadowy tendrils, there was a person who appeared to be female. However, it was hard to tell at first because the shadows almost completely covered the person. The only thing that the group could see clearly was the person's java-colored skin, waist-length box braids, and glowing golden eyes.

"Zorya?!" Amarok exclaimed when he saw the woman. Calliope could feel his confusion.

"Amarok? You know this... Shadow woman?" Dysnomi asked.

"I mean, yeah. And she's always been able to control shadows... But I've never seen her consumed by them like this," Amarok replied. "There has to be something else going on here."

As they all spoke, the shadows began to swirl around the men's ankles, tightening around each of them before pulling them all down to the floor.

"What the fuck?!" Dysnomi yelled as he hit the floor.

Zephyr whispered a spell to himself on the floor. A bright flash of light appeared inside his hand, forcing the shadows to retreat so he could stand again.

At the same moment, Amarok allowed his claws and teeth to grow. Then, he used them to tear at the shadows that were wrapped around his ankles, causing the woman who was controlling the shadows to let out a harrowing scream. There was a mixture of pain and anger in the noise.

"What do you want?" Calliope asked as she pulled her Blade of Light out of its holster—which was strapped against her thigh—and Dysnomi conjured his own blade to slice through the shadows that were wrapped around his ankles.

"Calliope..." Zorya said. She spoke slowly, but it was not only her voice that came out of her mouth.

It sounds more like... There's three or four voices speaking? Calliope thought. *What is going on here?*

'Don't listen to anything the shadow woman has to say,' Ember told Calliope in response.

Calliope asked the shadow woman, "What the hell do you want from me?"

"It's ya time," Zorya answered, using her many different voices. "Da other side... Dey're callin' for ya." She tilted her head to one side like she was listening to something that no one else could hear. "Take da siren," she then commanded the shadows that were swirling around her body. "Leave da rest. We don't need 'em."

"Yeah... That's not gonna happen," Dysnomi said, pulling up his Blade of Light. "Not while I'm around."

"Zorya, please. Just stop for a minute and listen to what you're saying," Amarok said in a worried voice. "This is not you. I KNOW you. You follow Baron Samedi, right? He might be the Loa of the Dead, but he's not the one that causes death. He just digs graves and walks souls to the other side. He heals people, and he even resurrects people if they ask him to. But he doesn't send his followers to murder people."

"Maybe he don't," Zorya replied. "But da Shadow Realm has been talkin' 'bout her. Dey told me it's her time to go. I don't know why. Maybe someone made a deal wit da Shadow Realm. But dey're in my head all da fuckin' time. Dey're all around me every fuckin' day. Dis is her fate. It has to be. And whether or not it seems fair, I have to do dis. If I don't, da Shadow Realm will neva let me alone. I'll jus' have to accept da consequences if da Baron has a problem wit it." When she finished talking, her hands shot out in front of her. The shadows crawled over her arms before leaping toward Calliope and the three men who were inside the bar.

A feral growl echoed throughout the room, louder than any that Calliope had ever heard. She looked to the side to see where the sound came from. Next to her, an eight and a half foot tall wolf was standing on its hind legs in the spot where Amarok had been. The wolf looked at her with its glowing golden-yellow eyes and nodded at her. It leapt at the approaching shadows. The wolf's claws tore into the shadows, causing all the different voices to scream in pain.

Zephyr whispered the same spell into his hand again and, just like the first time, a ball of light formed inside his palm. The shadows seemed to have learned from the first time, however. They dodged the light and quickly dove through the dark sections of the room. The shadows snuck up behind him and grabbed him by his ankles, pulling him down. He came crashing to the floor face-first and his nose slammed into the hardwood. He grunted in pain as his nose began to gush blood.

Calliope and Dysnomi pulled their weapons up, holding their blades in front of them defensively. They both slashed at the shadow tendrils, watching as the tendrils burned away where the warm glowing light from their blades had touched them.

The shadows changed then, twisting themselves until they looked more like leather whips than anything else. After the transformation, Zorya pulled her hands up with her palms facing forward. Then, she slammed her hands down, hard! The whips mimicked her exact movements, pulling upwards before slamming down toward Dysnomi's and Calliope's heads. Dysnomi jumped to his right, barely avoiding the hit, while Calliope rolled forward and jumped back up behind the shadows. They heard a loud *CRACK!* when the shadow whips struck the open air instead of the intended targets.

"This is getting really fucking annoying," Dysnomi grumbled as one of the whips wrapped itself around his ankle, yanking him into the air upside-down. He cut himself free and landed on his feet, laughing when he heard all the screams as the shadows burned.

Amarok growled and swiped at the tendrils that were advancing on him. The wolf's head was lowered and his ears were laid back, which was a sign of annoyance in wolves. He was splitting his time between dodging the shadows when the shadows were gaseous, since he couldn't hurt them in that form, and viciously tearing through the shadows when they became corporeal.

With the entire group distracted, Zorya seized the opportunity to push most of the shadows toward Calliope. Some of the shadows formed more whips, lashing out across Calliope's body and face. Others formed thick chains, wrapping themselves around her ankles and wrists. The shadow chains then held her in place as she continued to get lashed by the whips. She was getting deep cuts all over her from the whips, and her new outfit had become torn and bloody. It hurt... But mostly, it just made her angry.

Before Calliope could do anything to fight the whips that were hitting her and the chains that were holding her, Zorya walked over. The shadow woman pulled out a silver needlepoint knife as she did.

Calliope noticed that the knife had shadows slithering around inside the hilt. However, she didn't have much time to think about that before the Shadow's Edge blade was stabbed deeply into her abdomen. Although she knew that it wouldn't kill her, the pain that it gave her was unbearable—more so when it was pulled out of her. She couldn't hold back her sonic shriek then, so she tilted her head back and allowed herself to scream. Her scream was head-splittingly loud and it caused everyone to cover their ears. Even the shadows seemed to vibrate with pain. As she screamed, her hands and wrists ignited, becoming engulfed in flames and burning away her shadow restraints. The flames then moved down to her ankles and did the same to the shadow restraints that were there.

Zorya stumbled backward a few steps when the restraints burned away completely. She began gasping for breath like it had been her physical body that was being burned. As she backed away, she heard what sounded like a sudden thunderstorm start up. A loud thunderclap caused her to jump with fear. Her eyes widened when bolts of lightning came shooting out of Calliope's eyes and she thought to the Shadow Realm spirits, *No one told me she had dis many powers. I'm no match for all dis.*

'*You will do as you are told to do!*' the Shadow Realm spirits screamed at Zorya inside her mind, and she covered her ears.

The lightning bolts zipped around Calliope's head and her hair flew upwards in static waves. It was the same way that a person's hair would fly up after rubbing a balloon on the top of their head. One bolt shot out and hit Zorya, sending Zorya crashing to the floor. Her powers died out before she could strike again, however. The exhaustion caused her to fall onto her knees, and she clutched the gaping stab wound in her abdomen when she landed.

Amarok shifted back into his human form and ran over to Calliope. He was attempting to check out her wound, but the shadow tendrils interrupted him as they lashed out once again.

"Enough!" Dysnomi screamed, using his encompassing voice. The sound boomed throughout the small bar. Then, he held his hands out toward the shadows with his palms facing forward. His glowing golden magic swirled around his hands as he whispered, "Cleanse the darkness. Get rid of the shadows." He smirked once before sarcastically adding, "Let there be light."

Calliope rolled her eyes at Dysnomi's joke at the same moment that an incredibly bright light jumped from his hands toward the shadows. It became brighter and brighter, until it was so bright that everyone had to shut their eyes against it. When the light finally went out, Zorya was left in a heap on the floor and the shadows were almost all gone. She was gasping for breath and clutching her chest as she scooted herself backward until she hit the wall. She leaned against the wall heavily. Amarok ran over to check on her, leaving Dysnomi to monitor Calliope.

"What's wrong with her?" Zephyr questioned as he looked curiously at the young black woman and her glowing golden eyes.

After checking Zorya over, Amarok replied. Though, his voice wavered and he sounded uncertain. "I can't really be sure, but I think the Shadow Realm spirits were corrupting her from the inside out. Worse than that, though... I think she's gonna die without them."

"I... I'm sorry," Zorya gasped to Calliope. Calliope could see that the glowing lights were leaving her eyes.

Calliope thought quickly and forced herself up to her feet, still holding onto her abdomen with one hand. She drifted over to the bar, pain shooting through her body with every step. "Pass me... The best rum... That you have," she told Zephyr.

"What? Why do you want rum? Cher, you need to get to a hospital," Zephyr replied, looking at Calliope with bewildered eyes.

"I don't have time to explain," Calliope snapped. Zephyr simply sighed and passed her a bottle with two glasses. "I guess it's a good thing I'm badly injured. Otherwise, I don't think this would work," she said, sighing. She poured two shots out, whispering, "I'd like to offer you this rum, Baron Samedi. Please... Come and have a drink with me... And listen to my request... If you will."

"It's not gonna... Work..." Zorya gasped between breaths. Her breathing was becoming shallow and her eyes were beginning to droop. "The Baron has visited no living person... In ages..."

16. I'VE GOT FRIENDS ON THE OTHER SIDE

(THE LOA OF THE DEAD AND THE CROSSROADS BETWEEN LIFE AND DEATH)

"I wouldn't even dream of passin' over this gorgeous woman right here," said a voice from behind Calliope. It was a deep, masculine voice and it made her feel abnormally nervous. She shivered when the man who was standing behind her spoke again. He was so close to her that she could feel his hot breath against the back of her neck. Calliope turned, catching a glimpse of the dark ebony-skinned man, who had a skull painting on his face and raven-black hair, which was styled into long, luxurious dreadlocks. The man winked at her, then disappeared behind her once more. His hands, which had tattoos of the metacarpals and phalanges on them, tenderly caressed her shoulders. "You are a damn unique lil thing, too. You can't be...?" he questioned. "No... You're fuckin' kiddin' me, right? I never knew that old bastard

Shango had any game. La Siréne is not just ANY woman. And she's not easy to talk to. Trust me... I fuckin' tried."

"You're telling me," Calliope laughed—joking despite her pain. "Try living with her sometime." She took the Baron's hands and led him over to the barstool that was next to her, sitting him down gently and sliding him a glass of rum. He smirked at her and nodded gratefully as he picked the glass up and drank from it. "So... Here's the thing..." she started, attempting to sound nonchalant, though the truth was that he had made her feel on edge from the moment that he appeared. "I was kinda hoping I could convince you to heal Zorya... Over there." She pointed to the spot across the bar where Zorya was leaning heavily against the wall.

Baron Samedi let out a hearty laugh, then replied to Calliope in a husky voice that sent a pleasant chill down her spine. "Straight to the point... You must've learned that from your mother." He lifted an eyebrow at her and smirked, causing her to blush slightly. "Oh, but I DO fuckin' LOVE a woman who knows what she wants," he said, causing her to blush deeper. Then, he asked, "Her? You sure you don't want me to heal YOU? It would be a damn shame for the world of the living to lose such a beautiful young woman." He nodded at the wound in her abdomen, reminding her that she was hurt and had not begun to heal.

"My body will heal itself," Calliope assured the Baron. "But, unfortunately, her body won't be able to. And, according to Amarok, Zorya's served you for years. I really think she deserves another chance at life," she said, sticking her bottom lip out and looking at him with her wide iris-purple eyes.

"Hmmm..." Baron Samedi stood up, pinching Calliope's chin between his forefinger and his thumb, forcing her to look up at him and to meet his intense gaze. After staring into her eyes, his expression softened a bit. He sighed and walked over to Zorya, taking her hand in his and closing his eyes. His face contorted with flashes of what appeared to be anger and sadness. Then, he shook his head and walked back over to the bar. "That damn Shadow Realm has done too much damage to her. I can do a ton of fuckin' things, darlin', but I can't heal that by myself," he said.

"So, there's nothing that can be done for her?" Calliope asked, sounding miserable. Her lip quivered and she looked at the Loa of the Dead sadly.

"Oh, don't give me those damn cute-ass puppy-dog eyes..." Baron Samedi said, turning his head away from Calliope. After a moment, however, he looked back at her and his expression softened again. "Alright, shit," he said with a sigh. "There MIGHT just be one thing that I can try. I could... Ah, fuck me." He threw his hands up, frustrated. "I could TRY to fuckin' take her back to the crossroads that lie between the world of the living and the land of the dead. Now, keep in mind that I've never fuckin' tried takin' a living mortal there before, but since she's in a sort of... Let's say... *'In-between'* state of bein' at the moment... Sorta stuck somewhere between life and death... Then, theoretically... One of three things could happen if I take her. The first outcome is that the magic of the crossroads... Just fuckin' accepts her. She'd stay the way she is—minus the pain, of course—and she could stay there for as long as she liked, helping me direct the traffic to the land of the dead. The second outcome is... The magic of the crossroads realizes that she's NOT fuckin' dead, HEALS her, then sends her back HERE to the world of the living," he said with a nonchalant shrug.

"And the third outcome?" Calliope asked cautiously. She knew that if the Loa of the Dead did not say what the last outcome was voluntarily, it could not be anything good.

"Third..." Baron Samedi said, clearing his throat. He shifted in his seat, appearing uncomfortable. "Is that the damn... Magic of the crossroads realizes that she's SUPPOSED to be fuckin' dead, KILLS her, then sends her ass to the land of the dead."

"Ugh, that's way too big of a decision for me to make for her... Zorya needs to make this decision for herself," Calliope replied.

"I would normally agree with you there, beautiful, but I don't think she's gonna be able to talk," Baron Samedi said, shaking his head sadly.

"Maybe not out loud," Calliope said, thinking. "But, one of my siren abilities is that I can get inside people's minds to communicate thoughts and emotions telepathically. I try not to do it unless it's absolutely necessary... But, I'd say this counts as necessary." She closed her eyes, took a deep breath, and mentally felt around the small bar. It was always harder for Calliope to mentally connect to someone new than it was for her to connect to someone that she knew and had feelings for.

When Calliope was sure that she had found Zorya's consciousness, she mentally called out for Zorya in an attempt to talk to the young woman. *Zorya?* she asked.

Who are you? Zorya questioned in response.

My name is Calliope, Calliope answered telepathically.

Oh, no! I'm so sorry 'bout everythin'! Zorya cried inside her mind. Her emotions washed over her. It was a mix of many different emotions, but the most prominent emotions that Calliope could feel were guilt and regret.

Hey, it's okay! Really, it's fine! Calliope assured Zorya. *I'll live! I just wanted to let you know that you have options. Baron Samedi has agreed to help you... But, only if you want him to. It's pretty risky, though, so it needs to be your decision. I didn't feel right making a big decision like this for you.*

Zorya listened to Calliope carefully, took a moment to decide, then told Calliope her decision. She apologized to Calliope once more before Calliope severed the telepathic connection.

Calliope closed herself off from Zorya's mind, then opened her eyes and told Baron Samedi what Zorya had decided. "She seemed nervous," she told him. "But, she also seemed like she was pretty sure about it."

"Well, then..." the Baron replied. "As much as I would fuckin' love to stay and find out more about your damn fascinatin' self..." He winked at Calliope, and she blushed. "I guess I better get her to the crossroads in-between life and death before she just ends up dead. Thank you for the rum, beautiful... And for the pleasure of your charming company, of course." He ran the back of his hand along her cheek, making her shiver and leaving her cappuccino skin feeling like it was on fire. "You're so fuckin' adorable when you blush," he said, making her blush harder. "Please, feel free to call on me again... ANY damn time you need me, darlin', day or night." He smiled and winked at her again when he said that. Then, he placed a card in her hand, his thumb brushing over the back of her knuckles lightly. The contact made her skin burn again. He lit a cigar before he carefully lifted Zorya into his arms. Then, he just... Disappeared.

When the Baron was gone, Calliope flipped over the card that he had given to her, examining it. *It's not even a business card, or really any kind of card that could physically help me contact him,* she thought, feeling confused. *It's just a simple tarot card.*

Calliope heard Lyn's voice inside her mind then, telling her, *'There is nothing simple about that tarot card... The death card doesn't have to represent a literal death. It can represent change—possibly the end of a very important chapter of your life.*

Alternatively, it can also represent growth or rebirth—a new way of life.'

17. FAMILY AFFAIRS

(THE SPIRIT OF LIGHTNING AND FIRE/THE LOST GIRL)

"What the hell happened here?" Asmodeus asked when he stepped through the door of The Tipsy Piano. He looked around at all of the destruction. There were broken chairs everywhere, tables were knocked over, and there was a lot of blood on the floor.

It looks like a crime scene in here, Asmodeus thought, horrified.

'You'd know all about that, wouldn't you?' Asmodeus' demon half asked him while laughing.

Asmodeus yelled at his demon half inside his mind. *Shut up,* he said as his eyes landed on Calliope. She was sitting on a barstool, panting and appearing disheveled. He immediately noticed the blood that was staining her brand-new shirt. It was spilling out over her hand, which she had pressed as hard as she could against her abdomen. "Calli, are you alright?" he asked as he ran over to her, leaning down to cup her cheek and staring into her eyes. *"Mi amor, ¿qué pasó?"*[22] he asked her.

"This woman who had... All these shadows surrounding her... She attacked us," Calliope answered, her breathing labored. "But, it was worse than that... The shadows were, like... Alive? I don't know." It was taking a lot out of her just to speak, her breathing becoming more labored with every word.

"Um, okay... Does anyone wanna translate that?" Asmodeus asked, looking at the other men.

"Yeah, jus' what da hell happened here?" Xena questioned, readjusting the armful of tobacco that she was carrying so it was sitting on her hip. She was carrying it the way that a mother would carry a toddler.

"And how did Calli get hurt?" Nagaveni asked in a small voice, looking concerned for her best friend while simultaneously looking sick from all the blood. She glanced at Calliope nervously, then back toward the men who were in the room.

Amarok addressed Xena, asking her, "You know your friend Zorya?" Xena nodded in response. "Well," Amarok began. "It turns out... Some of the shadows that she had the power to manipulate... Were corrupting her from the inside

---

[22] "My love, what happened?"

out. They were from the Shadow Realm. The Shadow Realm spirits drove her insane and convinced her she needed to kill Calliope. I guess someone made a deal with the Shadow Realm to get Calliope killed."

"That woman was a gods-damn lunatic," Dysnomi added, crossing his arms. His jaw was clenched, showing that he was still annoyed.

"Okay, so where's Z now?" Xena questioned, glancing around the bar anxiously.

"Well... I sent out a big burst of magic light to kill all the living shadows," Dysnomi started.

"But, unfortunately, the shadows had corrupted her too much. She was dying... Quickly," Amarok added.

"So, I called Baron Samedi... And offered him some rum," Calliope finished. She grunted as she lifted herself and leaned forward, holding the *'death'* tarot that he gave her between two of her fingers.

"So, she's... Dead, den?" Xena questioned. She looked crestfallen for a moment as she thought about the woman.

"Not that we know of," Dysnomi answered with a shrug.

"She was dying... But, I convinced Baron Samedi... To take her to the crossroads... Between the world of the living... And the land of the dead. He said one of three things could happen," Calliope elaborated. "Either she'll stay there and help him... She'll be healed and sent back here... Or..." She hesitated. "Or she won't heal... And she'll end up passing on," she finished through labored breaths. "It's too soon to know which will happen."

"That's... Just wonderful," Nagaveni said uncertainly. "Calli, are you sure you're okay? Here, just let me look at your wound." She rushed over and pulled the bottom of Calliope's shirt out from where it had been tucked into the waist of her skirt. Then, before Calliope could protest, she pulled the shirt up further to inspect the wound.

"*¡Dios mío!*[23] That looks awful, *mi amor.*[24] Why have you not started healing yet?" Asmodeus questioned. Calliope could feel how concerned he was and she did not want to worry him more.

"Oh, you worry too much, Deus," Calliope replied. "I'll be fine. Don't fuss over me, my love." She quickly pulled her shirt down to cover the wound again, trying to avoid the concerned looks that were coming from all of her friends. She attempted to stand, but the pain quickly became too much for her and she stumbled backward.

---

[23] "My god!"
[24] "my love."

Asmodeus caught Calliope in his arms, steadying her before helping her sit down. "Calli, it's bleeding worse now," he mentioned, pointing at the blood that was seeping between her fingers, which were once again pressed against her abdomen. "What did she get stabbed with?" he asked, looking at Dysnomi and Amarok.

"A silver knife," Amarok answered.

"But silver shouldn't be bad for Calli. She probably just needs some rest," Dysnomi suggested.

"No," Asmodeus stated, his eyes watery. "No, I'm telling you that something's wrong."

"Maybe it just needs more time?" Nagaveni asked sweetly. "It's a pretty big wound, after all."

"No, dammit!" Asmodeus yelled as he slapped the top of the bar. "You're not fucking listening to me! I've seen her get big wounds before. They always start healing immediately. Something. Is. Wrong," he insisted.

"We really don't have time for this arguing bullshit," Calliope announced, forcing herself to stand on her own. "I'm assuming you figured out how to summon my father?" she asked, looking at Xena.

"Mais," Xena answered, holding up the armful of tobacco proudly. With a smile on her face, she said, "We're gonna take dis tobacco. Den, we're gonna take some rum. An' den... We're gonna set dis shit on fire! ...Outside, o'course." Xena added her last sentence when she noticed Zephyr's wide eyes. She pulled a folded piece of paper from her pocket and held it up, saying, "Dis should be da incantation I'll needa chant to summon him."

"Awesome. Let's go do that now," Calliope replied, stepping forward on shaky legs. She almost fell with every step that she took, until she felt strong arms wrapping around her. She looked up to see Amarok steadying her. He helped her walk over to the side door of the building.

Amarok looked down at Calliope and smiled, saying, "I figure if you're stubborn enough to do this right now, I might as well help you."

They all finally made it outside, and Xena set the tobacco on the ground in the middle of the alleyway. Amarok helped Calliope lean against the building while Zephyr walked out with a bottle of rum and poured it out over the tobacco pile.

"Thank you," Calliope expressed to Zephyr with a small smile.

"Of course, cher. It's the least I can do. After all, you did get stabbed in my establishment," Zephyr joked.

Calliope laughed, then coughed when pain hit her from laughing. She looked at Xena and asked, "So, um... I'm assuming you were told... How this all works?"

"Mais," Xena answered. "First... We gotta light it."

"I got it," said Asmodeus, stepping forward. He held his hands out toward the pile. Calliope could feel anger rising inside of him as flames formed inside his palms. He focused on his anger, strengthening it until the flames shot out from his hands. The pile of tobacco and rum ignited dangerously, shooting flames high up toward the sky.

"Now, I summon him... I guess..." Xena said, unsure. She took out the piece of paper and read off a few words in Latin, then stepped back.

Everyone stood around the alley for a few minutes, waiting impatiently. Then, Nagaveni asked, "So, um... Did it work? Or... Did we do something wrong?"

An unknown deep, authoritative male voice answered Nagaveni from the opposite end of the alley. The voice said, "Oh, it worked. Now... Who are you, and why have you summoned me?"

They all jumped, looking toward the voice to see a tall, muscular middle-aged man walking toward them. He was taking slow, menacing strides, and he had java-colored skin, short raven-black hair, and tattoos covering most of his upper torso. He was carrying a tall wooden staff in one hand, which he kept inches above the ground like he was proving that it was not used for walking.

Calliope struggled, but she eventually managed to push herself away from the building to stand tall and proud in front of the man who was supposedly her father. *This man who I look nothing like,* she thought.

"I summoned you," Calliope answered. "My name is Calliope. I'm the daughter of La Siréne."

"The daughter of La Siréne..." the man repeated, contemplating Calliope's words with a fond expression. "So, I suppose that makes you the daughter that I have never met?"

"I guess," Calliope replied, looking down and wringing her hands together. "I mean... I'm a siren, but... I can also do this." She held her hand out with her palm flat, then created a ball of fire. She allowed the fireball to stay for a moment before snuffing it out. "I have lightning magic as well, but it hurts to use it and I can usually only use it during high-stress situations."

"Yeah, um, this is a nice little family reunion and all, but we're here for a reason, Calli. And you need to rest soon," Asmodeus interjected.

Calliope knew that Asmodeus was worried about her, but she felt slightly annoyed by his interruption. It was her first time meeting her father. She did not want to be rushed.

Shango looked at Asmodeus, anger rising inside of him as he wondered who dared to interrupt his conversation with his daughter. He began to say something. However, he stopped when he noticed Calliope holding her abdomen, blood spilling out from between her fingers. "Daughter... You are hurt," he stated.

"Yeah..." Calliope replied. She shrugged despite the pain, and said, "That's kinda why I needed to talk to you. Someone's trying to kill me and I think it has something to do with the powers I inherited... Your powers." She jumped into it then, relaying the entire story while Shango listened intently. Her friends waited patiently behind her.

When Calliope finished, Shango remained silent for a while, appearing thoughtful. Then, he laughed. Through his laughter, he said, "Your brother always did have a flair for the dramatic."

"My brother?" Calliope asked. Her jaw dropped and her hand that was clutching her wound fell to her side. She asked, "Raiden?"

"But, Raiden should still be locked in the Demon Realm," Asmodeus interjected. "I haven't heard of him getting free." He looked at Calliope with a panicked expression. "Okay, so... I may have lied about my reasons, but when I said I was trying to protect you... I wasn't lying, *amor.*"[25]

"Wait, did you know Raiden wanted me dead?" Calliope asked.

"No. No! Of course not," Asmodeus answered. "But... I had a feeling that he resented you. It was like he wanted you out of his way. But I didn't know why. He found out I was trying to investigate that and he attacked me. THAT'S why he didn't like me. It had nothing to do with me being a cambion. I had demons take him because I didn't want him to attack me again. Or worse, for him to attack you... And... I found out that HE was the reason all your friends went missing... He wanted to isolate you... But, it came to a point where it was just easier to let you believe I was the bad guy. I mean, I had no proof. You never would've believed me. It left me feeling so much hate, though. When that letter about you came, I

---

[25] "love."

directed that hatred toward you. *Lo siento, mi amor.*"[26]

"Oh... You should have told me, Deus," Calliope replied. Her eyes watered as she wrapped Asmodeus in a hug. She winced when she pressed against him, though, so he pulled himself away.

"Yes, yes. Not to worry. He is still locked away... For now," Shango interrupted. "Though, I suspect he will be free soon. He gained his powers some time ago and I am certain that when he is free, he will come find you, daughter."

"I still don't understand why he hates me, though," Calliope replied, frustrated.

Shango looked amused for a moment. Then, he answered Calliope. He said, "It has nothing to do with hate, young one. It has EVERYTHING to do with power. Your brother wants more power... He wants to be stronger than me. He wants your power so he may take mine."

"What? He can't do that, though... Can he?" Calliope asked, shocked.

"It depends," Shango replied with a nonchalant shrug, like the whole thing didn't even bother him. "He can... If he gets his hands on the Compendium of Supernatural Powers. Inside, there is a large section on power absorption. It

---

[26] "I'm sorry, my love."

contains every piece of information about it—how to absorb powers, the rules of absorbing powers, which powers can not be absorbed, and much more. If you want to stop him, daughter, you will need to find it before he does. The last I heard, it was safe in New York... In the possession of a man called Dmitri. You should know, daughter, that your brother's powers are stronger than your own. If you have anything that could help you, I would suggest using it," he told Calliope.

"Wait, there are rules to absorbing powers? And powers that can't be absorbed?" Calliope asked.

Shango nodded, answering with, "I do not know the rules, but I know that certain abilities only appear in certain Supernaturals. Therefore, they can only be used by certain Supernaturals. For example, banshees and sirens are the only Supernaturals who have a sonic shriek. If another Supernatural were to attempt absorbing your scream, it would not work because you and banshees are the only Supernaturals capable."

"Thank you, father," Calliope said, smiling gratefully.

Shango nodded. He abruptly turned and walked a few steps away. Then, he stopped, turning back to Calliope with an expression that told her that he forgot to mention something. "Daughter?" he asked. "That wound of yours needs stitches. Shadow Realm silver is very dangerous." He paused before continuing with, "Do not let it get infected. You do not want to know what will happen."

Then, Shango vanished. "But... Now I kinda DO wanna know what happens if it gets infected," Calliope whispered to herself.

"C'mon. Let's get you inside so you can sit down," said Amarok, wrapping an arm around Calliope to help her walk.

"I'll put the fire out," Asmodeus stated, holding his hands out and pulling the fire into his body. It curled around his arms, licking at his skin before being absorbed.

Once inside, Amarok sat Calliope on a barstool. She whimpered, the movement hurting her and causing more blood to spill out of her wound.

Nagaveni rushed over, pleading with Calliope. "Please, Calli, let me look at it again," she said. Calliope allowed her to lift the shirt. The area around the wound was swollen, there was an angry crimson-red around the entry site, and Calliope's skin was deeply bruised. The inside of the stab wound was so deep that she could not tell exactly how worried she should have been. "Calli, it looks terrible. You've lost a lot of blood. I think you need to go to a hospital."

Calliope grunted. Then, she replied, "And tell them what, Nini? *'Oh, I was stabbed with Shadow Realm silver, but it's okay because the Shadow Woman—you know, the puppet master of the shadows?—may or may not be dead...?'* I would sound insane. They'd probably throw me in the psych ward."

Nagaveni rolled her eyes. "Well, if you won't go to the hospital, will you at least allow me to stitch it so you're not losing any more blood?"

Calliope threw her hands up, sighing. "Fine, fuck, whatever," she said. "Just be quick."

"Thank you," Nagaveni said in a sing-song voice, the way that she always did when she felt like she had won. Then, she looked behind her, asking, "Zeph, can I get the highest-content alcohol you have? I'll need it to clean her wound."

"Of course, ma chérie," Zephyr replied. "Anything for you." He winked at Nagaveni, then grabbed a bottle off of the top shelf and passed it to her.

"Holy shit, you actually have absinthe?" Amarok asked when he saw the bottle.

"Mais, brah, it's popular with the vamps," Zephyr answered. "Especially the younger vamps. They're always amazed by the amount of alcohol they can handle after being turned."

"Brah, you should've told me! It takes a lot to get werewolves drunk. I bet this would make it a hell of a lot easier," Amarok replied, laughing.

"I dare you... To try it," Calliope joked through pained breaths as Nagaveni dug a travel-size sewing kit out of her purse.

"Fuck it," Amarok said with a shrug. Zephyr lifted an eyebrow at him, but slid him a shot glass anyway. He poured himself a shot and shook his head, groaning. "Aghhh, this is gonna be awful," he complained before closing his eyes and tossing back the shot. He scrunched up his face in disgust, then growled, "I fucking hate absinthe..." He trailed off then, blinking a few times before announcing, "Hey, that REALLY works." He took a step backward and let himself fall into a seat.

Calliope laughed despite her pain, then asked Amarok, "Hey, are you good?" He gave her a thumbs-up, which caused her to laugh more, then gasp when she began to hurt worse.

"Okay, that's enough, mister. Give me that," Nagaveni scolded, snatching the bottle away from the bar. She then turned back to Calliope. "Hold this," she demanded, placing Calliope's hand on the hem of the shirt. Calliope grabbed hold of it with shaky hands. She noticed a small bit of sweat on Calliope's forehead as she poured the alcohol over the wound and Calliope clutched the shirt tightly. "Are you doing okay, Calli?" she asked as she began to stitch the wound.

"Yep. Just... Fucking... Great," Calliope answered through gritted teeth. Her fists were clenched and she was wearing a pained expression on her face. She breathed in deeply, trying to distract herself until Nagaveni finally finished.

"Alright, all done!" Nagaveni announced.

"Awesome," Calliope remarked, releasing the breath that she had been holding. She motioned to Zephyr and asked, "Hey, can I get something strong? Just... You know... Maybe not AS strong as absinthe."

"Of course, cher," Zephyr replied, pouring Calliope a double-shot of whiskey. She accepted it gratefully and drank it. When the alcohol finally hit her, it relieved some of the pain that she was feeling. She sighed, finally feeling content.

Dysnomi and Asmodeus walked up to Calliope as Nagaveni stood to the side, putting her sewing kit back into her purse. Asmodeus looked at Calliope with a guarded expression before asking, "Are you... Okay?"

"I will be," Calliope replied.

"Are you... Mad at me?" Asmodeus asked Calliope, hesitating before setting his hand on top of hers.

She should be, Dysnomi thought; he did not say that out loud, though. He knew that Calliope didn't need any more stress.

"I'm not mad, Deus," Calliope answered, looking up at Asmodeus with watery eyes. "I just wish you had told me. I treated you so unfairly... Just look where that's gotten us."

"You haven't treated me unfairly. I've still done many awful things... To others... And to you... I've hurt you so many times... And I hid the truth about Raiden, thinking it was the best thing for you... But I ended up making things worse," Asmodeus said. He looked down, feeling ashamed of himself.

"No, Deus. This isn't on you," Calliope assured Asmodeus. "It's not your fault. Okay?"

Asmodeus nodded sadly. Before he could speak again, Dysnomi interrupted. "Hey, uhh... So... What's the plan now?"

Calliope sighed, thinking. After a moment, she miserably threw her head down onto the top of the bar. "I don't know!" she wailed. "To find the Compendium of Supernatural Powers, ALL I have to go on is ONE name. And it's not even the guy's full name! It's just the FIRST name! How in all the hells am I supposed to stop Raiden if he's more powerful than me? I just... Man, I can't fucking do this anymore," she cried, letting her tears fall freely.

Amarok pushed himself off of his seat to stand next to Calliope. He threw an arm around her shoulders and leaned down to whisper, "It'll be okay, Calli. We're all here. And we're not going anywhere." She buried her face in his side, holding onto him tightly as he comforted her.

After a moment, Xena—who had been unusually quiet—waved the group over to her, saying, "I tink I figured out who got da book." Calliope wiped her tears and sniffled. Then, she hobbled over to Xena while holding her hand against her newly-stitched wound. Xena pointed at her open laptop screen, which she had sitting on top of the bar. "Dere really ain't much info 'bout him, but... From what I found? Mais... You ain't gone fuckin' believe dis..."

Everyone gathered around, staring at Xena's laptop screen with matching expressions of wonder. Then, they all began talking excitedly with each other except Dysnomi, who began laughing.

"So... Am I the only person who doesn't understand what's so important about... Whoever THAT guy is?" Nagaveni questioned, pointing at the laptop's screen.

"Oh, my gods... No way!" Calliope gasped when she looked at the picture that Xena had pulled up. "Are you serious?! *Dracula?!* Fuck my life. I mean, I guess I can send him a text... Never thought I'd say that again."

18. I THINK WE'RE ALL DAMNED

(PROPER PREPARATION AND PLANNING)

"Okay, so after two hours of being on the phone with him, you've got nothing?" Dysnomi teased Calliope, running a hand through his champagne-blond hair.

"Not... Entirely nothing?" Calliope said with a questioning, hopeful tone in her voice. "He confirmed that he DID have the Compendium of Supernatural Powers... At one point. He also confirmed that he DID go by the name Dmitri... The main problem now comes from the fact that he has absolutely NO fucking idea where the book is currently."

"And it took you two hours just to get that little bit of information out of him?" Dysnomi teased again.

"It TOOK me two hours to avoid us having to get STUCK at one of the legendary *Dracula's* parties, only for us to find out at the end of the night that he doesn't even have what we need,"

Calliope fired back, sticking her tongue out at Dysnomi the way that a petulant child would to their sibling.

"I still can't believe dat ya know *Dracula.*" Xena said as she laughed and shook her head. "I mean, *Dracula*... Da legend himself."

Calliope replied, "Yeah, I slept with him, too. Trust me, it's definitely not as cool as it sounds. The man can be quite the drama queen when he wants to be. He's a very... Theatrical person." She laughed, but her laughter soon turned into her gasping for breath. Tears rolled down her face when the pain from her stitched-up stab wound hit her.

"Calli, you need to be careful!" Nagaveni exclaimed, scolding Calliope with a motherly tone.

"Yeah, yeah," Calliope said. She waved Nagaveni off, then asked, "So, what are we even supposed to do now? My brother could get out of the Demon Realm at any moment, we don't have the book he's after—the ONE thing that he could use to steal my powers—and according to my father, Raiden's stronger than me."

"Yeah... I hate to say it, but it does kinda feel like we hit a dead-end," Amarok admitted.

Just as they all began to lose hope, Calliope's phone chimed with a notification. She sighed, picking it up. "It's Vlad," she said, confused. "He just... Sent me a list of every vampire that he thinks MIGHT have taken the book."

"Well... That's a start, at least," Asmodeus said, sighing. "Let's get to contacting them, I guess."

"Um, it might take us a while," Calliope replied. "I'm pretty sure that this is just a list of everyone he invited to his last party. It's like, ten pages long, and it's completely filled with names."

"Eh, just send us all a copy of it. We can split it into sections," Amarok suggested.

So, Calliope did exactly that. Much to her surprise, the group made quick work of the list of names. Within an hour, they had made it through all of the names on the list. When they were finished, they leaned back in their seats. Everyone felt exhausted.

"Well... That ended up just being an enormous waste of time," Calliope said, sighing and running a hand through her hair.

Asmodeus looked like he was going to say something to Calliope in response, but his phone beeped with a notification the moment that he opened his mouth. He paused to check the notification on his phone with a curious look on his face... Until he read—and fully understood—the text message that he had been sent. Then, his face fell and he looked up at the siren with a mix of terror, anger, and sadness in his piercing electric-blue eyes. "That was Amadeo... Um... Menoetius freed your brother... And, somehow... They already have the gods-damn book," he said.

Calliope knew that Asmodeus was telling her the truth. Between his facial expressions and his intense emotions, which flooded through her like a bursting dam, she knew that there was no possible way that he was lying to her. "Oh... That's fucking great," she replied, throwing her hands up. She stood with a grunt of pain. "I assume that means he's gonna be coming to get me? I guess there's not much I can do about it now."

"Don't say that," Nagaveni said, trying to sound encouraging and hopeful as she reached out to Calliope. "We could always still try—"

Calliope lifted a hand, stopping Nagaveni from finishing her sentence. "Nini, that gods-damned book was my only chance... My one shot. If my father was right and Raiden really IS more powerful than me... AND he really DOES have the Compendium of Supernatural Powers... Then, that's it for me. I'm probably gonna die," she said. She sighed before following that sentence with, "I'm gonna go enjoy what could very likely be my last night alive. You're all more than welcome to join me, but not if you're gonna keep talking about my brother. I just want to have some fun tonight... Okay?"

With those words, Calliope turned and walked out of The Tipsy Piano. She shivered when the cool night air caressed her exposed shoulders and legs. For a moment, she considered going back to the hotel that she had been staying at first, just to change out of her bloody, torn-up clothes. However, she didn't see the point in going through all the trouble of doing that if it truly was going to be her last night of life.

19. EVEN WHEN YOUR HOPE IS GONE

(LIFE OF THE PARTY)

Calliope walked slowly until she arrived outside of the crowded nightclub, Elysium, on Bourbon Street. She walked inside, where she immediately turned to head toward the bar. When she made her way over to it, she ordered herself the first drink that she saw that she had never tried—snake tequila, which definitely looked weird despite apparently being popular in Mexico. She closed her eyes as she tossed the drink down her throat quickly, swallowing the liquid without even really tasting it. As the night continued, she ended up doing many more shots of varying types of alcohol.

By the time that all of Calliope's friends made it to the packed club, they were greeted with the sight of Calliope doing a body shot off of some random hot woman. The woman was laying on her back on the top of the bar, and she was giggling as Calliope licked a line of salt off of her stomach.

Nagaveni giggled as well. *I guess I shouldn't be too surprised,* she thought. *Calli has always been able to make friends everywhere she goes.*

Calliope finally noticed her friends when she was finished doing her shot. She ran over to them after excusing herself from the hot woman, who had just given her phone number over to Calliope.

Calliope was smiling widely as she walked up to the group. When she was standing in front of her friends, she asked them, "So, did you all finally decide to come celebrate with me?"

Asmodeus stepped forward and asked Calliope, "What exactly do you think we should be celebrating, Calli?" He raised an eyebrow and continued. "The fact that you're gonna die?"

"We should be celebrating my life, buzzkill," Calliope retorted. Her voice was dripping with sarcasm, which she immediately felt bad about.

"Come on, Calli... We don't even know for sure that getting your powers taken away is gonna kill you," Nagaveni pointed out.

Calliope knew that Nagaveni was just trying to remain optimistic, but she didn't want to listen to it. She just wanted to forget about everything for one night. "Maybe we don't, but I still just have this nagging feeling that I'm going to die," she responded. "And besides, I thought I told you I don't want to talk about it anymore. At least... Not tonight." With that, she sighed, rubbing her face. Then, she grabbed Asmodeus' arm and pulled him toward the dance floor. "Come on... Come and dance with me, grumpy," she pleaded with him desperately.

Asmodeus reluctantly allowed Calliope to pull him to the middle of the crowded dance floor. He swayed to the rhythm of the loud music with her, growling in her ear when she began to grind against him. "Calli..." he groaned. Then, he pulled away slightly and said, "Hey, I'm really sorry about all of this... The trickster was right. I should've stayed behind so I could monitor that piece of shit brother of mine."

"Stop," Calliope said, placing her forefinger against his lips. "Please... Can you just please... Let me enjoy your company for one night? We may not have gotten the chance to see what would happen between us this time around, but... I need you to know that I DO love you, Deus. So... Fucking... Much. I just really, really want nothing more than to enjoy being here with you tonight," she pleaded.

'He doesn't even want to live if you're not going to be here for him to spend his life with... Even if he has to settle for only being friends, he wants you

in his life. That's so sad...' Lyn whispered inside Calliope's mind.

I know Lyn, Calliope thought in response. *But, he's probably going to have to live without me. There may not be any way around that, so he needs to learn to accept it.*

"*Te amo también,*[27] Calli," Asmodeus said. He lifted Calliope's chin using his forefinger and his thumb, forcing her to meet his soul-piercing gaze. *The purple color in her eyes is breath-taking,* he thought to himself. It made him want to kiss her more than anything. So, he leaned into her, kissing her round, full lips deeply. *Your lips are so fucking soft,* he said to her telepathically. *You're so gods-damn perfect to me, Calli.*

Calliope responded to Asmodeus' advances immediately, kissing him with an intense passion. Then, she wrapped her arms around his neck, tangling one of her hands in his thick off-black hair.

Asmodeus grabbed Calliope's slim waist, tightening his grip as he attempted to control his demon half. His demon half was screaming at him to get her alone so they could do much more than kiss, but he wanted to give her the night out that she had asked for. When he gripped her tighter, he

---

[27] "I love you too,"

heard her whimper into his mouth and he felt her bottom lip tremble from the pain she felt and a small amount of fear. He felt awful then, realizing that attempting to stop his demon half from hurting her had accidentally caused him to bruise her delicate waist.

"Careful," Calliope whispered against Asmodeus' lips. "You don't want my stitches to pop open, do you?"

"*Mierda,*"[28] Asmodeus responded, feeling ashamed of himself. "I'm sorry, Calli." He released his hold on Calliope, feeling a tsunami-sized wave of guilt washing over him.

"It's alright, Deus," Calliope replied. She smiled at Asmodeus, staring into his hypnotizing electric-blue eyes before hugging him. She nuzzled her face into his chest, taking comfort in the warmth that radiated off his body.

Asmodeus hugged Calliope back tightly, squeezing her into him. She could feel that he was terrified that she would just disappear the moment that he released her.

"Hey, lovebirds... Y'all wanna drink?" said a deep voice from beside Calliope and Asmodeus. They pulled apart to see Amarok standing there.

---

[28] "Shit,"

He was towering over both of them and offering them each a glass. "It's rum," he said with a shrug.

"Oh. Thank you," Calliope replied, accepting a glass. She then noticed that Amarok was looking down at her. His face was contorted with a mixture of sadness and concern for her.

Asmodeus accepted the second glass, looking uncomfortable for a moment. Then, he sighed and looked at Amarok, hesitantly telling him, "Hey man, I'm really sorry about calling you a mutt earlier. That, um... That wasn't me. I mean, it WAS me, but... Ugh... *Es difícil de explicar.*"[29]

Amarok laughed loudly, vibrations rumbling from his chest. He gave Asmodeus a friendly slap on the shoulder and told him, "It's all good, man. I get it, honestly. Your demon has a mind of his own, right? My wolf does, too. As do Calli's phoenix and thunderbird, if I remember correctly." He laughed again—a deep, hearty laugh.

Asmodeus chuckled and replied, "Well, it sounds like your wolf isn't too different from my demon, then."

"Hey, you know what we should do?" Calliope interrupted, practically bouncing with excitement. "We should go out on the town. We could listen to some street jazz and walk around,

---

[29] "It's difficult to explain."

seeing all the sights. I hear the streets of New Orleans really come alive at night," she suggested.

"I'm in, for sure," Amarok agreed. He smiled warmly at Calliope, then said, "I've always loved the streets of NOLA at night. It's an almost... Magical experience."

"I'll go see if I can find everyone else," Asmodeus offered. He took off, searching around Elysium for the rest of their friend group.

As soon as Asmodeus was out of sight, Calliope turned back toward Amarok and said, "Hey, um... I just wanted to say that I'm sorry... If it seems like I used you... You're honestly such an amazing man, and I've had so much fun with you the past few days. I probably should've warned you that I've slept with both Deus and Dys, rather than you finding out due to Deus getting jealous... I mean, I'm not with him or anything—not since we broke up three years ago—but apparently, he's still a little bit possessive."

"Hey, don't worry about that," Amarok replied, dismissing Calliope's apology with a scoff and an amused raise of his eyebrow. "I've had a lot of fun with you, too. You're a sweet, fun woman. And you're an amazing friend. But, I wish things had turned out differently... I wish I could've helped you more, or that there was something more I could do for you..." He paused, looking down at her with a deep sadness behind his golden-yellow eyes. Then, he whispered, "I really wish I had more time with you. I've loved every second of getting to know you."

"Oh, you really don't have to worry about how things turned out, Amarok. This was never your fight. I shouldn't have even dragged you into it. I'm really sorry about that... I was having a bad day after Dysnomi and Asmodeus got into an argument... But... If it makes you feel better, I also wish that I had more time with you," Calliope replied.

"Hey, I resent that," Amarok said in an argumentative, yet playful, tone. "You didn't drag me into anything, Calli. I chose to be a part of it. I mean... I like you, and I wanna help you in... Every way that I possibly can."

Calliope smiled as her eyes teared up and she hugged Amarok tightly. He returned her hug, enveloping her small body inside of his thick, powerful arms. *I feel so safe when I'm in your arms,* she said to him telepathically as he held her close to him.

Amarok kissed Calliope's forehead in response, then pulled back to tell her, "No matter what happens, I'll always remember you, Calli.

You're an amazing woman. I swear, I haven't had this much adventure in years. I still wish there had been more that I could've done to help you, but I'm so grateful for the moments I was able to spend with you. I know it's only been a few days, but I've had more fun with you than I've ever had with anyone else."

Calliope laughed. However, her laugh sounded slightly bitter as she wiped a tear away from her eye. "I'm glad I could help you have an adventure," she remarked. "Thank you for showing me around NOLA. I don't know how I could ever repay you for your kindness..."

At that moment, Asmodeus returned with the rest of the group in tow. Calliope ran up to each person, hoping to leave them all with a few words that they could remember her by.

First, Calliope walked up to Dysnomi and hugged him. She placed her delicate hand on his cheek and he leaned into her touch. She whispered to him, "You've been an amazing friend to me for the past two years, Dys... And we've shared so many wonderful moments with each other. I just want you to know that the night we shared did mean something to me. I know that I've seemed a little estranged from you since then, but I promise you... It meant something... I just... I would never wanna lose you as my friend."

Dysnomi smiled sadly at Calliope, then kissed her on the forehead. "I'll never forget that night, Calli," he whispered. He placed one of his hands on the back of her neck, then leaned forward until his forehead was touching hers gently. He whispered to her again, saying, "So... It turns out that even tricksters can find at least ONE person who they would never wanna deceive. Who would've guessed that?"

Calliope smiled and moved to stand in front of Nagaveni. She told her best friend, "You have been the absolute best friend that I could've ever asked for. Now... I know that *Hisstopher Walken* and *Benedict Cobrabatch* might not like this at first... But, please... Please promise me you'll take care of Nanuk. Thora and Wrath will be fine—they usually do their own thing regardless—but, I worry about Nanuk. She's gonna need a home when I'm gone."

Nagaveni cried softly as she responded, "I promise. You know I'll care for Nanuk, Calli. I can't believe I didn't know about her until recently, but wow... She's such a sweet little thing. Well, not exactly little, but still..."

Calliope nodded, grateful, then moved on. She stood in front of Xena next. She looked at the young hunter fondly and told her, "You've been an amazing help to me. Thank you so much for all that you've done. To try and repay you, I sent you a list of all of the health deities I think could help you out. You might wanna look into them, because one of them might be able to cure your magical disease. I've also given my witch friend, Salem, your phone number. She's gonna look into your affliction and if she can find any kind of healing spell—or maybe some kind of magical item—that she thinks will help you, she'll be in contact with you. That way, she can help you try whatever it is. I really hope you find a cure, Xena."

"Thanks, Calli," Xena replied. "Dat means so much to me. You got no idea."

Calliope stepped back, wiping the tears away from her eyes. She cleared her throat once, then announced to the group, "Alright, alright... That's quite enough of... Well... ALL of this... Let's go enjoy the night!" She plastered on a smile. It was obviously a fake smile, but no one questioned it. She led her friends out of Elysium and onto the streets of New Orleans, where she took in all of the sights and the smells of the Crescent City.

The group walked along, listening to the jazz music, which was filling the streets, and looking around at all of the gigantic neon signs, which lit up the night brightly. The bright lights seemed to dance over all of their bodies as they strolled around the city.

It wasn't long before Dysnomi noticed a small group of street performers. They were performing magic tricks, and he couldn't resist the temptation to join in on the fun for a few minutes.

"He loves showing his *'magic tricks'* off," Calliope told the rest of the group. "Which is actually just regular magic. You know... No tricks."

Dysnomi reached behind a young woman who was standing in the crowd of on-lookers and conjured a bouquet of flowers to give to her. She laughed with delight as she accepted the flowers and he bowed, winking at her. He continued with his *'performance',* creating wonderful illusions, which left even the magicians themselves speechless as they tried to figure out how exactly he was doing all of that.

When Dysnomi was finished showing off, Nagaveni walked up to a burly man, who was holding a massive yellow Burmese python. She pet the python and it cuddled into her as she talked to it in a soft voice. Her emerald-green eyes were beginning to glow, and the way that she spoke to the giant snake made it seem like she was having an actual conversation with it. The man watched her, utterly amazed as the heavy python slithered onto her shoulders and back off of them. The man told her that his snake, *Kaa*—named after the snake from *The Jungle Book*—rarely liked being around people. Nagaveni simply laughed, stroking the extra-large snake's scaly skin as she told the man, "I guess I've just always been good with snakes. You could say I'm somewhat of a snake charmer."

It was then Asmodeus' turn to choose something for the group to watch or to take part in. He levitated for a crowd of humans, though he only did so a few inches off of the ground so he wouldn't raise any suspicion. He blew the crowd out of the water when he disappeared in a black cloud of smoke, which he and Calliope created using their fire powers. Then, he reappeared behind the crowd after teleporting, bowing as they clapped for him.

Afterward, Xena noticed a group of tourists who were taking one of the many haunted walking tours, and she stopped them to spin a few of her fantastical tales about werewolves, vampires, witches, rougarous, and many other Supernaturals.

"The tourists all believe her stories are fictional, of course," Amarok whispered in

Calliope's ear after leaning down to her. "But, look how they all just eagerly consume it. Tourists will eat this up, but they'd freak out if they ever actually saw any Supernaturals."

  Afterward, Dysnomi conjured a beautiful saxophone for Amarok, which he thanked Dysnomi for. Then, Amarok used his shiny new instrument to join some of the jazz musicians who were playing on the street, making Calliope laugh internally as she thought of the scene from *The Lost Boys*. Some of the musicians seemed to already know him, greeting him warmly as he walked up to them. He played beautifully for a while, earning a loud round of applause from basically everyone on the street.

  Calliope stared at Amarok, taking in his tall, muscular body, his golden-yellow wolf eyes, and his shaggy, dark copper hair. After fully taking in his appearance, she stopped to think, *I wonder if he's just naturally this good at everything he does? I haven't seen anything that he hasn't been amazing at.*

  Then, Calliope danced into the streets, stopping to catch a set of beads, which had been thrown down to her from a man who was standing on a balcony overhead. She blew the man a kiss, then thought, *This is probably the closest I'll ever get to catching beads at Mardi Gras. I might as well enjoy it.*

Calliope continued her dancing, laughing, and twirling like she didn't have a single care in the world. Amarok took her hand, spinning her around elegantly. His motions were as fluid as a river, causing her to laugh with delight. He soon began leading her toward a group of performers, who were dancing and singing in the middle of the crowded street. She smiled while dancing along to the sound of their beautiful voices. She held a fondness for one song in particular, and before she even realized what she was even doing, she began harmonizing with them throughout the song. When the song was finished, she realized for the first time that the performers had stopped singing. They were all staring at her in complete awe, and she earned cheers from anyone who had been listening. She blushed, a part of her feeling embarrassed.

Then, Calliope looked down at her stomach, realizing that her stitches did not hurt nearly as bad as they had before. *The wound's still there,* she noted. *But it seems to have healed. At least, it has a little.*

The group kept their party of six going until they all practically fell onto their asses, laughing together. Then, they finally realized exactly how exhausted they all had become.

Xena and Amarok were the first to stand and say their goodnights and goodbyes. They walked off in separate directions, leaving the rest of the group to travel back to their hotel together.

Asmodeus walked Calliope to her room inside of the hotel, only stopping when they reached the door. He leaned into her, giving her a tight, desperate hug and kissing her cheek softly before finally leaving her for the night. She walked into her room, dressed for bed quickly, and fell asleep the moment that her head hit her pillow. She was exhausted from the long, emotional day that she had.

20. TWO MINUTES TO MIDNIGHT

(DON'T THREATEN ME WITH A GOOD TIME)

"Calli, wake up!" a voice yelled from outside of Calliope's hotel room door.

"Ugh, hang on, I'm coming," Calliope said. She slid out of the bed and rubbed her eyes, crossing her hotel room floor to open the door. All of her friends were waiting for her on the other side, dressed and ready to go for the day. "What's going on?" she asked them.

"Oh my gods, get dressed, Calli!" Nagaveni commanded in her best motherly voice.

"Yeah, *¿qué diablos?*[30] Asmodeus questioned. "You're not dead yet, are you? No? Okay then, we're gonna spend the day together."

"What are we even doing?" Calliope inquired.

"Zeph's keeping the bar closed for the day so we can hang out," Amarok answered.

---

[30] "what the hell?"

"Now, go get dressed!" Dysnomi exclaimed, practically shoving Calliope back into her hotel room.

"Okay, okay. I'm going!" Calliope said defensively, throwing her hands up. She walked back into her hotel room to find an outfit that she could wear. She threw on a *Nirvana* t-shirt, a pair of ripped black skinny jeans, and a pair of white high-top *Converse* shoes. She pulled her turquoise hair into a messy bun on the top of her head, then applied a layer of mascara to her already-long lashes and a layer of lip gloss to her plump lips. When Calliope came back to the door, all of her friends either whistled at her or teased her.

Then, Nagaveni asked, "Okay, but seriously, Calli, how do you always look so... Effortlessly perfect?" She gestured toward Calliope, moving her hands up and down as if that would prove her point. Calliope noticed that she was picking at the bottom of her shirt when she spoke, and Calliope wondered why she was so nervous.

"You're one to talk, Nini," Calliope responded, pointing out Nagaveni's look, which consisted of a loose t-shirt that had the words *'ride or die'* on it, a pair of light blue mom jeans, and a pair of gray *Nikes* sneakers.

"Oh, thanks," Nagaveni said. She blushed and looked down at the floor in the hallway of the hotel.

"Ready to go?" Xena asked.

"I'm all good," Calliope answered.

As the group walked down to the hotel lobby, Calliope slowed her pace until she was walking next to Nagaveni.

"Are you doing okay, Calli?" Nagaveni questioned. Her eyebrows furrowed, making her appear concerned.

"Huh? Yeah, I'm fine. Um, here," Calliope said, shaking her head. She spoke quickly before she pulled out her hotel room key-card and shoved it into Nagaveni's hands. "You should probably hold onto this."

"What? Why?" Nagaveni questioned.

"Just in case I don't make it back. That way, you'll be able to get my stuff," Calliope answered with a shrug.

"Um, okay..." Nagaveni mumbled. She stuffed the card into her purse before speeding ahead so Asmodeus could then stroll up next to Calliope.

Side-by-side, Calliope and Asmodeus walked through the hotel's front door, following the rest of the group. Calliope stopped when she felt the heat from the sun hit her face and body. She let it sweep over her, the warmth comforting her and making her feel strong for a moment. Then, she threw her arms straight out to the sides, mimicking the Jesus pose that Dysnomi stood in during Tartarus' opening night, which had been barely two weeks prior. She allowed her thoughts to wander, thinking to herself, *I'm really gonna miss having the sun wash over me. At least... I think I'm gonna miss it. I don't actually know if you can feel anything when you're in Purgatory.* A gentle tug on her hand brought her back to reality.

"What are you thinking about?" Asmodeus asked Calliope softly.

"Just enjoying the sun," Calliope lied. Then, feeling guilty for lying, she whispered a question to Asmodeus. She asked, "Can you... Feel... In Purgatory?"

"Feel?" Asmodeus inquired. "Feel what, exactly?"

"Anything," Calliope responded, shrugging and clasping Asmodeus' hand. "Like... Can you feel the sun on your face? I mean, is there even a sun in Purgatory? Can you feel... Fire? Or the dirt...? Or... If you pinch yourself?"

"Ah, I think I understand," Asmodeus said, nodding. "You're wondering if it'll actually feel like a life to you, right?" he asked. Calliope nodded. "Well, there is an artificial sun in Purgatory, and artificial seasons... So, you can feel those, although I've been told that it feels a little... Strange," he told her.

"How so?" Calliope questioned.

"I've heard it feels so real, but there's always this feeling in the back of your mind that tells you it's not. It's a feeling you have to learn to get used to. You really can't focus on it too much or you'll end up going insane," Asmodeus answered.

"That sounds... Wild," Calliope remarked.

"Yeah, definitely. Oh, and yes, you can feel it if you pinch yourself in Purgatory. You can also feel it if others pinch you," Asmodeus told her with a joking tone as he lightly pinched her arm.

"Well, that part's reassuring, at least," Calliope said, laughing.

"Calli! Deus!" Nagaveni called out, glancing over her shoulder at them.

"What's the hold-up?" Dysnomi yelled.

"Oh! Coming!" Calliope called back. She shared a guilty look with Asmodeus. Then, they both started laughing. She placed her hand on the back of Asmodeus' neck, pulling him down until their foreheads met. She leaned up to kiss his lips, melting into him and sighing.

Asmodeus returned Calliope's kiss, wrapping his arms around her. "Calli," he whispered, nuzzling his face into her neck and leaving a trail of gentle kisses there. *"Te amo más que a mi vida."*[31]

"I love you, too, Deus," Calliope whispered back. "More than life." She pulled away when she remembered that their other friends were waiting and she awkwardly told him, "I, uh... I guess we should, um... Catch up with everyone else."

"You're right... As always, *hermosa,*"[32] Asmodeus admitted, taking Calliope's hand and kissing it before holding it at his side. They walked hand-in-hand, not catching up with everyone else until they finally reached the front door of The Tipsy Piano.

"After you," Amarok said, holding the door open for Calliope and Asmodeus. Asmodeus let go of Calliope's hand and gestured for her to go ahead of him.

"What are you all up to?" Calliope asked suspiciously, though her tone was playful. She took in the scenery as she stepped inside the bar. Zephyr was standing behind the bar, as usual, with a huge smile on his face. They had all decorated

---

[31] "I love you more than life."
[32] "beautiful,"

the bar and taped up LED strip lights in the room. The lights framed the ceiling and changed colors regularly, lighting up the entire bar—red, orange, yellow, green, blue, purple, repeat. "Zeph, this is amazing!" she exclaimed as her friends began to walk into the bar behind her.

"It was nothing, cher," Zephyr replied. "Just took a bit of an elf's touch," he said as he winked at Calliope.

"Though, the drinks required a trickster's magic," Dysnomi said with a wink of his own, nodding toward the bar.

"Oh, you conjured the Fae alcohol to make the Cosmic Paradise?" Calliope asked excitedly.

"And he was kind enough to give me the recipe," Zephyr said.

"Well, it was only fair since you gave us the recipe for the Siren's Lament," Dysnomi told Zephyr.

"Oh hush," Zephyr said, waving Dysnomi off. "Nini earned that fair and square."

Nagaveni giggled and blushed, picking at the bottom of her shirt again. Calliope wished that she could make her friend feel more comfortable. *That's it!* she thought almost immediately. An idea came to her and she sprung into action. "Zeph, you're closed to the public today, right?" she asked.

"Of course, cher. What's up?" Zephyr wondered.

Calliope walked over and pulled the shades down over some of the windows, asking, "Xena, can you lock the front door? And pull the shades? Amarok—same with the side door?"

"You got it," Amarok said, making sure he locked the side door and pulled the shades down.

"Mais," Xena answered simultaneously, locking the front door and closing the shades. "So... You wanna tell us what dis is all about?" Xena questioned when she was finished.

"It's so Nini can take off the Serpent Tamer," Calliope answered honestly.

"What?" Nagaveni asked, turning to look at Calliope incredulously.

"You just seem so nervous," Calliope said, pointing to Nagaveni's hands, which were still fidgeting with her shirt. "I figured you'd feel more comfortable if you could let *Snake Lively* and *Justin Timbersnake* out to roam for once."

Nagaveni laughed. "Okay, I think you might be right," she said, pulling off the Serpent Tamer necklace and shoving it into her pocket. The snakes on her head hissed quietly as they woke up, slithering in all-different directions. "Hello my little Jörmungandr babies," she said happily, petting them.

"My work here is done," Calliope joked as she walked toward the bar.

Before Calliope could sit, however, Amarok said, "Not so fast." He grabbed her arm, his massive hand wrapping completely around it as he pulled her along beside him. "We hooked the lights up to the surround-sound speakers, and since this whole thing is for you, I need you to make a playlist."

"Oh, that's easy," Calliope said before laughing. "I listen to basically any kind of music, so it really won't be hard to make a playlist."

"A woman after my own heart," Amarok joked, leaning back and grabbing his chest dramatically.

"And here, I thought you already knew that," Calliope teased as she began making her chaotic music playlist.

"Oh, I did, but since you've come to town, I've found an additional reason to like you more every day," Amarok told Calliope.

"Aww," Calliope said, giving Amarok a quick hug. She turned back to her playlist and added a few more songs before saying, "And... Done!"

Amarok hit the *'shuffle play'* option and the first song to start was *'Come On Eileen,'* playing over the surround-sound system. Calliope grabbed one of Amarok's hands with both of hers, dragging him toward the bar. "Slow down," he told her, laughing.

"No way!" Calliope replied. "I still haven't had a drink and everyone here's waiting for me."

Amarok laughed and scooped Calliope up with one arm, surprising her and causing her to squeal with delight. He sat her down on a barstool when they made it to the bar.

"Alright," Zephyr announced. "Since it's Calliope's day, she gets to choose which of these drinks we each get." He made a sweeping gesture at three different drinks, which were all sitting side-by-side on the top of the bar.

Calliope recognized Dysnomi's galaxy-inspired Cosmic Paradise and Zephyr's turquoise Siren's Lament, but there was an ombré drink that she had never seen on the end. The last drink was red near the bottom, orange in the middle, and yellow near the top. "What's this one?" she asked, pointing to it. "I don't think I've seen it before."

"I'm so glad you asked, cher," Zephyr replied. "This is a new drink I've come up with—and yes, Dysnomi, I will give you the recipe," he said, holding a finger up in the 'wait one moment' symbol just as Dysnomi opened his mouth. Dysnomi stared at him slack-jawed for a moment before slowly closing his mouth. "Anyway, cher. I call this one Firestorm. It's pretty good, but you better be brave 'cause it'll be on fire when you drink it," he said.

"Fire doesn't hurt me," Calliope said, laughing. "I'm down to try it. Anyone else?"

"Count me in," Asmodeus said. "Fire doesn't hurt me, either. Prince of Demons here," he said, gesturing at himself and smirking at Calliope.

"Hell, I've never been one to back down from a challenge," Amarok said with a shrug.

"Yeah, I tink I'm gone pass on dat one," Xena replied. "I got enough scars from dis damn *'magical eczema'.* I really don't tink my body would like me to add a burn scar to it."

"Understandable," Calliope said. She turned to Zephyr and asked, "What about you, Zeph?"

"Oh, no, thank you, cher," Zephyr responded. "I'm too excited to try the drink from Dysnomi's club."

"That's a great idea, actually!" Calliope exclaimed. "You and Xena should definitely try the Cosmic Paradise. Trust me, it's amazing. You can never go wrong with Fae liquor. Deus, Amarok, and I are all gonna try the Firestorm, and... Dysnomi? Nagaveni? Do you two want the Siren's Lament... Or...?" Calliope questioned, looking over at the trickster and the gorgon, who were sitting next to each other.

"Yes, please!" Nagaveni exclaimed, her face lighting up with joy.

Once everyone had their drinks, Amarok lifted his Firestorm, the rim of which was flaming, in the air. Asmodeus and Calliope clinked their glasses against his. Then, he said, "This is just for you, Calli," with a wink before tossing the drink down his throat, swallowing it quickly. He made a face and let out a wolf howl, causing Calliope and Asmodeus to burst with laughter.

"Together?" Calliope asked Asmodeus when their laughing subsided, despite knowing that the fire that was leaping from their glasses wouldn't be able to hurt them.

"Together," Asmodeus agreed, and they downed their drinks quickly. "Holy hell, that's fantastic!" he yelled, slamming his glass down on the top of the bar.

Calliope laughed and asked, "Holy hell? Seriously, Deus?"

"Cállate,"[33] Asmodeus replied, laughing along with Calliope and rolling his eyes. "You know damn well that I didn't mean it like that."

---

[33] "Shut up,"

21. GIMME SHELTER

(CAUSE FOR CONCERN)

Calliope spent almost the entire day at The Tipsy Piano drinking and laughing with her friends. As she looked around at all of them, her heart filled with joy. She realized something at that moment... She realized that despite how dysfunctional her biological family was turning out to be, she still somehow ended up with her own chosen family—these people that she loved and would die for. She told herself, *As long as they're all alive at the end of this, everything will have been worth it.* Then, she added, *I will happily give up my powers—and even die—if that's what it comes down to.*

'No! You are NOT just going to give up! That's such bullshit! I will not let you give up!' Ember yelled at Calliope.

'What? Not even if that's what it takes to ensure that everyone else here is safe from her brother?' Lyn asked Ember.

'She will not be able to keep anyone here safe unless she is willing to fight for them! She can't ensure their safety if SHE'S already dead!' Ember roared in response.

Ember and Lyn continued their argument inside Calliope's mind, causing her to let out a deep sigh while rubbing her temples. *Please stop fighting,* she thought to the spirits. *You're both giving me a fucking migraine. I really don't want to hear this right now.*

A male voice called out from behind Calliope, asking, "Calli? Are you okay? Does your head hurt or something?"

Calliope jumped at the unexpected sound of the man's voice. "Shit, you scared me," she gasped, laughing as she turned around to look at Asmodeus. "Yeah, I'm alright, Deus. Ember and Lyn are just arguing right now. I love having the spirits of the phoenix and the thunderbird, but honestly, they're kind of giving me a headache at the moment."

"Ember and Lyn?" Asmodeus asked. "I don't think I've ever actually heard you say their names before."

"Oh, right," Calliope said. "I forgot you weren't there when I first learned about them, I'm sorry. Okay, so Ember is the phoenix spirit—she basically runs off of pure rage, and she's the reason that fire can't hurt me. Lyn is the thunderbird spirit—she thrives on emotional connections, sort of like... Well, you know how it feels when *'the sparks are flying'* between us? That's the kind of feeling that makes her strong."

"Oh, okay," Asmodeus said. "I understand. So, they're separate entities within you, right? Like the demon inside of me?" he asked.

"And like Amarok's wolf," Calliope added, smiling widely.

Asmodeus nodded his head and replied, "Right, right. Amarok actually did mention that last night when we were all talking. I remember now."

Before Calliope could respond, a familiar slow, romantic song started playing over the surround-sound speakers. "Oh! This is the song that I danced with Amarok to on our first day in New Orleans!" she exclaimed. There was a mix of slight nostalgia—despite the memory only being barely two weeks old—and sadness behind her eyes.

Amarok caught Calliope's gaze from across the bar. He stalked toward her with a wolfish grin. When he reached her, he bowed like a gentleman, making her playfully roll her eyes. "Do you mind if I cut in for a moment?" he asked Asmodeus.

"Oh, it's not up to me," Asmodeus answered, holding his arms out toward Calliope like he was offering her up—or maybe just showing her off—to

Amarok. "She's the boss over here," he said, laughing.

"In that case, would you honor me with this dance, Calli?" Amarok asked Calliope. He took one of her hands and pulled it up to his lips gently, kissing the back of it.

"The honor is all mine," Calliope replied, laughing. She pretended to be curtsying to Amarok, holding an imaginary dress skirt out at her sides.

Amarok laughed and took Calliope's hand, then led her to the middle of the bar's floor once again. She danced with him the way that she had on the first night, between the booths and the bar, feeling exhilarated. As the song ended, Amarok once again dipped her down low, although her hair did not get close to touching the floor the second time around since it was secured in a messy bun on the top of her head.

By the time Amarok pulled Calliope up, she was breathing heavily from both the dance and the tension that she had felt growing between them. "That... Always amazes me," she told him with a small, breathless laugh.

"YOU always amaze me," Amarok replied, kissing Calliope's cheek.

Calliope was about to tell Amarok how corny he sounded. However, he leaned down before she could speak and planted another light kiss on her, though it was her lips that he kissed then. When he finally pulled away, she had forgotten all about how she was going to tease him. She simply made her way back to the bar, where she could finally catch her breath. She sat down and began nursing another drink when she heard Asmodeus' voice inside her mind.

Asmodeus telepathically asked Calliope, *There's a small private room in the back of the bar. Will you meet me there? I promise I'll make it worth your time, Calli.*

Are we even allowed to go back there? Calliope telepathically asked Asmodeus in response.

Yeah, I already asked Zeph about it, came Asmodeus' reply. *He said it's fine with him since this might be the last night that any of us get to spend time with you.*

Okay, Deus. I'm coming, Calliope told Asmodeus. She excused herself from the bar and slipped into the small private room in the back, quietly closing the door behind her. The tiny room was dark, and she couldn't see much, so she called out to him. "Deus?" she asked, but there was no response.

Calliope was considering leaving when a pair of rough, hazelnut-colored hands covered her eyes. Then, someone walked her backward, pushing her onto a small couch, which was sitting against the far wall. "If you wanna be able to see me, you gotta promise that you're gonna kiss me," Asmodeus' voice whispered in her ear, making her shiver.

"Do I really need to promise you that, Deus?" Calliope asked with a pouting, bratty tone. "I think you already KNOW I'm gonna kiss you."

"You make a very good point," Asmodeus replied, removing his hands. "Very compelling."

Calliope turned around to face Asmodeus, wrapping her arms around his neck and kissing his lips passionately. She gasped when he pushed her down onto the couch and climbed on top of her. She slid her hands up the inside of his shirt, feeling his powerful muscles and causing him to gasp quietly at the feeling of her hands running softly along his taut abs. His skin felt electrified every time that she touched him.

Asmodeus pulled his shirt over his head, then did the same thing with Calliope's shirt, pulling it off of her. He groaned as his hands slid over her chest when he was removing her shirt. He pressed himself into her then, and she could feel his hard member throbbing insistently against her inner thigh.

Calliope moaned, telling Asmodeus telepathically, *Oh my gods, Deus. I need you right now. Please...*

That's all that it took for Asmodeus to comply with Calliope's wishes. He could never say no to her, even if he wanted to—which he never did. He pulled the rest of their clothes off as fast as he could, his need for her quickly consuming him. Then, he thrust his entire length into her, causing her to grab and hold onto his shoulders while moaning into his ear. They both quickly lost themselves in that moment, staying locked together in that way—her wrapping her legs around his waist and him with his arms enveloping her—until eventually... They finished together, both crying out in ecstasy.

'If you survive all of this shit, PLEASE tell me you're gonna get back together with him,' Ember said.

I don't actually know if I AM going to, though, Calliope thought to the spirit of the phoenix as she began to put her clothes back on. *I know you really like him, but we HAVE already played this game before and it didn't exactly work out. What guarantee do we have that it would work out any different this time?*

Asmodeus nodded at Calliope, letting her know that he was going to head back up toward the front of the bar. She nodded at him in acknowledgment.

'No, don't pick him. You should definitely choose Amarok, though. He's never hurt you, he's amazed by literally everything that you do, and there's this... Electric sort of passion in him,' Lyn argued.

I do really like Amarok as well, but... I live in Los Angeles, Calliope told Lyn as she walked toward the front of the bar after Asmodeus. *I don't know how I could ever make long-distance work for both of us.*

Calliope became so busy talking to Ember and Lyn inside her mind that she almost didn't feel the intense anger that was suddenly clouding the bar. She only noticed it after she saw all of her friends lying unconscious on the bar floor—each of them with what appeared to be electrical burns all over their bodies. Even Asmodeus—who had only walked back up to the front of the bar mere moments before she did—was lying there on the floor.

"Oh no," Calliope cried. "Please, gods, no." She quickly checked for their pulses, letting out a small, shaky breath of relief when she confirmed that they were all still alive.

'Raiden is going to fucking die for this! He could have killed them! Hell, Xena is only human! Her body can not take that kind of damage! We need to find him now and get rid of him!' Ember screamed inside Calliope's mind, preparing the siren for a fight. As Calliope looked around, she couldn't pinpoint anything that was out of place—other than her friends, of course—which seemed extremely weird to her.

If Raiden attacked them all using lightning, then why is there nothing else out of place around here? Calliope questioned. *Lightning is sporadic—you can't exactly control where it hits,* she thought. *I know my father said that my brother is more powerful than me, but to be able to fully control the lightning? That's an almost impossible power... It's god-level.*

Calliope heard something move behind her, and she quickly turned to see what it was. However, she wasn't quick enough to avoid the shock of a ball of lightning slamming into her face. It hit her nose hard, causing her immense agony. She fell to her knees, still looking around for her brother, when she finally heard his voice. She had not heard it in three years, but she would recognize it anywhere.

"Hello, sister," Raiden said to Calliope. "I see you're still in love with that half-demon piece of shit who locked me away. So... I guess this must be why you never tried to help me get out of that awful place."

Before Calliope could respond, a second voice called out from behind her. The man speaking was so close to her that she could feel his hot breath on her, and she could almost feel his lips brushing against the back of her neck. "The siren obviously has poor taste in men. I mean, she DID choose my weak older brother when she could've had me. Oh, well... Asmodeus can't save you now, you stupid little siren bitch."

Menoetius... Oh, gods... No... Calliope thought, panicking.

22. END OF THE ROAD

(INTO DARKNESS)

Hazelnut-colored hands wrapped around Calliope from behind, one moving to caress the inside of one of her thighs while the other began reaching for her throat to choke her. Menoetius said to Raiden, "To be fair to the little siren whore, she DID leave my brother when she found out what he had done with you... But, it doesn't really matter since it appears that she simply couldn't resist seducing him a second time."

"Oh, please," Calliope groaned, rolling her eyes. "Don't even try to fool yourself, Menoetius. You should know by now that you were never an option in my opinion. In fact, you weren't even on the back burner of my mind... I simply didn't think about you... At all... Ever."

"You stupid little slut!" Menoetius yelled. He grabbed Calliope by her hair, pulling her backward. Then, he moved around to stand in front of her, keeping his face menacingly close to hers as his ink-black eyes turned impossibly darker and his thick midnight-black horns grew from his head. His horns curved over and down toward the back of his head like a ram's horns. "You're a filthy fucking liar. You might claim that you never thought about me, but please... Be honest, little whore. I was the ONLY demon that you were ever afraid of and we both know why. If it hadn't been for my naive brother walking in that night... Three years ago... You wouldn't have been able to stop me from doing whatever the FUCK I wanted to do to you." He flashed her a sinister grin. "I had already broken you—you were bruised and bloody—and if he hadn't walked in, you would've fucking died that night... AFTER I had my fun with you, of course."

"Oh my gods, can you please shut the fuck up, Menoetius? I fucking get it, dude. You're this cool, edgy, bad-ass demon. You do horrible things to people simply because you enjoy hurting people. You're so fucking scary," Calliope said sarcastically, rolling her eyes. "Look, I know that your daddy didn't give you enough love when you were just a little baby demon because he only cared about the prince, but—"

Before Calliope could finish, Menoetius yanked on her hair with the hand that was still clinging to it. "Shut! The fuck! Up!" he screamed at her. Then, he slammed her down face-first as hard as he possibly could. Her head smashed into the hardwood floor with a loud *THUMP!* and bounced up again. He slammed her down once more, then held her there on the floor as she let out a small, pained groan. Blood began to run out of her now-broken nose and down her face.

"As much as I would enjoy watching you beat the shit outta my sister all night—I mean, she did leave me stuck in the Demon Realm for three years, after all—I'd really like to get what I came here for first," Raiden said to Menoetius. He stepped forward then, and Calliope could see the hatred and anger in his eyes when he finally addressed her again. "You left me to rot, dear *'sister'*. And you knew I didn't have powers like you do. After all, how could I possibly have your powers? I'm not female, so I wasn't able to inherit our mother's siren abilities. Yet, despite knowing that, you still didn't even try to help me. You didn't care enough to rescue me."

"I didn't know what happened... For a long time," Calliope replied. Her voice came out in a hoarse whisper. "When I finally found out, I left because I thought it was too late to help you." She paused, thinking about what Asmodeus told her. Then, she looked up at Raiden and said, "But FUCK you for trying to make me feel bad! Asmodeus told me that you already had feelings of resentment toward me, that you attacked him, and that you isolated me from all my friends."

"No, Calliope. Bullshit. You're lying and you know it. More often than not, you simply don't think of anyone but yourself. You're selfish... Just like every other siren. You're not even capable of caring about other people. Another person's emotions only matter to you if you can use them somehow," Raiden told Calliope. Hatred shot out of his words like snake venom. "If I resented you before, that's exactly why... And if I convinced your friends to leave you, it was only so you'd know what it felt like to be so alone. I only attacked your little boyfriend when he wouldn't leave me the fuck alone. I warned him multiple times. But I still thought that you would help your own brother," he scoffed, squatting in front of her. Menoetius grabbed her hair again and yanked her up into a sitting position. Her lip quivered when she felt some of her hair being ripped from her scalp; however, she refused to make a noise, not wanting to give Menoetius the satisfaction of knowing how badly he was hurting her. Raiden continued talking, saying, "But, you didn't help me. I was powerless, and you fucking left me. Well, sister... I'm not powerless anymore. The moment my powers appeared, I started working with them—learning how to use them. I've perfected my abilities now. I'm not weak anymore, and I never will be again. YOU will be, though. Trust me, dear sister, you're going to know how it feels to be weak and helpless. In fact, when I finally take your powers, I will be just about as strong as the father who wanted nothing to do with us, while you'll be weaker than ever. Then, I should finally be able to take our father out as well."

"But why?" Calliope asked. "I mean, okay, I get why you came after me, but why do you care so much about him?"

"You mean the man who decided he didn't give a shit about me?" Raiden replied with a scoff. "He never even bothered to meet me. He could have, at the very least, introduced himself and taught me how to use my abilities... How to be strong. But, he never even did that."

While Raiden was talking, Calliope noticed that he was holding the Compendium of Supernatural Powers. She could see the book shaking in his hands as he looked down at the floor, upset.

Menoetius seized the back of Calliope's neck, causing her to bleed as his nails dug into her and easily broke the skin. He leaned in close, his lips brushing along her earlobe, making her want to puke. He whispered to her, "You probably could've used a *'Daddy'* in your life. Who knows? Maybe you wouldn't have turned into such a little slut if you had ever had any form of discipline."

"I am so gods-damn sick of your shit, Menoetius," Calliope said, groaning and rolling her eyes in annoyance. "You're just mad because I'm the only woman who's ever told you no and gotten away with it."

Calliope heard a metallic sound resonate from behind her then. Menoetius laughed and wrapped an arm around her waist from behind, forcefully pulling her into him. He held his knife at her side with his other hand and pointed the bronze blade toward one of her eyes. She looked at it, noticing that there were siren scales covering its hilt. "See this?" he whispered in her ear. She could tell that he was excited, and it took all of her willpower to not recoil away from him. "I made this knife extra-special... I had it enchanted just for you."

In front of Calliope, Raiden scoffed. Then, with an arrogant smirk, he said, "Yes... Not only would your wounds never completely heal if you got cut with that, but they would always be agonizing. The pain would never end for you, sister."

"Personally, I can't fucking wait to test it on you," Menoetius whispered into Calliope's ear with a small laugh. He then brushed his lips lightly over her neck before he whispered, "I like to call it... The Siren's Suffering."

I'm so fucking sick of him! Come on, let's just fight already!' Ember yelled to Calliope.

Calliope thought, *You're right. Let's just do it already.* She leaned her head forward a bit, then slammed it backward. Her head hit Menoetius' nose, and the shock caused him to release her. Then, she slammed forward into Raiden's nose before either of the men could react.

"You little fucking bitch!" Menoetius screamed, holding his broken nose.

That's the second time I've broken his nose, Calliope thought, beaming with pride.

Raiden attempted to grab Calliope as she rushed forward, but she was faster. She dodged his grasping hand and managed to put some distance between her and the two men.

However, Calliope was stopped in her tracks when Menoetius suddenly teleported in front of her. However, she wasn't able to halt her movements fast enough, and the blade of the Siren's Suffering became embedded deeply into her shoulder. She grunted from the pain while

Menoetius laughed. He pulled the blade out quickly, causing even more pain.

Sparks of lightning darted between Calliope's fingertips as the agonizing, white-hot pain took hold of her. Thunder rumbled in the distance before a horrendous screeching sound ripped through the air. Calliope didn't realize what the sound was until she saw Thora flying in. Wrath flew in behind Thora, flames shooting high off of her wings.

Menoetius' arrogant smile faded when he finally processed the scene that was beginning to play out around him. He backed away from the lightning, which had begun to dart wildly around Calliope's arms, but he stopped when he bumped into something. He turned around in time to see Nanuk materialize directly in front of his eyes. Nanuk let out a low growl. "Raiden... Now might be a good time to take away your bitch sister's powers!" Menoetius called out.

"No!" Calliope yelled, throwing her arms out so the lightning jumped off and hit both Menoetius and Raiden. After the strike, Nanuk pounced, clamping her powerful jaws around Menoetius' arm and dragging him viciously to the floor. With him down, Calliope turned to face her brother.

Raiden stood with the Compendium of Supernatural Powers in one hand. It was open to a spot near the middle, and he looked down at the page before him. He began reading from it in a language that Calliope could not understand.

'It's probably Latin again,' Lyn guessed.

Yeah, you're probably right, Calliope thought in response.

Thora and Wrath swooped down, attacking Raiden with their thunder and fire abilities, though it didn't appear to hurt him at all. *'Hey, can your brother steal their powers, too? I really don't think they should be here if he can,'* Lyn said, worrying for the birds.

Calliope stopped to think, *You're right. If there's even a chance that he can steal their abilities, they shouldn't be here.* She addressed Wrath and Thora next, telepathically telling them, *It's too dangerous for you two to be here. Please get out while you can so he can't steal your powers.*

The two birds stopped when they heard Calliope speaking to them. Then, they both nodded at her in thanks before flying out.

Calliope addressed Raiden last. She begged him, "Raiden, please stop this. This is insane. You don't have to do this." He just looked up at her as he continued to read. Lightning and fire both began to pull away from her body.

The spirits of the thunderbird and the phoenix were screaming inside Calliope's mind. It sounded like they were in as much pain as she was, despite them not having physical forms.

The lightning and the fire continued to get pulled away from Calliope, swirling around and twisting together while being absorbed by Raiden. She then found herself unable to stop the scream that was clawing at her throat, desperate to escape. When the agonizing pain that she was feeling became worse, she released her sonic shriek, shaking the entire building.

Raiden had trouble keeping himself steady as Calliope screamed, but he forced himself to power through it. He continued to read, pulling her abilities away from her. Blood poured out of his ears as the last of Calliope's lightning and fire abilities were eventually absorbed by him.

Calliope fell to her knees, her scream trailing off as her throat became hoarse. She heard Nanuk yelp loudly behind her. Menoetius yelled, "Stupid fucking mutt!"

Raiden shook his head and walked over to Calliope, saying, "You're right, sister. I didn't have to do that... But, I wanted to." He smiled and looked over at Menoetius, who Calliope realized was extremely close to her. Then, he said, "I'm done. Kill her."

Menoetius laughed as Raiden walked out of the building. Then, he moved behind Calliope, wrapping one arm around to grab her throat, pulling her onto her feet.

Without her fire and thunder powers, Calliope felt more weak than she ever had. Her legs were shaking and she was having trouble standing on her own.

"I guess it's my turn with you," Menoetius whispered in Calliope's ear, tightening his grip on her throat. She tried to keep her emotions in check, but she couldn't stop the small whimper from escaping. She was afraid, and the demon loved it. He nipped at her earlobe, which made her feel disgusted. Then, he said, "You've always been such a pretty little thing... Oh, don't worry though, whore. I'm not going to touch you... I don't think I even want you anymore. You're weak and pathetic."

"Fuck... You," Calliope choked out through gasping breaths.

Menoetius took the Siren's Suffering knife and sliced a deep gash across Calliope's stomach before she could move away from him. She shouted from the pain, almost falling. She was only being held up by his hand at her throat and he soon realized that as well. He released his hold on her and her body fell, crumpling on the floor while he laughed. Then, he noticed that her friends were waking and he leaned over her to whisper, "They can't save you now." He stabbed the knife deeply into her side, causing her to cry out in pain. Then, he grabbed her hair, twisting the turquoise strands through his fingers and walking backward with her as her friends rose.

"Menoetius!" Asmodeus yelled when he noticed his brother with Calliope. "Don't you dare fucking touch her!"

The rest of Calliope's friends watched in abject horror as Menoetius replied, "Too late for that, brother. Say goodbye to your little slut." He then stabbed the knife into her chest.

"¿*Mi amor?*"[34] Asmodeus screamed, running over to Calliope. She gasped as the knife pierced through her heart, and she fell to her knees. She heard Menoetius laugh one more time before he disappeared. "Fuck!" Asmodeus yelled as he looked over her wounds.

"No, no, no," Nagaveni cried. She buried her face into Dysnomi's chest.

---

[34] "My love?"

Dysnomi held Nagaveni. To Calliope, he whispered, "I'm so sorry, Calli. I can't fix that... The consequences would be too severe..."

"It's okay, Dys," Calliope choked out.

Zephyr was looking at Xena sadly without saying a word. Amarok was holding Xena, who was lying limp in his arms after being struck by the lightning. He looked between her and Calliope, his face appearing unimaginably torn when he realized that the only thing that he could do for Xena was to get her to the hospital quickly... And that there wasn't anything that he could do for Calliope. "I..." he started as a tear fell down from his golden-yellow eyes.

"Go on," Calliope gasped, nodding toward the door. So, with tears in his eyes, he nodded back at her and ran outside with Xena.

Asmodeus dropped to his knees in front of Calliope as the others surrounded her. He and Dysnomi helped to ease her against the bar. "Calliope," he said, reaching out to touch her face. She leaned into his touch, closing her eyes. "Stay awake," he told her. "Please... *Abre tus ojos, mi amor.*"[35]

Calliope forced her iris-purple eyes open to look into Asmodeus' electric-blue ones. She could

---

[35] "Open your eyes, my love."

feel the sadness inside of him, bursting out of him like a burst dam. His despair was consuming him. "It's okay, Deus..." she whispered. She forced herself to speak, even though it was painful. "It'll be okay." She looked at all of her friends then and choked out, "I love you," as blood bubbled out from between her lips.

Nagaveni cried softly into Dysnomi's chest. He wrapped his arms around her, staring solemnly at the floor.

Asmodeus caressed Calliope's cheek as tears fell from his eyes. She gave him a small smile as her vision faded to black and the lights in her eyes dimmed.

Calliope's eyelids drooped and her hands fell to her sides harshly. The intense pain that she felt subsided as her breathing became more labored. Her entire body soon became numb. She could almost hear her friends pleading with her to stay awake, but all of their voices sounded muffled to her, like she was underwater while they were talking.

She no longer felt scared or upset as she lay there against the bar. She felt at peace for once, like she had nothing in the world left for her to worry about. She released one last breath with a smile on her abnormally-pale lips. Then, every other sound around her faded away, her eyes finally closed, and everything just... Faded to black.

23. AT DEATH'S DOOR

(WHEN THE DEAD COME KNOCKING)

"My, my, my... What do we have here?" said a masculine voice behind Calliope. "You're here so much sooner than I ever expected you to be."

The man's voice caused Calliope's eyes to shoot open and her body to jerk upright. She looked around, feeling terrified as she tried to make sense of her foreign surroundings. She was sitting in the middle of a dirt road, which appeared to be in the middle of nowhere. *There aren't even any signs near the road,* she thought. *In fact, there doesn't seem to be much of anything around here. Where the fuck am I?* she wondered as her eyes scanned the horizon. She tried to look for any visual clues about where she was or why she woke up there... Or even how she woke up at all.

"Alright, calm yourself down now, gorgeous. I don't know what you're looking for around here, but you're not gonna find anything. It's pretty gods-damn borin' 'round here," the man who was standing behind Calliope said.

Calliope jumped when she heard the man's voice again. She turned around to look at the man, who was still standing behind her. The person that she saw surprised her, but she was relieved to know that it was him rather than Menoetius or Raiden. "Baron Samedi?" she questioned. She had an incredulous look on her face, as if seeing him then—standing in front of her—had to be some kind of dream. "Where... Are... We?" she asked him.

"Where the hell do you think we are, doll? This, my dear, is the crossroads, which lie between the world of the living and the land of the dead. This is where I meet all the newly-departed souls and send their asses on to the land of the dead..." Baron Samedi replied. "Although... Sometimes... If I feel like someone really needs to go back... If I feel like they aren't done with their life... Like they have more they need to do... Well... Then, I'll just send their ass back to the world of the living."

"So then, this is where you... Um, work? Or... Preside?" Calliope asked, stuttering and wringing her hands together. She was staring at the ground and lightly kicking at the dirt in the middle of the crossroads.

"That's right, darlin'. It's fucking boring 'round here sometimes, but all of this... Is my domain," the Baron replied, stretching his arms out wide with a sly smile. "So... Would you like me to show you around? Give you the whole... Fancy-ass grand tour?" he asked, holding one of his arms out for Calliope. She smiled and looped one of her arms in his as he lit a cigar with his free hand. Then, he led her along the road in front of them, telling her, "Now... Over here is how the new souls come in... If I've got an empty grave, of course. A new soul can only come if I've got an open one. But hey—if I'm being honest with you, honey... No one ever really fuckin' uses one—not for long, anyway—so I've almost always got the whole damn graveyard empty."

Calliope looked up at the Loa of the Dead as he inhaled a long drag from his cigar. She admired the painting skills that it had to have taken to decorate the upper part of his mature, handsome face so intricately. "So, how many souls DO you deal with everyday?" she questioned.

"Ah, hell, doll, I don't fuckin' know. Too goddamn many to keep track of, that's for damn sure," Baron Samedi replied with a slight laugh before taking another drag from his cigar.

As they got closer to the graveyard, Calliope noticed all of the empty graves that were around them. There were a handful of graves that were occupied, but most sat open and appeared to be undisturbed. "Do the souls just... Appear in the graves?" she asked. "Is that why you need the empty ones?"

"That's right," Baron Samedi answered, amused. "Though, the moment a soul wakes up, they get transported to the middle of the crossroads... Just like you did."

"Oh," Calliope exclaimed as the Loa of the Dead began to lead her in a new direction.

"Now... This—" Baron Samedi told Calliope as they walked closer to the new area. "Is where I stay when I'm not too busy..." He puffed on his cigar once more before he finally flicked it to the ground, stomping it out completely. "Or when I'm not getting called up there to the damn... World of the living. I mean, don't get me wrong... I do fuckin' love partyin' up there. The rum, the cigars... The beautiful women..." he said as he laughed. "I don't really get to use... This," he said, gesturing to a Gothic-style house that was looming over them.

"It's so gorgeous," Calliope breathed with a look of awe adorning her delicate facial features. She was going to ask the Baron how often he actually got to use the house when she spotted a familiar-looking woman. The woman sitting on the front porch steps had flawless java skin, waist-long box braids, and brightly glowing golden eyes. "Zorya?" she called out, waving.

"Calliope?" Zorya asked, running over to Calliope from where she had been sitting. "What're ya doin' here? I... I didn't cause dis, did I?" She looked away, feeling guilty and sad.

"Nah, this isn't on you," Calliope answered. "My ex-boyfriend's brother fucking stabbed me." She rolled her eyes, then she told Zorya about her own brother being the person who wanted her dead, and how Menoetius had stabbed her in the chest with a bronze knife after Raiden stole her powers. "It was all just a huge mess," she joked. "But what about you? How's your progress going here?"

"Well, I seem to actually be healin', so hopefully I'll be good 'nough to go back to da world of da living soon. I really miss Xena," Zorya answered with a small, almost sad, smile.

"I have no doubt you'll be better in no time," Calliope said encouragingly.

Baron Samedi cleared his throat and said, "I hate having to break up this lovely reunion, but we really should finish the tour before another one of those damn souls wakes up."

"Mais. Don't let me keep ya," Zorya responded. She and Calliope shared a quick hug before the Baron whisked Calliope off down the third dirt pathway.

The Baron led Calliope using one of his tattooed hands, which he was resting on the small of her back. The sensation oddly caused her to blush and turn her face away from him. She was still avoiding eye contact—her cheeks still warm from blushing—when they finally arrived at a new area of the crossroads, which had been only a short walk down the third path. He looked down at her with a soft, seemingly empathetic, expression. "This path would lead you to the land of the dead," he whispered. "After going into the land of the dead, the souls get sorted into... Whatever fuckin' afterlife they belong in."

"So... I guess that means this is my last stop before I get sent off to Purgatory," Calliope replied awkwardly. "Thank you for showing me around first."

"Oh, you sweet lil thing," Baron Samedi said with a smile. "This is only your last stop if you would like it to be. I am the Loa of the Dead. Now, that's true... But... I am also the Loa of fuckin' resurrection!" He laughed, throwing his arms out theatrically.

"What?" Calliope asked, furrowing her eyebrows in confusion.

"Did you keep that card I gave you?" Baron Samedi asked Calliope. He lifted an eyebrow, then narrowed his eyes at her.

"Of course I did," Calliope answered. "But... I mean, it's not like I have it ON me." She laughed before saying, "I mean, I don't exactly have a physical body here."

Baron Samedi smiled widely and leaned down to whisper in Calliope's ear, making her shiver. "Check your pocket, siren," he said, smirking.

Calliope looked up into the Loa's deep brown eyes as he smirked at her. She thought, *He's so mischievous... I wonder where he's getting at with this.* She reached into her back pocket, making a mental note that her *'spirit-self'* was still wearing the *Nirvana* t-shirt and ripped skinny jeans that she had been wearing when she died. *Huh,* she thought. *I guess that means that you DO get stuck in the same clothes you were wearing when you died. I'll have to remember that whenever I wanna be lazy about my outfits from now on.* Calliope noticed that she could see her bright lavender and turquoise scales through the rips in her jeans, despite having legs in the spirit world rather than her tail. *That's kinda weird,* she thought.

Calliope then felt something in the back pocket of her jeans and pulled it out. It was the *'death'* tarot card that Baron Samedi had given to her the night that they had met. "How—?" she started to ask.

"Ah, ah. I can't reveal all my secrets now, can I?" Baron Samedi asked, laughing. "This card is my personal assurance that you'll have passage back into the world of the living whenever you fuckin' need it... That is... IF you would like to go back, of course," he said, looking at Calliope with a kind and patient expression.

"I..." Calliope started, holding the card close to her chest. It comforted her to have it so close. "I... Honestly don't know." She felt conflicted. She could remember feeling at peace when she died, but she also knew that her friends must have been hurting, and she did not like the idea of her friends hurting because of her. *And,* she thought, *Raiden's still out there with the powers he took from me. He's probably working on becoming stronger than our father already. He'll be too strong for me to fight head-on.*

"As I said, it's your choice," Baron Samedi said with a shrug. Then, he placed his hand on Calliope's chin, tilting her face up with his forefinger and his thumb so that she would look at him. "Just remember what I told you... It really would be a damn shame for the world of the living to lose such a beautiful soul."

Calliope smiled a bit, blushing, then turned her face slightly away from the Baron. She took a deep breath to give herself the confidence that she needed... Then, she looked into his eyes and told him, "I think I'm ready to go back to the world of the living... I have some things I need to take care of."

"Oh, I was really fuckin' hoping you'd say that," Baron Samedi replied, pulling away from Calliope and laughing. "Come! Let's fuckin' bring you back to life now!" He offered her his arm and she accepted it once again, allowing him to lead her to the only path that he hadn't given her a tour of—the path that led to the world of the living.

"Oh my gods, I'm so nervous," Calliope said, laughing. "So, um... Got any tips for how I can defeat my brother when I get back now that he's stolen my powers?"

"Just a little bit of advice, gorgeous," Baron Samedi replied, winking. "He might have those powers of yours... But he doesn't know that you've made your own goddamn POWERFUL friends on the other side..." He looked down at Calliope.

"Which means he doesn't know that you'll be fuckin' coming back. Correct?"

"...Right..." Calliope answered, using a suspicious tone of voice, almost as if to ask the Loa, *What are you trying to do?*

"Good," Baron Samedi said. "Keep it that way until the time is right. If you can surprise him, the powers he has won't fuckin' matter. He's still a mere mortal... He can still die easily if you can just fuckin' catch him off-guard."

"Baron Samedi, you're an absolute genius," Calliope said, laughing. "Thank you for everything. Seriously."

"Ah, I don't wanna hear none of that shit," Baron Samedi replied, laughing. "You just go on now and kill that bitch-ass brother of yours. Show him that you are not the woman to fuck with."

"Yes, sir," Calliope said, giving the Baron a surprised smile and a slightly sarcastic salute. She then turned toward the dirt path that was laid out in front of them. "Well... Here goes nothing," she said. She took a few unsure steps forward, then turned to look over her shoulder at him. He gave her an encouraging nod and she steeled herself again, squaring her shoulders. She was trying her best to be confident.

One step... Two... Three... Just a few more steps to go now, Calliope thought. *One... Two... Three... Four.*

On the fifth step, she was bathed in a warm, bright light. The light seemed to get brighter and brighter with her next steps, until it was eventually blinding Calliope. She had to shut her eyes tightly for her last few steps and it became so hot around her that it was starting to hurt her, but she continued onward.

One... Two... Three... One last step, Calliope thought, kissing the tarot card that she had and holding it in the warm light. The warmth faded then, along with the bright light... Leaving Calliope alone in the dark. She felt around for a moment, noticing that she seemed to be stuck inside of something that was barely big enough for her to move in. Calliope could feel wooden walls on every side of her, and a wooden lid above her. She pushed on the lid, but it didn't budge, even when she pushed on it as hard as she could.

Oh, my gods, Calliope thought, trying to not panic. *Oh my gods, I'm stuck inside a fucking coffin.* She tried to keep herself calm for as long as possible, but she did not last very long. Instead, she began to punch and claw at the inside of the coffin, screaming for help.

24. PULL YOURSELF BACK TO CREATION

(OF GRAVE IMPORTANCE)

Okay, Calliope... Calm down and think about this rationally, Calliope told herself. *How do I even get out of this situation?* The siren took a deep breath, pulled her arm back as far as the tiny space inside the coffin would allow, clenched her fist tightly, then slammed her closed fist into the lid of the coffin as hard as she could. The coffin shook, but nothing else happened. She punched it again. Still, nothing. So, she punched again, and again, and again, until finally, she heard the wood from the lid above her splinter. *Yes!* Calliope thought excitedly to herself. She pulled her arm back and punched again. She continued that process until dirt fell from above the coffin lid, landing on top of her.

Shit, I didn't think about this, Calliope said inside her mind. Acting quickly, she pulled her shirt over her face, using it to block the dirt from getting in her mouth or nose.

When the broken opening above Calliope was wide enough, she reached up, clawing at the lid, and at the dirt above her. She was then able to begin pulling herself up toward the surface. It was an agonizingly slow process, and she was beginning to realize how badly her hand was actually hurting, but she continued to make her way up. She eventually felt the cool night air the moment that it hit her skin when her hand finally broke the surface.

At the top of the grave, Calliope took a moment to rest after she pulled her shirt back down. She noticed that she was wearing a really nice, plain, watermelon-pink shirt and a pair of faded jeans. *Thank the gods for Nini dressing me in casual clothes for my funeral. I really love that woman,* she thought. She took a moment then to look at her hand, noticing the bruises and blood that were all over her knuckles, and how swollen her hand had become in the short amount of time. *Broken again,* she pouted. *Funny how this keeps happening.*

With a pained grunt, Calliope pushed her sore body up to her feet and checked her surroundings to try and figure out where she was at. Once she gained a vague understanding of her location, she made her way out of the graveyard—which she saw was called Obsidian Cemetery—and onto the streets of NOLA, wandering for what felt to her like forever. She finally came up to a familiar street, sighing as a huge feeling of relief washed over her.

Finally! Calliope thought as she made her way through the crowded street. A few people—humans—around her looked at her curiously. They were all noticing her disheveled appearance, her broken and bloodied hand, and the dirt that was all over her body and staining her clothes. She didn't pay attention to any of the people, however—didn't show that she was in need of help in any way. She was a woman on a mission, quickly making her way to the Tipsy Piano, where she hoped that her friends were waiting... *Or at least still up and drinking there,* she thought. *Since they don't even know that I'm coming back.*

After walking a few more blocks, Calli was finally walking up to the front door of the bar. The lights inside the bar were dim, but she noticed that they were definitely on. However, the front door to the bar was already locked. She tried knocking on the door, but no one answered. She sighed and knocked again—louder and more insistently. Again, there was no answer. Then, she tried once more. Just as she was about to completely give up hope, the door opened. The voice of the person who was answering the door came from the other side of it, saying, "We're closed, okay? Come back tomorrow—Oh!"

"Hey, Zeph," Calliope said, giving the elf an awkward wave.

Zephyr stared at Calliope with a dropped jaw. He let his hand fall off of the handle of the door, allowing the front door to swing open. Amarok, Xena, Nagaveni, Dysnomi, and Asmodeus were all inside the bar with drinks sitting in front of them, but when the front door opened and revealed Calliope standing there, they all stopped drinking and talking. They were all staring at her incredulously, which made her feel very uncomfortable.

Calliope smiled awkwardly at them all and said, "Hey, guys."

25. SURVIVAL OF THE FITTEST

(TOUGHER THAN THE REST)

"Calliope? Is it really you?" Nagaveni asked as she quickly stood up from her seat.

Calliope opened her mouth to respond. However, before she could say anything, Asmodeus disappeared from his seat, only to reappear in front of her. He grabbed the siren by her throat and slammed her into the front door of the bar, slamming it shut in the process. He growled, "I swear to all of the gods in existence that if you're some shapeshifter—or any other gods-damn type of Supernatural—pretending to be *mi amor*,[36] I will murder you right where you stand."

The others came running over to Asmodeus and Calliope quickly. Amarok grabbed Asmodeus by the shoulders, pulling him off of Calliope with ease. She sucked in a sharp breath of air when the cambion's hands released her throat and she gasped out, "It's really me, Deus." She took a moment to catch her breath before locking the

---

[36] "my love,"

door to the bar behind her. She then turned back to her friends and told them, "If you don't believe me, just ask me something only I would know."

"Okay..." Amarok said slowly. "Tell me... What was the first thing you said to me and Zeph when you found out we're not human?"

"I said..." Calliope sighed and let out a small laugh before continuing. "I said that only in New Orleans could you find a werewolf, an elf, and a siren hanging out together in a bar," she finished with a smile.

Zephyr pulled Calliope into a tight hug and said, "Cher, how are you back? What happened?" He let go of her then and began walking toward the bar, saying, "Wait, you're gonna need a drink. Then, you can tell us everything."

As Zephyr worked on making a Cosmic Paradise for Calliope, the rest of her friends came up one at a time to hug her tightly. Asmodeus was the last person to approach her.

"So, uh, I'm sorry about how I reacted," Asmodeus said shyly, rubbing the back of his neck. As Calliope looked at him, she realized that he was still wearing his funeral clothes—as were all of her other friends.

Calliope wrapped Asmodeus in a warm hug and whispered, "It's okay, Deus. It's perfectly understandable." She then took his hand and led him toward the bar. They sat next to each other and Zephyr slid her the drink that he made for her. "So, were you all just sitting around and drinking away your misery?" she joked.

"Hey, that's not funny," Dysnomi told Calliope. He gave her an annoyed glance, although it seemed half-hearted. "We thought you were dead. It's been three days, Calliope. We had to bury you."

"I understand that, Dys," Calliope responded quietly. "And, to be fair, I WAS dead. So, I suppose that in most cases, it would've been time for the funeral."

"If you were dead, then..." Nagaveni started to question, but she trailed off, biting her lip.

"Den, how da hell are you even here?" Xena asked, finishing the question.

Calliope found the *'death'* tarot card—which was still in her back pocket—and pulled it out for everyone to see. Thank the gods for Nini, she thought for the second time that night. "Well," she said with a smile on her face. "Let's just say that I've made some friends in high places."

"Baron Samedi sent you back?" Amarok asked, looking shocked.

"Fascinating, cher. Tell us more," Zephyr pressed.

"He did send me back. Though, it was a choice that he gave me and allowed me to make for myself. I thought about moving on, into the land of the dead," Calliope responded. "I really, really thought about it... Everything just felt so hopeless at the time."

"What changed your mind?" Asmodeus questioned, a look of concern flitting across his face.

"Thinking of all of you changed my mind," Calliope answered. "Well, that and... The Baron helped me realize something about my brother."

"What?" Nagaveni asked curiously.

"He reminded me... That my brother may have a longer life span, but he's still ONLY human," Calliope replied, laughing. "He may have powers now, but if I can get close enough to him... I can kill him easily."

"Why don't you just shoot him?" Dysnomi suggested. "You don't even have to get close to him to do that."

"Eh, guns can bring a lot of unwanted attention," Calliope said, shaking her head. "It would probably be better to do it quietly. Though, first, we'll have to figure out where exactly he's hiding and where he's planning on summoning our father to fight him."

"Not to mention, we'll need a plan to distract my brother," Asmodeus responded. "If Menoetius gets in your way again, it'll be that much harder for you to get to Raiden."

"Yeah," Calliope said as she sighed. "Though, that motherfucker has something coming for him, as well."

"He does," Asmodeus agreed. "But, I want you to let me handle him. I know how my brother works and I know how to fight him better than anyone."

"Are you sure you can fight Menoetius on your own?" Calliope asked Asmodeus, remembering how Menoetius had left him with a scar on his face the last time that they fought. "Nanuk couldn't even keep him down for long." She gasped when she remembered Nanuk then, and she asked, "Oh my gods, Nanuk! Is she okay? I heard her yelp, but I didn't get to see what happened to her before I died!"

"She's fine!" Nagaveni assured Calliope. "She's a little banged up, but mostly okay. I sent her back to Salem. Salem's working on getting her back up to speed."

"Oh, thank the gods," Calliope said, breathing a sigh of relief. She grabbed her glass and took a drink, calming her nerves.

Asmodeus noticed Calliope's bloody and bruised hand when she set down her glass and he asked her, *"Mi amor, ¿qué pasó con tu mano?"*[37]

"What? Oh!" Calliope exclaimed, looking down at her hand. "Well, I had to break the coffin I was in to get out of it. It may or may not have broken my hand as well." She looked down at her hand again, noticing that the swelling had reduced a bit and that the skin had knitted itself back together, though it still looked bad. *Well, at least it's healed a bit,* she thought.

"Oh, here," Nagaveni said, digging through her purse. She pulled out the Hand of Restoration and tossed it across the bar to Calliope.

Calliope caught it and said, "Thanks, Nini. You're honestly the best friend I could ever ask for." She slipped the ring on her finger and watched with a small smile as her wounds began to heal. "So..." she started. "I guess the biggest question now is... How in all the hells do we figure out my brother's next move? We can't warn my father because we don't want to summon him and have Raiden show up while we're unprepared. Plus,

---

[37] "My love, what happened to your hand?"

it kinda seemed like my father already knew Raiden was coming after him."

"I dunno 'bout figurin' out his next move," Xena said. "But, maybe dat witch frienda yours knows some kinda trackin' spell? You'd at least know where he hidin' at den."

"Good thinking," Calliope responded. "I'd text her myself, but uh... I don't seem to have my phone," she said as she checked her pockets.

"Oh!" Nagaveni exclaimed. "I've got that, too!" She pulled the phone out of her purse and slid it across the bar to Calliope.

"Again I say... You're the best friend anyone could EVER ask for," Calliope said as she laughed. She sent a quick text to Salem before turning to look at Xena. "So, Xena... You'll be happy to hear that I saw Zorya," she said to the young hunter.

"Ya did?" Xena asked excitedly. She jumped a bit from the excitement. Calliope noticed that when she jumped, the movement also caused her to wince.

"Yeah, I saw her at the crossroads... She's been staying in this giant house. The house is supposed to be for Baron Samedi, but he doesn't get to use it much anyway, according to him," Calliope explained.

"Well?" Xena asked, pressuring Calliope to continue. "How she doin'? She stayin' dere? She healin'? Please don't tell me it's da bad option..."

"No, Xena, she's doing amazing!" Calliope exclaimed. "She said she should be back up here in the world of the living really soon!"

"Oh my god, I'm so glad to hear dat," Xena responded, breathing out a sigh of relief. "I was so worried 'bout her."

"Yeah, I could tell that you're close with her," Calliope said. "Wait though, how are YOU doing? Honestly, I'm surprised you're not still in the hospital."

"Mais, I did get a nasty electric burn from da lightnin'," Xena answered, rolling up her sleeve and pulling up part of her shirt to show Calliope.

Calliope could see that Xena had a lightning flower—also known as a Lichtenberg figure—burned all along her side, with some nasty-looking blisters over certain parts of it.

Well, that's definitely going to leave a scar, but at least it will make a good story, Calliope thought. *It's not as bad as I thought it would be, though.* She glanced at Xena as Xena pulled the shirt down again, and she said, "It looks like you got lucky, all things considered."

"Right?" Xena agreed. "I can't believe it, but hell, I'll take it. I'd rather have dis cool fuckin' scar den to be stuck in da hospital for who knows how long."

"Yeah, that makes sense," Calliope said. "I'm glad Amarok got you to the hospital and made sure you were okay."

"I'm sorry I had to leave you to do it, Calli," Amarok said with a sad expression.

"It's okay," Calliope responded. "I told you to go, remember? Now come on, let's just celebrate being alive!"

The whole group of friends cheered and laughed as Calliope pulled Amarok to the middle of the floor to dance with her. They all joined in on the dance before long. Then, they drank and joked with each other for the rest of the night. When the group finally decided to leave and get some sleep, she pulled Asmodeus to the side.

"This is going to sound pathetic," Calliope started. "But... Can I sleep with you tonight? I don't want to be alone," she admitted.

Asmodeus stroked Calliope's cappuccino cheek with his thumb and kissed her forehead. "Of course you can sleep with me, *mi amor*.[38] That

---

[38] "my love."

doesn't sound pathetic at all. You went through a lot. *Es comprensible querida,*[39] he answered.

"Thank you, Deus," Calliope said with tears in her eyes as Asmodeus took her hand. He then led her to his hotel room for the night.

---

[39] "It's perfectly understandable."

26. NO REST FOR THE WICKED

(THE CHOICES WE MAKE)

"Calliope, wake up," Asmodeus said the next day, while gently shaking Calliope. "Salem found out where your brother's been hiding."

"Really?" Calliope asked, sitting up and smoothing down her wild turquoise hair. "That was fast. What time is it, anyway?" She reached over to the nightstand and grabbed her phone to check the time. "Holy shit, Deus, why in all the hells did you allow me to sleep until four in the afternoon?"

"You needed the rest," Asmodeus replied, shrugging nonchalantly. "But, apparently, your brother's still in New Orleans. In fact, it doesn't appear that he ever even left," he said. "Come on and get dressed so we can all get together to come up with some kind of plan. Nini brought your clothes over to the room this morning."

Calliope nodded at Asmodeus and stretched before standing. She then rifled through her clothes to find an outfit that she could wear for the day. First, she pulled on a tight long-sleeve black crop top, which gave her some serious *Kim Possible* vibes. Next, she pulled on a pair of black skinny jeans, which had a belt around the waist and more belts strapped around the thighs—perfect for her to attach her daggers to—and a pair of black combat boots. Then, she pulled her hair into a giant messy bun at the top of her head. Turning to look at Asmodeus, she said, "I'm ready," with a wide smile.

"Alright," Asmodeus said as he took Calliope's hand. *"Vamos,*[40] everyone's waiting for us at the bar."

Hand-in-hand, Asmodeus and Calliope walked down to the hotel lobby, out of the front door, and all the way down the street. They eventually ended up at The Tipsy Piano, where all of their friends were waiting for them inside.

Asmodeus and Calliope walked inside the bar, giving each other's hands a squeeze before breaking apart. Calliope sat down at the bar next to Amarok, who immediately wrapped her in his giant embrace, squeezing her tightly.

"I missed you," Amarok whispered in Calliope's ear as he hugged her.

"I missed you, too," Calliope whispered in response. "It's been crazy since the first day I got to

---

[40] "Let's go,"

this city, but I'm so glad to be back here with all of my friends." She looked around at the entire group then, and asked them all, "So, does anyone know what the plan is?"

"Well," Xena began as Zephyr slid a drink—the Siren's Lament—to Calliope. "Salem say ya brother don't take da book everywhere wit him. She put a trackin' spell on it, too. Jus' to know for sure."

"Yeah, so, she's supposed to text me the next time he goes somewhere without it," Nagaveni added.

"Salem also mentioned that he rented a house around here rather than getting a hotel," Dysnomi added. "So, it really shouldn't be too hard to break in undetected once he's gone."

"Or..." a voice said. The voice was coming from the door of the bar, which had just opened. Everyone quickly turned their heads toward the voice, where they were greeted with the sight of Zorya standing in the doorway. Baron Samedi was standing behind her and smirking. "Ya could lemme do my ting with da shadows," she said. "Ya don't have to break in at all if I just use da shadows to unlock da front door."

Calliope noticed that Zorya still had a few shadows emanating from her body. The young woman no longer looked consumed by shadows, however, and the few that remained no longer seemed to whisper to her.

"Zorya?" Xena yelled, jumping up and hugging Zorya fiercely. "What're ya doin' here so soon?"

"Well, I got better, so he brought me back," Zorya responded, nodding her head toward Baron Samedi, who was still standing behind her.

"I just came to make sure she made it here," Baron Samedi said. "And... To check on how you're doing, gorgeous," he added, looking Calliope up and down slowly. His gaze sent a shiver down her spine and caused her to blush slightly.

"I'm doing amazing... Thanks to you, of course," Calliope replied, smiling. "I definitely could've used a warning about how I was gonna wake up in a coffin, though. I broke my hand punching my way out of it." She laughed then as she shook her hand, which had healed completely overnight.

"Ah, shit," Baron Samedi said, throwing his hands up in frustration. "I knew I was forgettin' to tell you somethin'. I'm sorry, doll. I do hope you can forgive me." He gave Calliope a feigned sad face, causing her to giggle.

"Of course I forgive you, silly," Calliope said to the Baron. "You fucking resurrected me!"

"Well, I am the Loa of fucking resurrection," Baron Samedi replied teasingly, flashing Calliope a smirk. "But, I better get my ass back to the crossroads. You know there's always more work to be done. I do hope I get to see you soon, though, beautiful." He turned and began to walk away. Then, he stopped and turned to look at her once more, saying, "But, uh... Not too soon, alright? And... Preferably not in my domain next time." He then winked at her before he disappeared.

Zorya stepped fully into the bar then, closing the front door behind her. "So, ya tryin'a get an important book back from ya brother, right?" she asked Calliope.

"Yeah, the Compendium of Supernatural Powers," Calliope answered. "Do you really think your shadows will still be able to unlock the door?"

"I believe so, yeah," Zorya responded. "My natural powers may not be nearly as strong as da powers da Shadow Realm gave me, but I should still be able to pull off sometin' like dat. It's actually a pretty simple process."

"Then, that sounds fine to me," Calliope said, shrugging. "So, who's gonna come inside with me and who's gonna stay outside to keep an eye out in case Raiden comes back while we're in there?"

"I'll go inside to help you look," Nagaveni offered, raising her hand.

The movement reminded Calliope of the way that Nagaveni had done it when she had been asking Wrath a question on the opening night of Tartarus. She felt a sudden pang of sadness then, realizing that she hadn't heard either Ember or Lyn in her mind since before she was resurrected. Their presence could no longer be felt within her mind, either. It was just... Empty.

"After I unlock da door for ya, I should prolly stay outside in da shadows," Zorya said. "Da Baron told me I prolly need a few days to rest before I'll feel like I'm at full strength again."

"That's fine," Calliope said, shrugging.

"We should probably keep the group inside the house to a minimum," Asmodeus suggested. "That way, if anything goes wrong, it'll be easier for you to get out of the house without being detected."

"Yeah, and honestly—I think Nini and I should be able to handle it just fine," Calliope said in agreement with Asmodeus.

"Now that we have the plan figured out," Dysnomi started. "I suggest we drink... You know, to calm our nerves."

Calliope laughed then, noticing that Dysnomi had already begun drinking. She took her seat at the bar, taking a huge drink from her glass, which was filled with the drink that had been named after her—the Siren's Lament. Then, she leaned her head against Amarok's shoulder after he sat down next to her.

Amarok kissed the top of Calliope's head and whispered to her, "You know I won't let anything bad happen to you if I can help it... Right, Calli?"

"I know you won't, Amarok," Calliope replied, sighing contentedly. "You're amazing, you know that?"

"Nah, I think you must be confusing me with yourself," Amarok replied to Calliope jokingly as she took another drink. "So, you down for another drinking game with me?"

"Always," Calliope answered, laughing as Zephyr poured a long row of rainbow shots in front of her and Amarok.

"These are my favorite shots to make," Zephyr said with a slight laugh. "It is officially pride month, after all. What better time to make rainbow shots?"

"Oh, shit, I totally forgot!" Calliope exclaimed, her face lighting up with joy. "Everyone! Come do a round of shots for pride month!"

"Hell yeah!" Asmodeus yelled as he, Dysnomi, Nagaveni, Xena, and Zorya all gathered around where Calliope and Amarok were sitting. They each grabbed a shot—including Zephyr—and waited for Calliope to make a toast.

"Here's to taking the Compendium of Supernatural Powers so that Raiden can't use it against our father," Calliope began. "And, of course... Here's to spending pride month in New Orleans!"

Calliope held her violet shot in the middle, and the rest of the group cheered and laughed as they crammed together to tap their shot glasses against hers. Then, they all put their rainbow shots against their lips, throwing their heads back and drinking quickly.

"You know," Calliope began to say as the group dispersed. "I'm gonna be highly disappointed if I don't get to see the biggest, gayest parade for pride month while I'm here."

"Oh, you just stick around and see for yourself, cher," Zephyr responded, laughing.

"Yeah, NOLA parades are always the best, Calli," Amarok told her. "I'm pretty sure our pride parade will blow you away."

"Gods, I hope so," Calliope said. "If I'm not gonna be here for Mardi Gras, I'd say pride month would definitely be the next on my list. I mean... Speaking as a bisexual female." She gestured to herself then, shaking her head as she laughed.

"And as a pansexual male," Asmodeus said, walking up to Calliope and throwing an arm around her shoulders. "I'd definitely have to agree with you on that one."

Calliope laughed, and telepathically said to Asmodeus, *I really hope we get to enjoy the parade together.*

Me too, Calli, Asmodeus telepathically sent to Calliope in response.

Calliope opened her mouth to speak again, but before she could, Nagaveni exclaimed, "Oh!" Asmodeus pulled his arm off of Calliope and turned to look at Nagaveni, along with everyone else. "Salem just texted me," she said. "It looks like your brother just left the book at his rental house while he went out."

"I guess that means it's go-time," Calliope said as she stood. "So, who has the address of this rental house?"

"I do," Nagaveni answered, raising her hand again. She showed Calliope the address then.

"Oh, I know where that's at," Amarok announced when he saw the address on her phone screen from where he was sitting. "It's a cabin at the edge of the city. It's kinda secluded, but it's actually not too far from where I live."

"Alright," Calliope started, thinking. "Could you show us the fastest way to get to it?"

"Yeah, I can do that," Amarok replied to Calliope. "But, we don't know where exactly your brother's going, so if we're gonna do this, we better go now and be quick about it."

"I guess we better go, den," Zorya said, making her way toward the door.

Everyone followed behind Zorya except Zephyr—he was keeping the bar open as the group's meeting spot—and Xena, who had been told to stay behind in case things started going wrong. No one wanted her to get hurt again. It did upset her a little, at first, but she realized that she was way out of her league when it came to dealing with a literal demon and a deity's son.

27. BLOODLINES

(THE MAN WHO KNEW TOO MUCH)

The group found their way to the cabin that Raiden had been staying in right as the sun went down. Amarok had been correct—the cabin was secluded. It might have been perfect for Raiden to hide out in, but it was also perfect for Calliope and Nagaveni to sneak into.

Asmodeus, Dysnomi, and Amarok posted up around different areas outside of the cabin, while Zorya walked right up to the front door. She seemed nervous as she stepped forward, holding her hands out in front of her with her palms facing forward. The shadows shot out from her palms and made their way into the lock, working it until there was the unmistakable click of the door unlocking.

Then, Zorya stepped back and smiled, giving Calliope and Nagaveni a theatrical bow. "An' dat's how it's done," she said.

"Good work, Z," Nagaveni said to Zorya.

"Yeah, seriously," Calliope agreed. "That was awesome." She stepped up toward the door as Zorya stepped down and slipped into the shadows.

"I guess it's time," she said as she slowly opened the door.

Calliope stepped inside of the house cautiously, and Nagaveni stepped inside moments after her. "I'll take this side of the house," Nagaveni said, nodding toward the right side.

"Sounds good," Calliope replied, nodding before walking off toward the left side of the house.

Calliope walked into the first room that she saw, which seemed to be used as a study or an office. She checked the desk on the far side of the small room, opening all of its drawers and rifling through them. When she found nothing inside, she whispered, "Fuck," before moving on to the next room.

Calliope opened the door to the second room, which she quickly realized was a bedroom. However, she couldn't tell whether it was her brother's bedroom or Menoetius'. She looked through the closet first, searching every space that she could. After not finding anything inside of the closet, she released a frustrated sigh, then began to search underneath the bed. She pulled out a few boxes, which were all filled with what appeared to be a few sentimental items.

After searching through the last box, Calliope pushed all of the boxes back under the bed. She was becoming more and more frustrated when she suddenly had the idea to check between the mattress and the box springs of the bed. *If I had to hide something so no one would find it while I was gone,* she thought. *I'd definitely hide it in the mattress, or somewhere similar.*

Calliope lifted the unwieldy mattress as much as she could, reaching an arm under it. Her hand grazed something hard and she grabbed the item, pulling it out. "Yes!" she whispered when she was able to see that it was exactly what she had come there looking for.

"Hello... What do we have here?" a man's sinister voice asked, scaring Calliope. The voice came from directly behind her, causing her to jump and turn around to face whoever the voice belonged to.

"Menoetius," Calliope said, breathing heavily from her fear.

"How the hell are you even alive?" Menoetius asked Calliope. Then, he shook his head and said, "Nevermind. I'm not even going to ask. After all, this is my lucky day. I was just sitting there in my room when I suddenly heard a noise. I came here to check it out... Only to find you—alive and well—trying to take something that doesn't belong to you."

"Shut the fuck up," Calliope said, her voice laced with venom. "It doesn't belong to Raiden, either. It was stolen from Vlad, and I intend on giving it back to him."

Before Calliope could say anything else, Menoetius disappeared. He reappeared inches away from her face, grabbing her throat tightly. He pinned her against the bedroom wall, causing her to drop the Compendium. Then, he leaned forward. With his face in the crook of her neck, he inhaled the scent of her shampoo deeply as he asked, "Vlad? You mean the vampire? *Dracula?* He never would've noticed it was even missing if it weren't for you... Now... What in the world am I going to do with you while I have you pinned like this?"

"You could always try keeping your disgusting fucking hands off of me," Calliope replied, lifting a hand and hitting Menoetius in the face.

Menoetius growled and said, "Don't even fucking think about hitting me again, you little slut." His grip on Calliope's throat tightened. He brought his other hand up to grab her hip, squeezing it tightly with his demonic strength and bruising it as he pulled her a few inches away from the wall only to slam her against it again.

"Don't fucking touch me," Calliope choked out.

Menoetius laughed as he slid his hand upward from Calliope's hip. He began playing with the bottom of her crop top as he asked her, "And what exactly are you going to do about it without all your big, bad powers?" She reached up and hit him again as hard as she could. However, that only made him angry, causing him to slam her head into the wall using the hand that was still gripping her throat. His other hand slipped underneath her shirt, then underneath her bra, grabbing one of her breasts painfully as he growled, "Keep fighting me, bitch. I like it even more when you fight it. I'm gonna take my time and enjoy finally getting to do everything I've always wanted to do to you. Then, I'll get to have the absolute pleasure of making sure you fucking die this time."

"I said... Get the fuck off of me," Calliope choked out. She noticed a picture hanging on the wall beside her then, and she reached up to grab it. When the picture was securely in her grasp, she pulled it off of the wall, slamming it down on top of Menoetius' head.

"You fucking bitch!" Menoetius yelled. The force of the picture slamming into him caused him to release Calliope as he stumbled backward.

"See, that's your problem, Menoetius," Calliope commented, picking up the Compendium of Supernatural Powers for the second time. "You get so caught up in the things you want to do to me that you fail to keep me restrained. Every. Time. It really is a shame that you're such a disgusting asshole, though, because you're honestly pretty cute. I'm sure you wouldn't have these female problems if you were a little nicer." Menoetius stepped forward, his eyes ink-black. His midnight-black horns were growing and curving toward the back of his head. Before he could speak, she punched him in the nose, then pulled out the Hell's Scream dagger, which had been strapped to one of her thighs. "See this?" she asked. "It was forged in the deepest pits of the Demon Realm. It's specifically designed not only to kill beings made of pure light such as angels or seraphim, but also beings made from pure evil such as nephilim and... Well... Demons like you." She smiled sweetly at him then.

"You little bitch," Menoetius growled. He pulled out his own weapon then, and Calliope recognized it immediately. She tried not to have a panic attack as he told her, "Well, I'm sure you remember my little friend here. The Siren's Suffering is finally about to live up to its name. I'm going to kill you slowly. I want to watch as you feel every bit of pain this will give you."

The two Supernaturals began to circle each other slowly. Calliope watched Menoetius' every move intently, trying to decipher when he was going to strike. Finally, he made his move, stabbing the knife toward her shoulder. She was ready for it, however, which allowed her to dodge his attack before making her own move. After dodging the blade, she stabbed her dagger in his direction, catching him in his arm. He cursed and grabbed his sizzling wound after she pulled the dagger out of him.

Calliope attempted to attack Menoetius again, but he disappeared. He teleported behind her, stabbing his knife deeply into her shoulder blade. As the pain shot through her, she yelled, "Fuck!" She spun around, knocking his hand to the side and slicing him across his bare chest. She watched as his skin seemed to boil and sizzle around the wound. *So, that's what the Hell's Scream does,* she thought. *Gods, I love Salem.*

Menoetius growled at Calliope again and stepped forward menacingly. "I can't wait to fucking kill you," he said.

"Yeah? Well, you're gonna have to try a lot harder than this if you wanna kill me again," Calliope said, gritting her teeth against the pain that she felt in her shoulder.

"Oh, don't worry. I intend on making sure you're dead for good this time," Menoetius replied, lunging at Calliope. She jumped out of his way, narrowly avoiding his knife.

Frustrated, Menoetius began teleporting rapidly, leaving Calliope scrambling to avoid his attacks. He sliced her already-wounded shoulder, causing her to cry out in pain. A voice from the doorway screamed at him then.

"Hey!" Nagaveni yelled. Calliope noticed the anger in her eyes, which Calliope had never seen before. Calliope turned away from her eyes, while Menoetius made the mistake of turning to look directly at her. "Leave my friend alone," she said, using her best attempt at a menacing voice.

"Or what?" Menoetius asked, laughing. Calliope tried not to laugh at his mistake then. He severely underestimated Nagaveni at that moment, obviously not knowing what kind of Supernatural she was.

Nagaveni looked at Menoetius angrily, then pulled off her Serpent Tamer necklace. Menoetius' eyes widened with fear as he finally realized what type of Supernatural she was. Her snakes were waking up, immediately hissing at him as they did. "I tried to warn you," she said, shrugging and moving her eyes up to stare directly into his.

Menoetius released a terrible demonic scream as his entire body began turning into stone. It started at his fingertips, continuing to spread until he was nothing more than a stone statue.

The men from the group that had been outside ran inside of the house when they heard the scream. Dysnomi was the first to reach Nagaveni, asking, "What the fuck happened?" as she placed the Serpent Tamer around her neck again.

"Is... Is that statue my brother?" Asmodeus asked then. His electric-blue eyes were wide with shock, flickering to their ink-black color occasionally as he tried to make sense of the situation.

"That... WAS your brother," Nagaveni replied, biting her lip. "Now, it's just a statue." She felt guilty, but she knew that she had no choice.

Amarok ran over to Calliope, helping her stand on her feet as she grabbed the Compendium of Supernatural Powers again. She attempted to ignore the pain that was shooting through her shoulder, even though it was horrible. "We need to get out of here, now," he said to her.

"Agreed," Calliope replied through her labored breaths. She grabbed the Siren's Suffering dagger off of the floor where Menoetius had dropped it, ignoring the way that it hurt her to hold it—the burning sensation that she felt. She said, "The Siren's Suffering is coming with me. I don't want this gods-forsaken thing ever being used against me again."

28. BEFORE THE STORM

(UNFINISHED BUSINESS)

The entire group ended up running as fast as they possibly could away from the secluded cabin. Looking back, Dysnomi yelled, "What the fuck just happened?"

Calliope could feel fear and anger all at the same time. Menoetius had scared her since the first time that he had tried to force himself on her three years earlier, and their most recent interaction had left her shaking.

Asmodeus could feel Calliope's emotions mixing within her and he wished that he could hold her, or at least tell her that everything was going to be okay. His demon half, on the other hand, was only feeling pissed that Calliope and Nagaveni had gotten Menoetius killed. *Well, maybe he's not dead,* Asmodeus thought to his demon. *I don't exactly know how Nini's whole 'turning people to stone' powers actually work.*

'It doesn't matter!' Asmodeus' demon half yelled to him in response. *'That was your brother! She had no right to do that to him!'*

Better for Nini to do that to him than for me to have been forced to kill Menoetius, Asmodeus argued. *It would've been really hard for me to kill my own brother, no matter how awful he was. I was going to though, because of what he did to Calliope. He killed her! He deserved to die.*

"We did tell Salem!" Nagaveni yelled in response to Calliope as they all continued to run. "Menoetius shouldn't have been there!"

"My brother could teleport just like me!" Asmodeus yelled. "He must have gotten bored of whatever the fuck Raiden's doing and teleported back to the house."

"This is just fucking great! My brother's gonna know we were there a lot sooner than we anticipated now," Calliope yelled.

The group continued to run until they made it to the middle of the city. They then slowed to a walking pace so they wouldn't look suspicious to anyone around them. They continued making their way back to The Tipsy Piano, trying to act normal.

When they were all safely inside the bar, Calliope hurriedly closed and locked the door. She ignored the questioning looks that she and the others were getting from both Xena and Zephyr.

"What da hell happen to y'all?" Xena asked when Calliope finally looked at her.

"Apparently, Menoetius teleported back to the house while we were still in it," Calliope said breathlessly.

"And... He attacked Calliope," Nagaveni explained. She sounded nervous and guilty.

"He was trying to assault me... Again," Calliope added, sounding annoyed and scared. She looked at Asmodeus, shaking with fear. He looked back at her with a mix of anger toward his brother and fear for Calliope's life. She could feel those emotions, along with how much he loved her and how thankful he was that she made it out mostly unharmed.

"So, I had to turn him to stone," Nagaveni finished. "I didn't really have much of a choice."

"And now," Asmodeus said, sighing and rubbing his temples. "Raiden's gonna know we were there... A hell of a lot sooner than we anticipated."

"Will we even be ready in time?" Amarok asked, looking at Calliope with worry written across his face.

"We're gonna have to be," Calliope told Amarok as calmly as she could manage. "We don't really have any other option now."

Calliope then sighed, laying the Compendium of Supernatural Powers on top of the bar. She climbed onto a barstool and laid her head down on top of the large book. She felt a reassuring hand gently squeeze her knee as someone sat down next to her, and she glanced up to see Amarok looking down at her. His face clearly showed his concern for her safety.

"Are you okay?" Amarok asked Calliope. "I know that had to have been a lot for you to go through tonight... Dealing with Menoetius trying to..." He trailed off, too disgusted by the thought of what Menoetius was going to do to even say it.

"It was a lot," Calliope replied, her voice wavering. "And... I thought he was gonna kill me again." Tears began to fall out of her iris-purple eyes and her lips began to quiver.

"Oh, Calli... It's okay now," Amarok said softly. He pulled Calliope into him, hugging her tightly against his chest. "Come here. It's alright. I've got you," he whispered soothingly in her ear.

"I don't know if I'm gonna be ready," Calliope admitted to Amarok in a whisper. "I don't even have a plan anymore."

"It's okay, Calli," Nagaveni said as she walked up behind Calliope, resting a hand on Calliope's shoulder.

"Mais, we'll come up wit sometin' together," Xena said.

"I mean, you saved my life... You know I'm gonna help you," Zorya added, shrugging nonchalantly.

"Whatever we plan," Calliope began to say, looking between the shadow woman and the hunter. "You two can't be there when everything goes down."

"Like hell we can't!" Xena yelled, looking at the rest of the group for support. The group of Supernaturals all just sadly shook their heads at her.

"Look, I appreciate everything you've done for me, Xena, but you're HUMAN," Calliope explained. "You BOTH are. I can't have you two dying because of me."

"I might be human, but I have powers," Zorya pointed out defensively. She was determined to be stubborn about it.

"None of which include rapid healing," Calliope countered, giving Zorya a pointed look with a raised eyebrow.

Zorya nodded, realizing that there was no sense in arguing. Calliope was not going to change her mind. Not about that, at least.

"So..." Dysnomi started to say. "Does anyone have any bright ideas about what we're gonna do?"

"Maybe..." Asmodeus said, thinking. "We could hide Calli? Then, when Raiden shows up, we'd just have to distract him long enough for her to sneak up behind him and kill him."

"Could we even distract him long enough?" Nagaveni asked. "I mean, all it took last time was one hit from his lightning powers to make all of us pass out... And he's even stronger than that now."

"I mean, I've always got a few *'tricks'* up my sleeve," Dysnomi replied, pulling Nagaveni close to him and smirking at her as she groaned from his awful joke.

"That... Actually could work," Calliope commented, holding one finger up toward Dysnomi. Her mind suddenly felt like it was running a mile a minute as she began to think of a plan. "You could create some projections to distract him or confuse him. I don't think he's ever seen anything even remotely close to your magic before. At the very least, I bet it would throw him off."

"That's good enough for me," Dysnomi replied, shrugging.

"Well, it's not exactly the best plan ever," Asmodeus said reluctantly. "But, it is... A... Plan...

Which, I suppose, is better than not having one at all."

"Yeah..." Zephyr said. "On that note, I'm gonna suggest some strong alcoholic drinks." He poured a line of rainbow shots then, like he had before they left. Everyone gathered around the bar and drank their shots quickly.

After three rounds of shots, Amarok made his way up to the raised stage, where he sat at the piano. Calliope walked over and sat down next to him, softly singing along to the song that he was playing as his fingers pressed each key expertly. The two Supernaturals shared a few longing glances at each other as the song continued. When it ended—*Too soon,* Calliope whined to herself—she laid her head on his shoulder. He kissed the top of her head gently, breathing in her scent.

She smells just like the ocean, Amarok thought. Calliope's scent reminded him of the vacations that he used to go on with his family when he was a young child. He longed for simple pleasures in life again... Such as playing in the ocean waves the way that he did when he was younger. *Even if she doesn't want me romantically,* he thought. *Even if she doesn't want to be with me... I swear, I would do anything for this woman. I would die to protect her.*

'Fight for her!' Amarok's wolf yelled at him, which he thought was extremely odd. His wolf was usually quiet and reserved, even avoiding conversations with him most of the time.

I'm not gonna fight Deus for Calli's affection, Amarok thought to his wolf. *If Calli wants to be with him, that's her choice. And it's fine with me... As long as he treats her well.*

Calliope leaned into Amarok, pulling him out of his thoughts. She felt safe every time that he wrapped his arms around her. "Thank you," she whispered, looking up at him.

"For what?" Amarok asked, looking down at Calliope with confusion on his face, furrowing his eyebrows and pursing his lips.

"For always making me feel safe," Calliope replied. She leaned up and kissed Amarok on the cheek, brushing her lips over his skin lightly. "I don't know what it is about you," she said, shaking her head. "But, when you hold me... I feel like no one could ever hurt me."

Amarok smiled down at Calliope and held her for a while longer. It was beginning to get late and he knew the moment that she looked up and signaled Asmodeus to wait for her that she would soon be leaving. He looked back down at her in time to see her open her mouth like she was going to ask him a question. However, she quickly closed her mouth again, appearing conflicted.

"Would you like to dance with me one more time before things get really crazy around here?" Amarok asked Calliope. His boldness at that moment shocked him. He normally would have simply watched her leave with Asmodeus, not daring to ask and keep her from leaving if she wanted to.

Calliope nodded at Amarok and he noticed that her mesmerizing iris-purple eyes seemed to glow as she became excited. He stood and held his hand out to her, bowing deeply.

Calliope giggled as she took Amarok's hand. She loved dancing with him. *It always makes me forget about all my worries for a while,* she thought.

Amarok pulled Calliope to the side of the stage, and as he did, Dysnomi smirked at Nagaveni.

Then, Dysnomi asked Nagaveni, "Would you like to dance, too?"

Nagaveni nodded as Xena walked up to Zorya, who had been standing next to Dysnomi and Nagaveni. Xena tucked a strand of hair behind her ear and asked, "What 'bout you?"

"What do ya mean?" Zorya asked, furrowing her eyebrows in confusion.

"Um... D'you wanna dance?" Xena asked, feeling more nervous as she stood there longer. "Wit me?"

"Mais!" Zorya exclaimed. "Y-yeah." She took Xena's hand and Xena led her onto the floor.

"I guess that leaves me and you," Zephyr said to Asmodeus. He laughed and slid a shot toward Asmodeus, who drank it quickly. "You wanna dance, too, brah? I don't know about you, but I don't really wanna be left out."

Asmodeus glared at Zephyr, his eyes turning ink-black for a fraction of a second. He quickly calmed his demon half and the electric-blue returned to his eyes. Then, he curtly nodded, his expression unreadable.

When everyone was on the floor—other than Amarok and Calliope, who were on the stage—Dysnomi smirked again. He snapped his fingers and the entire group became clothed with ballroom attire. They all looked down at their new outfits with expressions of excitement and wonder.

Calliope and Nagaveni were both wearing princess-style ballroom gowns. The main difference in their dresses was that Calliope's dress was lavender, while Nagaveni's dress was emerald-green. Xena and Zorya were not wearing gowns, which surprised no one. They were instead wearing flowing black jumpers that could almost pass as dresses, with flowing black capes on their backs.

The men in the room were all wearing expensive-looking black suits. Under their suit jackets, however, they each had on different colored button-up shirts. Asmodeus was wearing crimson-red, Zephyr wore royal-blue, Dysnomi had on emerald-green, and Amarok was wearing gold—much like the shirt that he usually wore. However, Amarok's golden shirt at that moment seemed even fancier than his normal one.

Calliope gasped when she reached out to touch him. The contact made her realize that his shirt was a fine silk. In fact, as she looked around, she realized that all of the men were wearing fine silk shirts.

"Dys," Nagaveni whispered, in awe of him and his magic.

"What?" Dysnomi asked. "If we're all gonna do this, we should do it the right way." He snapped his fingers a second time. The lights in the bar dimmed and a spotlight appeared, shining down on Amarok and Calliope.

"Oh!" Calliope exclaimed, surprised by the sudden flood of light that was bearing down on her.

Dysnomi snapped his fingers one last time, enchanting the piano to play a romantic melody by itself. That was their cue to begin dancing.

Amarok first led Calliope gracefully into a box step, gliding around the stage with her. He carefully avoided the piano, which was sitting in the middle of the stage. The other pairs copied their movements, though not everyone could be as graceful as Amarok was.

Amarok led Calliope into an elegant spin away from him, then spun her back toward him. She landed forcefully into his chest, gasping from the contact. He looked down at her and his golden-yellow wolf eyes filled with hunger, causing her to whimper softly.

"You're beautiful," Amarok whispered to her. A low growl escaped his throat as his wolf fought him for control.

"Thank you, handsome," Calliope said, blushing from Amarok's compliment.

As the song that the enchanted piano had been playing ended, Amarok picked Calliope up, spinning her in his arms. He then put her down, dipping her low the moment that her heels touched the stage floor. She hadn't noticed that Dysnomi had changed her hairstyle for the dance until her turquoise locks brushed against the stage floor behind her.

Amarok leaned down close to Calliope. He could hear—then, he could feel—her heart beating rapidly beneath him as he pressed his chest against hers. A strand of his shaggy dark copper-brown hair once again fell against her cheek, and he whispered in her ear, "Thank you for dancing with me, darling. It was almost as lovely as you are."

"You're very welcome," Calliope breathed. She shivered when Amarok's lips touched her cheek as he gave her a quick, sweet kiss.

The lights brightened in the room then. Everyone's hair and clothes reverted to their original form, like *Cinderella* when the clock struck midnight. Before Amarok could pull Calliope up, they both heard cheering and whistling from their friends below them.

Blushing furiously, Amarok pulled Calliope to her feet, then stepped away from her. He sheepishly rubbed the back of his neck. Calliope, who was unfazed by the teasing, stood on the tips of her toes to give him a gentle kiss on his cheek. "Thank you," she whispered before climbing off of the stage to take Asmodeus' outstretched hand.

Calliope noticed, as they began walking to the hotel, that Nagaveni had slipped her hand into Dysnomi's. Their fingers were intertwined, and Nagaveni was leaning her head against Dysnomi's arm gently.

Calliope nudged Asmodeus. When he looked at her quizzically, she nodded toward the couple walking in front of them and smiled at him. It took him a moment to understand what she was nodding at, but once he did, he looked down at her and returned her smile. Telepathically, he said, *Well, ¿no se ven acogedores?*[41]

Calliope smiled back at Asmodeus as they walked in the hotel door and replied, *Very cozy.* She lifted her eyebrow at him and giggled quietly before telepathically saying, *They actually look pretty cute, though.*

Yeah, they do, Asmodeus agreed.

---

[41] "don't they look cozy?"

29. LIVING THROUGH IT WAS JUST A LUXURY

(THE LAST FIGHT)

"Okay, so... Does everyone know what you're gonna be doing when the time actually comes?" Dysnomi asked the next day.

Calliope looked around at the group of people who were surrounding her, taking in their serious faces as they nodded to show that they understood. *Gods, I love these people,* she thought as she tried her best not to cry.

"Are you okay, Calli?" Asmodeus asked, laying a comforting hand against Calliope's lower back.

Calliope nodded, then gratefully accepted a drink from Zephyr—the Siren's Lament. He had noticed how nervous she looked, and made her a drink in an attempt to help her calm her nerves.

"Hey..." Zephyr said softly. "It's gonna be alright, cher."

Calliope nodded again before picking up her drink and pressing it against her lips. She drank deeply and desperately. Her hand shook as it held the glass and she finished the entire drink quickly. She felt like it was the only thing that was keeping her from going insane. She breathed in a long, shaky breath as she placed the glass on top of the bar once again. "Dys?" she asked then, looking down the bar toward Dysnomi.

"Yeah, Calli?" Dysnomi asked, leaning forward so he could see Calliope from the other end of the bar.

"So, whenever Raiden shows up... No matter how off-guard he catches us... We'll be okay... Right?" Calliope questioned nervously, her voice wavering.

"Yeah, of course we will be, Calli," Dysnomi responded. "Don't worry. The moment your brother appears, I'll use my magic to hide you—along with Xena and Zorya, if necessary—before I conjure a realistic projection of you. That should buy you enough time to sneak around and do what you need to do."

"You really think it's gonna work?" Nagaveni whispered to Dysnomi from her seat next to him. Calliope noticed that she sounded as nervous as Calliope felt.

Come on, Asmodeus whispered inside Calliope's mind as he looked at her intently. *Let's go get some air? It might help you calm your nerves.*

Are you sure that's such a good idea, Deus? Calliope responded using her telepathy. *What if Raiden finds us? We'd be by ourselves, with no contingency plan.*

Calli... Asmodeus responded sadly. *You know I wouldn't let anyone hurt you, right? I'd do everything—and I do mean everything—within my power to keep Raiden away from you... Para mantenerte a salvo.*[42]

Calliope nodded. *I know, Deus,* she thought. She meant it; she did know that Asmodeus would do everything in his power to keep her safe... She just worried that it wouldn't be enough.

Asmodeus held his hand out to Calliope as he whispered, "Do you trust me?" She nodded. "Come on, then," he said, giving her a small smile.

Calliope took Asmodeus' hand and allowed him to lead her through the front door of The Tipsy Piano and into the streets of New Orleans. The once-overwhelming sights, smells, and sounds of the city actually comforted her then. It all comforted her so much, in fact, that she soon found herself beginning to relax despite everything that was happening in her life. "Thank you for this," she said. "I didn't even realize how badly I needed this."

---

[42] "To keep you safe."

"That's what I'm here for, mi amor," Asmodeus responded. "I'd do anything for you, Calli."

Calliope held Asmodeus' hand tightly as they walked the streets with no specific destination in mind. At least, no specific destination that she knew of.

Asmodeus, however, had other plans. "Let's go in here," he said, pointing to a tiny shop that was advertising voodoo.

"What? Why?" Calliope asked, laughing nervously.

"It'll be fun," Asmodeus said with a shrug, but Calliope could tell that there was more to his decision than that. "Come on... Trust me?"

"Okay..." Calliope replied slowly, giving in to Asmodeus.

Asmodeus smiled as he pulled Calliope into the small shop. A bell rang loudly when he opened the door. "Good afternoon, ma'am," he said to an older woman inside of the store, who was standing behind the cash register.

"Oh, hey dere. Welcome," the woman said. "I'm da owner here, so if y'all need anytin', you jus' lemme know. Name's Ziana. Most people call me Miz Ziana... Now, what exactly... Are... You...?" she asked curiously, squinting her eyes as if doing so would help her see what Asmodeus really was.

"I'm sorry, ma'am," Calliope said, confused. "But, don't you mean to ask, 'Who are you?' You asked him 'what' he is."

"I know what I asked him, child," the older woman, Ziana, replied. She laughed before saying to Asmodeus, "Ya seem like a sweet kid, but... Dere's sometin' dark in you... Is dat why you're here?"

"No, ma'am," Asmodeus answered, attempting to suppress a chuckle. "Unfortunately, I can't exactly get rid of my demon half that easily... See, I'm a cambion. I had a human mother, but my father's an incubus. Anyway, I'm actually here on her behalf," he said, pointing toward Calliope.

"Me?!" Calliope exclaimed. She was bewildered not only by Asmodeus saying that he was there for her, but also because he openly told the woman what kind of Supernatural he was. He just laughed softly and turned back to the woman who owned the shop.

"So, you're half-incubus?" Ziana asked Asmodeus. He nodded. "Hmmm..." she hummed, thinking to herself. She slowly walked around the counter to stand in front of Calliope, gently taking Calliope's hands. "Dere's sometin' real bad comin' for ya, darlin'," she said, closing her eyes. "Sometin' angry and dark... Like a thunderstorm ana wildfire rolled into one."

"Yeah, that sounds about right," Calliope said, sighing. "That would be my brother. He's gonna bring a literal storm down on me, and there's nothing I can really do about it."

"I wouldn't be so sure 'bout dat," Ziana replied. She shook her head, appearing confused for a moment. "I'm sensin' dat you're far more powerful den ya give yourself credit for. I tink you could win against dis brother o' yours... But, I'm not quite sure if you can win on your own... Or if you're gone need help."

"Thankfully, I'll have plenty of help," Calliope said. "I was lucky enough to meet a handful of amazing people, and even luckier to be able to call them all my friends."

Ziana shook her head then, like she was clearing her thoughts. "You're... Well, ya gotta be sometin' unique," she said, furrowing her eyebrows.

"What do you mean?" Calliope asked, giving the older woman a questioning look.

"I'm sensin'... Dis energy in ya... It's da same energy dat comes from lightnin' or fire... At least, it's da same energy as dat kinda lightnin' and fire dat Shango gifts us with... And I can sense dere's parta you missin' now... Is dat what killed you?" Ziana asked.

"How did you—?" Calliope began to ask, but the woman raised a hand, stopping her.

"It's jus' a feelin' I get," Ziana said. "Ya must be highly favored by Baron Samedi if he resurrected you, though."

Calliope smiled awkwardly and pulled one of her hands away from the older woman. She reached into the back pocket of her ripped skinny jeans, pulling out the *'death'* tarot card, which the Baron had given to her the night that she first met him. She had kept it somewhere on her body ever since that day. "Yeah... I think Baron Samedi might favor me a bit, Miss Ziana," she said politely.

"Mais..." Ziana replied. "Now I know you gotta be sometin' special."

Calliope gave Ziana another awkward smile, and Asmodeus sighed. "She's nervous," he said. "But, Calliope is the daughter of Shango."

"And... La Siréne," Calliope added meekly.

"The daughter... Of La Siréne and Shango?" Ziana asked, shocked. Calliope nodded.

"Yes, ma'am, she is," Asmodeus answered. "But... Her brother stole her powers... And we think he's coming back for her now that he knows she's alive."

"You poor ting," Ziana said sympathetically, patting the back of Calliope's hand. "I tink I might jus' have da perfect ting for ya." She began frantically searching behind the counter, mumbling to herself the entire time. Calliope and Asmodeus shared a quizzical look, but neither said anything. "Ah-ha!" she exclaimed after a few minutes of searching, holding a tiny mermaid trinket in the air.

"What is that?" Calliope asked curiously.

"Dis lil ting?" Ziana questioned. "By itself, it's notin'. But... If you crush a single scale from a siren, open da top, pour in da dust, den sing a short tune into it and close it... Well... Den, it can provide you with a decent amount of protection. You'll still have to be careful, o'course, but it's betta den nothin'. It might even help heal dose cuts on your shoulder," she said, pointing at the painful wounds that Calliope had due to Menoetius slicing her.

"Oh, thank you, but these were cut into me using a special dagger... It was enchanted for me, specifically... Enchanted so any wounds I received from it would never heal, and would always hurt. I guess that doesn't count if I die and come back though," Calliope said, laughing. "It's what killed me, but when I was resurrected, my original wounds from it were nothing but scars."

"Well, you can neva go wrong wit extra protection, anyway. Take it," Ziana said, holding the trinket out toward Calliope.

"Oh, thank you," Calliope said.

"How much?" Asmodeus asked.

"Ah!" Ziana exclaimed, waving Asmodeus off. "Jus' put in a good word for me wit da Loas... And da Loa o' da Dead... Before I die," she said, laughing.

"I can definitely do that," Calliope replied with a smile. "Thank you, Miss Ziana."

"Oh, no needa tank me," Ziana replied. "Now, you two have a good night. I'm gone close up here." She waved Calliope and Asmodeus forward, effectively waving them out of the door the way that most people 'shoo' away cats.

Outside, Calliope placed the trinket into the front pocket of her jeans, then held Asmodeus' hand tightly in hers. They walked hand-in-hand all the way back to The Tipsy Piano. Although they didn't talk much, they were both enjoying each other's company more than anything.

Almost the exact moment that Calliope and Asmodeus walked inside the bar, Nagaveni jumped up and began ushering Xena and Zorya out of the side door. Before she followed them in case they needed protection, she announced, "Salem just texted me and said Raiden's on his way here... And he's moving fast." She managed to get the human women out through the side door while Calliope pulled out her Blade of Light.

"Where should I hide?" Calliope asked.

Dysnomi found a spot for Calliope to hide, shrouding her with his trickster magic and making her nearly invisible to anyone who looked. He then created an almost-perfect projection of her at the bar.

Before Calliope even had much time to think, the door to the bar slammed open and Raiden walked inside. She could hear the loud booming of thunder as it crashed behind him. "Hello again, sister," he said to Dysnomi's projection.

Yes! Calliope thought to herself. *It's working!*

The projection of Calliope rolled its eyes and asked, *'What do you want?'* It was using a tone of voice that suggested that it was already bored of the entire situation.

"What I want, dear sister, is for you to explain how the fuck you're even alive. Then, you can explain what the fuck you did to the demon," Raiden replied to the projection of Calliope.

'I don't know what you're talking about,' the projection said.

"Don't try to play dumb with me, sister," Raiden hissed with a sneer.

'I honestly have no idea what you mean,' said the projection, releasing an exasperated sigh.

"So, you have no fucking clue how the demon got turned into stone?" Raiden asked as he began to stalk toward the projection. "And you have no idea where the Compendium of Supernatural Powers suddenly disappeared to?"

Dysnomi stepped in-between Raiden and the projection of Calliope, saying, "That's close enough."

"Oh?" Raiden questioned. "And what exactly are you going to do?"

Dysnomi smirked and snapped his fingers, trapping Raiden in a sea of projections that looked exactly like Calliope. The chaos was enough to overwhelm Raiden and he began throwing fireballs—along with ball lightning—wildly around him. It was a pathetic attempt to snuff out the real Calliope.

Calliope smirked from her hiding spot, then carefully crept up behind Raiden. She crept closer and closer, until she was directly behind him. She matched his every move so he wouldn't catch her as she stood only inches away from his back.

Just as Calliope pulled back her Blade of Light, Raiden turned to face her directly. "Did you really believe I'd fall for that?" he asked her. He laughed and she thought he sounded insane. Then, he slammed a ball of lightning directly into her chest.

Calliope gasped, then screamed in pain as electricity coursed through her heart. However, she didn't drop down to her knees on the floor the way that she so desperately wanted to as her body became weak. Instead, she forced herself to continue standing.

30. STORM KILLER

(THE HOUR OF DEATH)

Calliope forced herself to continue standing on her shaky legs as the electricity ran directly through her heart. There were many times in that brief moment when she was positive that her heart was going to stop, but to her surprise, it didn't. She wasn't sure why, but she wasn't going to question it, either.

Raiden used his lightning powers on Calliope until he became exhausted. It took a lot of energy out of him, but he did his best to not show any signs of weakness.

Breathing heavily, Calliope held her hands out in front of her, the Blade of Light shaking in her grip as she rapidly lost strength. She continued holding the dagger defensively as she backed away from her brother. She moved backward until she hit the wall behind her.

"Are you going to kill me, sister?" Raiden asked Calliope with a sneer. She could tell that he was working hard to keep his breathing under control.

SILENCING THE SIREN
SARA REYNOLDS

Calliope smirked at Raiden after realizing how exhausted he was. Instead of answering him, she only shook her head and asked, "Brother... That was a lot of lightning power you used against me. Do you feel okay?" A sarcastic smile formed on her face. Dysnomi, Asmodeus, Amarok, and Zephyr all regarded her with confusing looks.

Raiden was giving Calliope a scorching glare, almost like he was daring her to say more and make him appear weak in front of everyone again. "What are you trying to say, sister?" he asked her through gritted teeth.

"Oh, nothing at all," Calliope replied, attempting to sound innocent. "Just... Remember what *Rumpelstiltskin* said, like... All the time... On the show, *Once Upon a Time*...? He said, *'All magic comes with a price...'* Are you sure you're willing to pay the price of using so much of your magic?" she asked.

"I'll be fine, dear sister," Raiden hissed at Calliope. "Don't start worrying about me now. Gods know you never did before."

"That's not true," Calliope replied calmly. "At all."

"Oh, it's not?" Raiden asked sarcastically, rolling his eyes at Calliope. "Well, it's clear you didn't worry enough to actually try to help me or anything."

"Are you fucking kidding me?!" Calliope shouted, holding the Blade of Light in front of her dangerously. "I looked for you! For months!" she yelled, anger rising inside of her. She moved forward and slashed at Raiden with the warm, glowing dagger, forcing him to jump backward. "I asked everyone if they had seen you... And I do mean everyone," she said, slashing at him a second time. Through her anger, she could barely hear the *'whoosh'* of the blade slicing through the air. "I placed missing posters on every street!" she yelled, slashing at him two more times.

"Stop fucking swinging that dagger at me!" Raiden yelled, throwing a ball of lightning at Calliope.

Dysnomi jumped in front of Calliope. He used his magic to place a barrier between them and Raiden, so the ball of lightning only hit a shimmering, translucent-blue wall rather than hitting Calliope.

Raiden's energy seemed to completely deflate after he used his magic again. Calliope scoffed at him, bouncing the Blade of Light in the air and catching the hilt in her hand each time that it came down. "I told you, brother... Magic always comes at a price. There's a reason they use that phrase in the show." She allowed her dagger to bounce in the air a few more times while she smirked at him. She caught the hilt when it came down the last time. Then, she tossed it at him like a dart—the warm, glowing golden blade embedding itself deeply into his chest.

Raiden grunted loudly from the pain, stepping backward until he hit the wall behind him. He looked down at the dagger with an expression that appeared to be a mix of confusion, anger, and immense agony. The Blade of Light began to glow brighter then, prompting Calliope to turn toward Dysnomi with a questioning look as Asmodeus, Amarok, and Zephyr were forced to shield their eyes.

"Okay, so I've never actually seen it do this before," Dysnomi admitted in response to Calliope's raised eyebrow.

"What?!" Calliope yelled. "Dys!"

"Okay, okay!" Dysnomi exclaimed, throwing his hands up defensively. "I've never personally watched it do that before, but I know that it gets brighter when it burns away darkness. We saw it with the Shadow Realm spirits—the way the daggers burned the shadows and made the shadow spirits scream. I assume it's doing the same thing with your brother right now, trying to cleanse whatever darkness he's got inside of him."

Calliope watched helplessly until Raiden slid down against the wall, feeling many conflicting emotions warring inside her. After all, he was still her brother... *Even though he had me killed once and was just trying to kill me again,* she thought.

Raiden was breathing heavily, and the dagger was still sticking out of his chest. He looked at her and said, "Well, sister... If I'm going to die... I'm going to bring you with me." He tried to summon his lightning again, attempting to shoot it at her. However, all that came from his fingertips were a few measly sparks—hardly anything at all.

"Ooh," Calliope hissed, leaning over Raiden. "Looks like you don't have the power you need, brother. Good. I don't wanna keep fighting. I feel like I've had a heart attack. Or five." She slid down against the wall next to him, but just out of his reach. "For what it's worth, I'm sorry it had to end like this."

"Yeah, I bet you are, sister," Raiden replied with a grimace. He straightened his back against the wall and asked, "Can someone take this fucking thing out of my chest now?"

"If we pull it out, you're just gonna die faster," Asmodeus warned Raiden. "...It won't exactly feel pleasant, either."

"I don't care," Raiden growled. "Take it out."

Asmodeus shrugged and moved toward Raiden so fast that it was almost impossible to see him move. He grabbed the hilt of the dagger, attempting to pull it out of Raiden's chest. As he touched the hilt, however, it sizzled and burned against his skin. It caused him to hiss in pain and pull his hand away like he had just touched a hot stove top. "Fuck!" he yelled.

"You're half-incubus, idiot," Dysnomi said, chuckling.

Meanwhile, Calliope stood and grabbed Asmodeus' hand, asking, "Are you okay? Lemme see."

"I'm fine," Asmodeus growled, quickly pulling his hand away from Calliope.

"You're obviously NOT fine. Lemme see it," Calliope insisted, reaching for Asmodeus' hand again.

"I said I'm fucking fine!" Asmodeus growled, pulling his hand back again. "Get away from me!" His voice changed and his eyes turned ink-black as he harshly pushed Calliope away from him.

Calliope stumbled backward, hitting the wall so hard that it knocked the breath out of her lungs. "What the fuck, Deus?" she asked. Her voice sounded more hurt than angry.

"I told you to get away from me," Asmodeus whispered before walking away to deal with his hand by himself. To his demon, he thought, *Why did you have to hurt Calli like that?*

'She should have just left you alone!' the demon screamed at Asmodeus.

Amarok put his hands on Calliope's shoulders and asked, "Are you okay?" She nodded, but he could see that she was close to tears, so he pulled her in for a tight hug. She allowed her tears to fall as she returned his hug, grabbing at the back of his shirt and pulling him closer to her.

"Alright, I'll get the dagger," Dysnomi announced as he sighed. He walked over and pulled the Blade of Light from Raiden's chest quickly, causing Raiden to yell from the pain. "Oh, hush," he said to Raiden, rolling his eyes.

Calliope pulled away from Amarok and dried her tears. Then, she asked, "So... What do we do now?"

"Now?" Dysnomi asked. "We wait." He shrugged and sat down at the bar.

Calliope sighed and sat down against the wall again. Amarok sat next to her and put his arms around her, holding her tightly. She leaned into him, finding a small bit of comfort from the feeling of him holding her.

Asmodeus' jealousy flared dangerously inside of him at the sight of Amarok holding Calliope. She could feel it rise within him, but she could also feel his guilt. His conflicting emotions only confused her in that moment, so she tried to keep them out of her mind completely as she waited for the end.

31. PICKING UP THE PIECES

(...AND YET, I SMILE)

"I still can't believe it's finally over," Calliope said, sitting at the bar inside of The Tipsy Piano. It had been a week since Raiden died, and she was still reeling from everything that she had been through.

"I can't believe it's been a week already," Nagaveni said in response.

"I can't believe you're gonna be leaving soon," Amarok said sadly, wrapping an arm around Calliope's shoulders.

Calliope laid her head on Amarok as he held her, and she said, "Well, you have my number. Plus, I'm obviously gonna come back to visit. After all, I'm still alive, and I still haven't bore witness to the beauty of Mardi Gras."

Amarok let out a deep, rumbling laugh. "You definitely can't miss Carnival now," he said. "Though I'm pretty sure the festival craziness won't be anything compared to this past month for you."

"It has been quite the month," Calliope said, laughing with Amarok. Zephyr slid everyone a drink then, and she picked hers up with a grateful smile.

"I'd like to propose a toast," Nagaveni announced, standing up. She smoothed her short pink flower-print dress, which matched Calliope's. Then, she said, "To New Orleans—apparently the city where you can find answers to any and all of your questions!"

Amarok stood up next, raising his glass. "To meeting amazing new people... People who make you feel as if you've known them your whole life," he said, winking at Calliope.

Dysnomi stood, wrapping an arm around Nagaveni. He looked down at her, smiling, and said, "To relationships no one would've ever seen coming... Long may they last." He kissed the top of her head then, causing her to blush.

Xena stood with Zorya. The two women were holding hands as Xena said, "To bein' reunited."

Zorya smiled and said, "To gettin' rid'a the Shadow Realm's hold on me."

Zephyr raised a glass, laughing as he said, "To the most interesting group of people I've ever met... And that's sayin' a lot when you live in the Crescent City, brah."

Asmodeus stood and cleared his throat, saying, "To Calli... I know we've had more than a few ups and downs over the years, but my life wouldn't be the same without you in it. *Te amo, hermosa.*"[43]

Calliope stood then. As she did, she noticed a familiar figure appear in a dark corner of the bar behind her friends. She smoothed her flower-print dress, winked at the figure, and said, "To Baron Samedi... For helping me believe in myself, and for allowing me to finish what my brother started. I could never thank him enough for his generosity."

They all drank from their glasses before laughing and talking with each other. Calliope grabbed two glasses of rum from Zephyr and walked over to the man who was hiding in the shadows.

The man's dark ebony hand reached out, accepting a drink from her. "Darlin', you really do know the best way to a man's heart, don't you?" he asked with a mischievous smile. "See, this is what I like so fuckin' much about you."

"Really?" Calliope asked with a sly smile. "And here, I thought you liked me so much because of my beauty and uniqueness, Baron Samedi," she joked.

---

[43] "I love you, beautiful."

"Oh, I do love your uniqueness," the Baron replied. "It's not every damn day you learn that La Siréne and Shango have a child together. And as for your beauty," he continued, trailing his dark fingers along Calliope's jawline and making her shiver. "Well... I would never lie about that. You are one of the most beautiful young women I have ever fuckin' met. ...And I do so love making you shiver and blush like this," he whispered in a husky voice as she looked away, blushing.

"Can I ask you something?" Calliope asked. Baron Samedi nodded, finishing off his entire glass of rum. She gave him her glass then, and asked, "Why did you give me this?" She held up the *'death'* tarot card. "Did you know I'd need it? ...Did you know I'd die? And if you didn't, then why did you decide to give it to me? I really can't be that special... And it can't all come down to you thinking it would be a shame for the living world to lose someone beautiful."

"Honestly, doll?" Baron Samedi asked. He drank the second glass of rum, then said, "I just had a feelin' you'd need it. I wasn't sure why, but between that feelin', and how selfless you were—askin' me to help the woman who fuckin' attacked you rather than askin' me to help yourself—I felt like you fuckin' deserved it."

"Well, thank you," Calliope responded before wrapping her arms around Baron Samedi tightly. He was shocked, but pushed his emotions aside and returned her embrace.

The Baron lifted a tattooed hand to grab Calliope's chin, holding it between his forefinger and his thumb while she hugged him. He tilted her face upwards, forcing her to meet his dark, scrutinizing gaze. She gasped as she once again noticed how handsome he was. *Especially with the way he always paints his face,* she thought.

Baron Samedi asked Calliope, "This is really your last night in New Orleans, then?"

Calliope answered the Baron, saying, "Yeah, I think I've already spent too much time here." She let out a small laugh before adding, "If I don't go home tomorrow morning, I'm not sure I'd ever go home."

"Well, it's pretty damn disappointing... But, I understand," Baron Samedi said with a smile. "You just hold onto that card, doll... And let me give you one more thing to remember me by."

"Oh, no, you don't have to do that. You've already done so much for me," Calliope said, beginning to protest. Baron Samedi silenced her with a deep, passionate kiss on her full garnet-pink lips, causing her to feel like she was melting in his arms. Locked in the embrace, he reached one hand to the back of her shoulder, placing it over the wounds that she had been given by Menoetius. She gasped as she felt a slight tingling sensation blocking the pain, but when he removed his hand, she no longer felt any pain at all. She realized then that he had healed her wounds. Breathless and embarrassed, she blushed deeply when he finally pulled away from her.

"There," the Baron said, giving Calliope a devilish grin as his eyes sparkled with mischief. "Now you'll never fuckin' forget me, doll."

Before Calliope could respond, Baron Samedi winked at her and disappeared. She released a small, breathless laugh, picked up the empty glasses that had once been filled with rum, and walked over to the bar. She set the glasses down on top of the bar, thinking, *I'm really gonna miss it here. I don't think I've ever been in any city as exciting as New Orleans has been. Los Angeles may be crazy, but NOLA is magical.*

"What would y'all say to one more night out on the town?" Amarok suggested. There was a hopeful gleam in his eyes as he looked around at the group. The hopefulness grew when his golden-yellow wolf eyes landed on Calliope. Her breath caught in her throat as he stared at her, and she found herself unable to answer him.

"I think that sounds like an amazing idea," Dysnomi said. "But this time, we're gonna do it right." He snapped his fingers, and everyone looked down to see that their clothes had changed and they were all wearing near-identical clothes.

Everyone in the group was wearing matching black shirts, which read, 'NOLA' on the front. The shirts also had retro 90's style art behind the lettering. However, everyone still maintained their own style. Nagaveni was wearing faded 90's style mom jeans with hot-pink *Converse* shoes. The Serpent Tamer necklace was concealing the snakes on her head, which—as usual—left the illusion of long, wavy jet-black hair flowing down to her waist. Calliope, on the other hand, was wearing a pair of extremely ripped and faded skinny jeans with a pair of fishnets underneath, along with a pair of black ankle boots—the same pair that she had worn on her first day in New Orleans. Her hair was also flowing freely down to her waist, the turquoise color complementing the retro colors on the front of the shirt. Asmodeus and Dysnomi were both wearing black skinny jeans—though Dysnomi had pulled on a pair of sunglasses and was wearing a pair of black combat boots, while Asmodeus wore a pair of black *Vans* shoes. Dysnomi's champagne-blond hair was half-up in a man-bun with the rest of it hanging down to his shoulders, while Asmodeus' off-black hair was down and flipped to one side. Xena and Zorya both wore black skinny jeans and black combat boots as well, although Xena had a black-leather jacket over the shirt. Amarok wore a nice pair of jeans and a pair of really nice-looking black *Nike* shoes. Amarok's long, shaggy dark copper-brown hair fell to his shoulders, looking as wild as it always did. Lastly, Zephyr wore an impossibly tight pair of skinny jeans with a pair of white *Adidas* shoes.

"I swear, you know us all too well now, Dys," Calliope joked.

"You and Nini are the easy ones, Calli," Dysnomi said in response. "I've known you the longest, and I've gotten to know her really well recently." Amarok, Calliope, and Xena cheered and whistled at him when he said that, which left Nagaveni blushing. "Yeah, yeah, whatever," he said, waving off their teasing. "Anyway, I was pretty much guessing when it came to everyone else. I mean, I know roughly the kind of clothes everyone wears, but that's all."

"You did pretty good," Xena responded. "So, what exactly are we gettin' up to tonight?"

"Whatever the hell we want to," Dysnomi said, shrugging. The group laughed then, and Calliope said goodbye to Zephyr, who wanted to stay behind to keep the bar open. Then, everyone walked out of the front door of The Tipsy Piano, heading back to Bourbon Street. It was their favorite place to party during the long nights that they had spent in New Orleans.

As the group began their walk, Asmodeus nervously grabbed Calliope's arm and slowed his walking pace until the two of them were behind everyone else. Before she could ask him what he was doing, he looked over at her. There was an obvious pain behind his electric-blue eyes. "Calli," he started to say. "About last week... *Lo siento por la forma en que te traté.*[44] I have no excuse for yelling at you... Or for shoving you. I'm not gonna ask you to forgive me. I've asked that from you too many times over the years. Please just know... *Lo siento, y te amo.*"[45]

"I love you, too, Deus," Calliope responded as tears filled her iris-purple eyes. Asmodeus felt heartbroken when he saw her eyes looking so sad.

---

[44] "I'm sorry for the way I treated you."
[45] "I'm sorry, and I love you."

He wanted to wipe her tears away, but he forced himself not to touch her as he waited for her to finish speaking. "I know it's hard for you to control the demon when you're really upset, or when you're in pain. I understand that more than anyone. You've never had to explain that to me. Is this why you haven't been speaking to me much lately?" she asked. He nodded, and she pulled him in for a tight hug, whispering, "Oh, Deus. I'd never abandon you over something like that. It may hurt me at the moment, but I promise you, I understand. I do appreciate your apology, though. Just... Please know that when I say I love you, I really mean that I love every part of you... Even the demonic side."

Asmodeus hugged Calliope back, allowing a single tear to slip out of his eyes before pulling away from her. *"Gracias,*[46] Calli," he said, lightly tracing her full, round lips with his thumb. He held her hand then, and they started walking again—moving a bit faster to catch up with the rest of the group.

As they came upon the crowded street, Calliope couldn't help thinking, *It looks more magical every time I come here.* She gawked at the neon lights and smiled as she adjusted to the

---

[46] "Thank you,"

sights, smells, and noises that were surrounding her.

As the couple began to walk past a group of bored-looking teenagers, Calliope gave Asmodeus a mischievous grin and pulled him closer. *What are we doing?* he asked her telepathically, looking at her with a questioning expression.

I don't know how these teens look so bored, Calliope answered telepathically. *But I say we entertain them.* Walking up to one of the teenagers—a young male with shaggy sandy-blond hair and sable-brown eyes, who was wearing a flannel shirt and torn skinny jeans—he tapped him on the shoulder politely.

"Yeah?" the teen asked, barely glancing up from his phone at first. When he saw Calliope, however, he quickly forgot his phone as he stared, wide-eyed. "You're... You're really pretty," the teenage boy stuttered.

Calliope simply laughed and said to the teenage boy and his friends, "I bet you my friend and I can read your minds." She lifted her eyebrow, challenging the group.

"No way," the teenage boy said, eyeing Asmodeus suspiciously. "I don't believe in that shit."

"Yeah, no one REALLY believes in magic," a teenage girl with long caramel-brown hair and baby-blue eyes said, stepping out from behind the boy.

"Oh?" Calliope questioned, once again raising her eyebrow in a silent challenge.

"Prove us wrong then, kid," Asmodeus said, smirking. "Think of something—something that's not obvious, so you know we aren't just guessing—and we'll tell you what you're thinking."

"Fine," the teenage girl said as the boy shrugged. Asmodeus listened to the girl's thoughts, finally catching her thinking, *I can't believe Mom made me come here. I wanted to go to Florida.*

"Why are you so hung up on Florida?" Asmodeus asked the girl, leaving her looking shocked. "I mean, there's just as many alligators here as there are in Florida. But twice as much culture as any beach you wanted to visit."

Calliope laughed as she looked at the girl's shocked expression, then turned to the boy. "Your turn," she said happily.

"Okay," the teen said, shrugging. He began to think then, and Calliope listened intently. Finally, she heard the boy think, *I wonder if I should order a pizza for dinner, or if Dad already has something planned.*

"You know, you could just text your dad and ask him if you're worried about what you're doing for dinner," Calliope said. The teenager stared at her, and his jaw dropped.

"How did you—?" the teenage boy began to ask, but Calliope just shrugged and laughed.

Asmodeus put his arm around Calliope's shoulder then, leading her away while they laughed. The Supernatural couple made it back to their friend group just in time to watch Dysnomi impressing a crowd with his magic once again.

Dysnomi waved his hands theatrically, then conjured a small stuffed animal for a young woman standing in front of him. The woman smiled and laughed in delight, accepting the small pink bear from him. He then moved over to a tall man—who looked fairly unimpressed—and conjured a drink for him. The man accepted it, took one drink of it, and nodded respectfully while smiling.

"He really knows how to work a crowd, doesn't he?" Amarok asked as he walked up behind Asmodeus and Calliope.

"It's his specialty as a trickster," Calliope replied with a small laugh.

A band of street performers were playing nearby, and as they began a slow song, Amarok held a hand out for Calliope. "Would you do me the honor of dancing with me one last time?" he asked her.

Calliope glanced at Asmodeus, not wanting to make him feel jealous, or for him to get upset with her. Asmodeus simply smiled and nodded, so she took Amarok's hand, saying, "The honor would be all mine." She giggled as Amarok brushed a kiss lightly across her knuckles before pulling her into the middle of the street.

Amarok had one of his hands enveloping one of Calliope's and his other hand was placed at her lower back, pressing her body firmly against his. Leading her in the slow dance, he had a hard time keeping his wolf from coming out, but he managed to force it down. He spun her out, then back into him—ending with her pressed tightly against him. She rested one hand on his muscular chest, her other hand still securely held in his. "I could never get enough of this," she whispered as he looked down at her. He watched her lips move with every word that she spoke.

"I'm really gonna miss having a partner to sing while I play the piano, and a partner to dance with," Amarok admitted as the song was coming to an end. He dipped Calliope down, keeping her lifted just far enough from the ground that her hair would not brush against the street. He looked down at her lips, then up to her eyes. "Promise to keep in touch?" he asked.

"Of course," Calliope replied in a breathless whisper. Before she could say anything more, Amarok placed a brief, gentle kiss against her soft lips. She sighed, almost forgetting where she was. She was only brought back to reality by the sound of the crowd surrounding them cheering and whistling, causing her to blush.

Amarok pulled Calliope up, stepping back from her and rubbing the back of his neck sheepishly. Then, he led her toward their friend group, smiling as they walked up to discover that Xena once again was telling her hunting tales. The crowd may have believed that her stories were fictional, but Calliope and the rest of her friends knew that the stories were very real, which made them all the more interested in hearing her tales.

Before long, everyone in the group had become tired. Although they were dreading it, they all reluctantly bid each other goodnight. Calliope hugged Zorya and Xena, promising Xena that she'd help Salem look for a cure for Xena's magical skin condition for as long as it took. Then, she stepped up to Amarok with tears in her eyes. He wrapped her in his powerful arms, allowing her to bury her face in his broad chest as she held onto him tightly.

After the Supernaturals all said their goodbyes, Calliope, Asmodeus, Nagaveni, and Dysnomi walked back to the hotel that they were staying at and packed their belongings for their return trip to Los Angeles.

32. THE STRONGEST FORM OF MAGIC

(THE SONG IN YOUR HEART)

Calliope, Asmodeus, Nagaveni, and Dysnomi left on an early flight to Los Angeles the next morning. They found themselves landing at L.A.X. after four hours of flying.

After dropping off their belongings inside their shared apartment, Calliope and Nagaveni called a car to pick them up. The two Supernaturals navigated their way straight to Tartarus. On the exclusive upper floor of Dysnomi's nightclub, none of the Supernaturals had a need for enchantments to make themselves appear human. Nagaveni took her Serpent Tamer necklace off of her neck when she stepped out onto the balcony, where Dysnomi, Salem, and Asmodeus were already waiting for her and Calliope in the seating area.

Before taking a seat, Calliope walked over to the private bar on the balcony. The flower nymph, Nasrin, was standing behind the bar, making drinks for everyone the way that she had been when the group had left.

Thank the gods that Zephyr gave us all of his special recipes, Calliope thought as she accepted a turquoise-colored Siren's Lament from the cute, baby-pink bartender. "I hope you didn't miss me too badly, goddess," she said to Nasrin with a wink, causing the nymph to blush. She placed money on the bar for Nasrin, despite knowing that Dysnomi would not allow his bartenders to ask anyone in their friend group to pay for their drinks.

Calliope then walked toward her friends, who were already sitting on the couches. She sat next to Asmodeus and cuddled into him as he wrapped his arms around her. At the same moment, Nanuk materialized on her opposite side, cuddling into her gently. She smiled and scratched behind the hellhound's ears, smiling as she felt the stinging sensation of Nanuk's coarse fur as it left small papercut-like scratches all over her hand. She spent the evening enjoying her friends' company. Though, she hadn't really been paying attention to all of the conversations that were happening around her until something that Salem said caused her to perk up and listen to the witch intently.

"I think I might be able to cure Xena," Salem mentioned proudly. "Now... I'm not completely sure just yet, but it does seem likely. And I'll spare you all the boring 'witchy' details, but I really do think that we've got a good shot."

"That's amazing, Salem!" Calliope exclaimed. "And once again, thank you so much for doing this. You're honestly the best witch in L.A. and I knew that if ANYONE could come up with a cure, it'd be you."

"Aww, thanks, Calli!" Salem replied. She tossed her wild, curly ginger hair over her shoulder, smiling brightly.

Calliope looked up at Asmodeus just as everyone began talking and joking with each other once again. "This month has been so insane," she whispered in his ear. He smiled, then tightened his grip around her waist as she added in a whisper, "I never would've made it this far without you. I love you so much, Deus, and I wanted to ask you... Do you think we could officially try again? As a couple, I mean..."

"*No me gustaría nada más.*[47] Thank you, Calli," Asmodeus whispered in response to Calliope. "You know that I love you. I will always

---

[47] "I would like nothing more."

want you to be mine, mi amor. There will never be a time when I don't want you."

Calliope hugged Asmodeus tightly when he said that to her. Before long, she was so tired that she could feel her eyes beginning to drift closed while she lay in the warmth and comfort of his strong arms. She eventually couldn't stop herself from drifting off to sleep.

However, only moments before the restful darkness of sleep completely overtook Calliope, she heard a familiar voice speak to her inside her mind. The voice almost sounded like Lyn—the spirit of the thunderbird—as it told her, *'Oh, I was really hoping that you were gonna pick Amarok... But... I guess that Asmodeus has grown a lot in the past few weeks.'*

Calliope was almost certain that the voice could not have been Lyn. She had not heard a word from either Lyn or Ember since the day that Raiden had taken her powers. The voice did sound like Lyn, though. Before she could think too much about it, however, she drifted off to a deep sleep in Asmodeus' arms.

ABOUT THE AUTHOR

Sara Reynolds is a wife and mother from Kentucky who has always loved escaping into fantasy worlds. She loves learning about mythology, and she put many hours of research and development into every mythological or supernatural creature that she wrote about. All of the research and development was done to help mix the myths with reality. There's nothing she loves more than helping others escape into a fantasy world, away from the monotony of everyday life. For updates on all future books—in this series and others—you can visit her webpage: https://sarareynoldsauthor.com/ or follow her on Twitter @ChaoticStupid96

Made in the USA
Columbia, SC
13 March 2023